Charmed Again

ROSE PRESSEY

DEDICATION

This is to you and you know who you are.

ACKNOWLEDGMENTS

To my son, who brings me joy every single day. To my mother, who introduced me to the love of books. To my husband, who encourages me and always has faith in me. A huge thank you to my editor, Eleanor Boyd. And to the readers who make writing fun.

CHAPTER ONE

The idea of vampires had rarely crossed my mind until now. I'd been too consumed in improving my witchcraft skills to give it much thought. That had all changed the night two gorgeous brothers showed up at my front door. They both claimed they had come to protect me, but for different reasons. That was how I'd ended up in a sleek black car headed for New Orleans in the middle of the night.

Fog had settled over Enchantment Pointe, making visibility difficult. I held on tight as the car sped along, hugging the curves of the road. Nicolas Marcos sat in the back seat of the car and Liam Rankin navigated the wheel. Unfortunately, I had no idea where we were headed. All I knew was that Nicolas had been accused of stealing another witch's powers. As the new leader of the Underworld, apparently this was my problem now. That put me in a bit of a pickle because Nicolas' sexy eyes and gorgeous body had distracted me for some time now. What did they want me to do about it anyway? Was there some kind of punishment for stealing powers? I had no idea.

My name is Halloween LaVeau and up until now the most exciting thing that had ever happened to me was that I'd been named Worst Witch of the Year for the past few years running. Yeah, I was that bad. Luckily, my skills were improving thanks to the Book of Mystics, but more about that later. Honestly, sometimes I wondered if my mother's decision to name me Halloween had been more than just a cruel invitation for me to be teased while growing up. Had my name somehow sent the paranormal powers-that-be directly into my path? Heck, maybe I was putting too much thought into it, but nevertheless, my world had been turned upside down just a few short days ago.

Nicolas and Liam had shown up on the doorstep of LaVeau Manor under mysterious circumstances. It hadn't been a coincidence that I'd just discovered a strange old book written in an unknown language right before their arrival. Much to my chagrin, I still hadn't figured out most of what was written in the book. The words and spells appeared of their own free will. Anyway, this old book had unleashed a power within me that I'd never come close to possessing before. Apparently, whoever owned the book was the leader of the Underworld. Lucky me. Heck, I still didn't know what the Underworld was— how was I supposed to lead it? But as we headed away from town, barreling into the night, I knew I was about to find out. My heart beat faster at the thought.

"Do you want to tell me more about these charges?" I asked, looking at Liam, then over my shoulder at Nicolas.

Tension emanated from the backseat. Nicolas' strong jaw was set in a straight line. He glanced down, avoiding my stare, and I took that as a message that he didn't want to discuss the matter. But if I was the leader now, I had to set some rules, right? I had to push the lust-filled thoughts of Nicolas to the back of my mind and ask for answers. I might be new at this gig, but I wanted to take the duties seriously.

I couldn't deny my feelings for both of the men. But for some strange reason I felt as if Liam would be just fine without me. Nicolas, on the other hand, seemed as if he needed me. I wasn't sure what had given me that impression. Wishful thinking maybe.

I studied Liam's handsome face, half lit by the sliver of moonlight coming through the car window. Liam and Nicolas were both amazing specimens of masculinity. Not to mention they exuded irresistible levels of charm. They had the same high cheekbones, dazzling smiles with full lips, eyes the color of a bright summer sky, and thick dark hair that you just wanted to sink your fingers into.

It was no surprise that they looked alike though because I'd recently discovered the two men were half-brothers. There was one thing that set them apart from each other. Yes, they were both witches, but Nicolas was a vampire too. I still didn't know the full circumstances of how that had come about. But his mother and aunt had been turned at the same time back in the 1800s. Now that I thought of it, why hadn't Liam aged? That thought hadn't occurred to me until now. Yes, witches lived long lives, but we aged. Liam looked to be around the same age as Nicolas.

It was funny now I realized just how little I truly knew about them. I'd have to ask more questions. Nicolas' mother had been the leader of the Underworld... but that was a story for later too. Right now I had to find out why Nicolas was being charged with such a ridiculous crime.

"Who is the witch who's accusing him?" I shifted on the leather seat. It was impossible to get comfortable with the waves of apprehension flowing through me.

Liam steered around a curve. "Her name is Sabrina Stratford. She's from the New Orleans Coven. Her brother is the leader of that Coven."

Nicolas remained tight-lipped in the back seat. Was this too stressful for him to talk about or was there truth to the allegation?

"Do you want to give me your side of the story before we get to wherever it is we're going?" I asked as sweetly as possible.

Nicolas ran his hand through his thick black hair. "I'm not sure where to begin…"

"How about you start from the beginning?" I said, forcing myself to remain calm.

After exhaling, he said, "She was being attacked and asked me to turn her into a vampire."

Whoa. That was a little more serious than I'd expected. I exchanged a look with Liam. He must have read my mind because he frowned in response.

"When did this happen?" I asked, keeping my tone deceptively composed.

"It was just a day before I came to LaVeau Manor." A look of discomfort crossed his face.

This was almost too much to wrap my mind around. I'd had enough to deal with learning about my new leader status and now this. I knew my Great-Aunt Maddy had just been trying to help me by leaving me her beautiful home, but it had been nothing but a disaster since I'd moved in. LaVeau Manor was an imposing structure with a large veranda and three stories. The manor stood near the river with a creepy old family cemetery nearby. Not knowing what else to do with the place, I'd decided to run the it as a bed-and-breakfast. Shortly thereafter Nicolas and Liam had shown up.

"Aren't you supposed to stay with her or something after turning her?" I asked.

I had no idea how the whole vampire thing worked. Clearly now that I was the leader of the Underworld I needed to learn a few things.

"You've been watching too many movies," Liam said with amusement in his voice.

"Well, excuse me for not having the paranormal handbook memorized." I didn't know what to do with myself so I nervously tapped my fingers against my seat.

After all, until recently I had been the butt of all the witches' jokes. My lack of powers had been famous for miles around. Enchantment Pointe Coven members had even written a pamphlet about my abysmal witchcraft skills.

"She didn't give me a chance to help her. After I turned her, she took off. I hadn't heard a word about it until Liam called just now." Nicolas' voice was smooth, but resolute.

"You said she asked you to turn her? What does that mean?" Maybe I should have read those *Twilight* books because I had no idea how any of this worked.

He let out a deep breath. "I went out for a jog by my house and that's when I heard a lot of noise, then a scream."

"What did you do?" I pushed.

"I ran toward where I heard the noise. That's when I saw the woman with a beast hovering over her..." Nicolas' voice trailed off.

My eyes widened. "What kind of beast?"

A grave look fell over Nicolas' face, as if he didn't even want to picture the thing in his mind.

"A demon beast," Liam answered for him.

I must have led an extremely sheltered life because I'd never heard of such a thing until now.

"A demon beast? What is that? How is that different from Isabeau?" I asked.

Isabeau was a demon I'd accidentally brought back with my substandard spell-casting. Looking back, I guessed I understood why the Coven had named me Worst Witch of The Year.

"A demon sent here from hell," Liam offered.

I shivered at the thought. "What does it look like?"

I probably didn't want to know, but I asked anyway.

"The demon is big and midnight black. The thing looks like a shadowy figure until you get up close."

"Have you been close to this thing?" I asked with wide eyes.

He hesitated, then nodded. "I came closer than I'd have liked once."

"What else does it look like?"

"The demon has long arms that reach almost to the ground and claws that curl under like hooks," Liam said.

I tried to seem unfazed by the startling description, but there was no way to hide the fear in my voice.

"What does it want?"

He shrugged. "Who knows? It wants different things, I guess. But mostly it just wants power and to take a soul back to the devil."

"Kind of like a token or prize?" I never wanted to be one of their prizes.

"You could say that, yes," Liam said, as he negotiated a curve in the road.

"But why would she want you to turn her just because this beast had attacked her? Couldn't you just save her from the demon? If it took off, then what was the need to turn her?" With each question I grew more confused.

"The beast had tried to kill her. She was dying and I was her only hope of survival." Nicolas' voice lowered.

No doubt the scene was playing on loop in his mind. I hated to remind him of what had happened, but I needed to know the details.

"So she knew you were a vampire ahead of time. It wasn't like you'd flashed your fangs at her or anything," I said, shifting in my seat again.

"No, I wasn't showing off my fangs." Nicolas tried to sound casual, but I wasn't convinced. He looked out the window into the darkness.

We sat in silence for a few moments while we all contemplated the situation. I had no idea what I was getting into. What did they want me to do about this? I couldn't make it all better. I couldn't un-turn the woman. Or could I?

I'd recently figured out that I had the power to reanimate the dead. I'd mistakenly brought a demon back to life. Thank goodness the demon I'd dealt with looked nothing like what Liam had described. Isabeau Scarrett had popped up at LaVeau Manor, a demon disguised as a beautiful blonde. Needless to say, bringing demons back was a power I didn't want and I certainly didn't want to start bringing vampires back from the other side as well.

We'd made it to the outskirts of Enchantment Pointe, yet I still had no idea where we were headed. The darkness of night coupled with the fog had left me disoriented.

"When are you going to tell me where we're going?" I asked, turning my attention back from the window.

"It's a place just outside New Orleans. We'll be there soon," Liam said without glancing at me.

"Well, that's a vague answer. I don't think it's fair to toss me into this situation without telling me what I should expect to see," I said, not hiding the frustration in my voice.

"She's right. She needs to know," Nicolas said softly as he leaned his head back against the seat.

"Nicolas' fate is in your hands now. You'll hear the charges against him and decide what happens next," Liam offered.

"What? I'm supposed to decide his punishment?" I asked with a high level of excitement coloring my words.

When I looked at Nicolas he offered a half-hearted smile. "Everything will be fine, Hallie."

I didn't agree. Things would be far from fine. How could I decide something like that when I had feelings for Nicolas? We'd just fought off another demon together. Well, with the help of Nicolas and Liam I'd fought off the demon at the annual Enchantment Pointe Halloween Bash. It would be All Hallows' Eve soon, my birthdate and the reason my mother had named me Halloween in the first place. Call me crazy, but I'd rather go back to celebrating the holiday by passing out candy to the cute kids than going to New Orleans and deciding another witch's fate.

"We'll hear what this witch has to say," Liam said.

"You mean we're going to meet this woman?" My chest tightened and heaviness sat like a weight in my stomach.

"Yes, like I said, her brother is the leader of the New Orleans Coven. She has been an outstanding member of the coven for many years," Liam said.

I rubbed my temples. "Why did she just take off after this happened? It doesn't make sense."

And they expected me to sort this mess out. Had she been afraid of Nicolas? I supposed that made sense. But didn't she recognize Nicolas right away? The brothers had been around the coven members often.

"With any luck, that's what we'll get to the bottom of," Liam said, tapping his fingers nervously against the steering wheel as he drove.

I expelled a long, tired breath. "Yeah, with any luck. So we're going to this plantation. What happens once we get there?"

"You'll meet all the coven members. They'll share the charges and then it's in your hands."

Liam glanced at me as if to say he was sorry. No reason to be sorry. It wasn't his fault.

My stomach sank again. Was it too late to turn back? I needed to speak with Nicolas more. And face to face, not over my shoulder. I couldn't discuss this with him sitting in the backseat of this darkened car as we sped down the highway. Would he look me in the eye and tell me the truth? I'd always believed he was honest.

"I understand that vampires are trying to steal witches' blood. But that's not me and that's not what I'm about. Liam can tell you that," Nicolas said as if he'd read my mind.

There had been a tension between the brothers from the moment they had arrived at LaVeau Manor. Heck, they'd kept the fact that they were brothers from me until earlier tonight. I'd thought for quite some time that they might kill each other. Liam was a detective with the Underworld and had been in charge of protecting Nicolas' mother. But she'd been murdered by her own sister while on Liam's watch. That had caused a great deal of animosity between the brothers. They were far from mending fences and I wasn't positive that Liam would vouch for his half-brother.

I looked to Liam for his response.

After a pause, he nodded, then said, "Nicolas hasn't done that as far as I know. Of course we haven't exactly been on speaking terms until recently."

At first, Liam had led me to believe that Nicolas had been at LaVeau Manor only to collect my blood. Had he been? I didn't know who to believe.

"So this beast was attacking the witch and she asked you to turn her." I felt as if I was interrogating Nicolas, but the questions had to be asked.

Apparently I wasn't getting out of this Underworld leader thing tonight.

"Just before she took her last breath she asked me to turn her." He shook his head as if he was trying to get rid of the memory.

His response sent a chill down my spine. I was envisioning the scene in my mind and it wasn't a pretty sight.

I braced myself for the next question I was about to ask. "Can you tell me more about this demon beast? What does it do? Can you tell me more about what it looks like?"

Nicolas scrubbed his hand across his face. "I'm not an expert on these creatures. But it looked like a giant werewolf and attacks like one too."

"How do you know it wasn't a werewolf?" I asked.

"It disappeared as soon as I approached. Meaning it didn't run away, but disappeared into thin air," Nicolas said.

I contemplated this for a moment. "I wonder why it vanished."

Nicolas nodded. "I couldn't begin to guess."

Picturing Nicolas biting anyone's neck was tough, although since he was a vampire I knew he'd done it before. But had he ever killed anyone in the process? Just because he was a vampire didn't mean that he'd caused anyone harm, right? Was that just wishful thinking on my part? Probably. He had come close to biting my neck, but I'd thought of that as more of a nibble… a love bite.

"Did you experience anything from turning her?" I asked, unsure of my wording.

Like I said, I'd never dealt with this. How was I expected to know the correct terms?

"Are you asking if my powers increased?" He met my gaze.

A pang of sympathy ran through me. "Yes, I guess that's what I'm trying to ask."

Nicolas looked down and didn't respond. He didn't have to answer. His silence was all I needed to know. This wouldn't help Nicolas' side of the story.

In the distance lights came into view. My heart rate picked up and my stomach turned. I didn't have to ask to know that the lights came from our destination. They must be waiting for me. I had no idea if the Coven would consist of two members or two hundred. But I assumed since it was New Orleans then it would be quite a bit larger than Enchantment Pointe's Coven.

As we turned onto the tree-lined pebble driveway, I knew I'd soon find answers to some of my questions.

The driveway seemed to stretch out forever as the plantation came into view at the end. Moss-draped oak trees dotted the landscape. For a moment the thought of alligators popped into my mind. I knew the area was surrounded by the bayou. Alligators might be the nicest thing I'd encounter tonight.

Clouds completely cloaked the black night sky now, blocking out the last slivers of moonlight. Two large porches wrapped around the home on both the bottom and top floors. Massive columns decorated the front of the white façade. Light shone brightly from every window, casting an eerie glow into the vast and foreboding black sky. If not for the lights, it would have been unnervingly dark. Was I really ready for this? I knew the answer to that question after one second—no.

When we pulled up in front of the house, several people stepped out onto the porch. Obviously they'd known I was coming and they hadn't wasted any time in coming outside to check me out. By the expressions on their faces, I knew this visit wouldn't involve eating cupcakes and playing with puppies.

CHAPTER TWO

The small group of people greeted us as we stepped out of the car. All eyes were on me as if I was some kind of novelty circus act. If my count was correct, there were three men and three women. They must have been the head members of the New Orleans Coven.

Most people might picture coven members dressed all in black, but that wasn't the case. Dressed in casual business attire of slacks and dress shirts, they looked more like they were there for a homeowners' association meeting than a coven gathering. That was the thing—witches had special powers, but looked and dressed just like everyone else. No green skin or warts. The smell of approaching rain hung in the air. Warm night air wrapped around me, but nothing comforting came from this situation.

A man stepped forward and stretched his hand toward me. "You must be Halloween LaVeau. We've been eagerly awaiting your arrival."

Something about his clipped tone made me uneasy. How long could they have been awaiting my arrival? We'd only learned of the charges against Nicolas an hour ago.

I shook his hand. "Pleased to meet you."

He gestured toward the beautiful home. "Won't you come in? My name is Jacobson Stratford."

This had to be the brother of the victim. What would be his reaction to seeing Nicolas? This was more than a little awkward.

The Coven members glared at Nicolas. Obviously, he wasn't their favorite person right now. Everyone in the group was tall, making my insecurities as the new leader even grander. I was like a tiny scrub in a forest of redwoods. Liam gestured as if to say he would follow me. Nicolas' eyes were blank. Was it worry darkening his expression? I had no idea what must be going through his mind.

How bad could this really be? I mean, the woman was okay, right? No harm done? Well, other than the fact that she was a vampire now. That was kind of a big deal, I guessed. But she'd asked him to turn her, right? Maybe she was telling the truth though. What if Nicolas had turned her against her will in a botched attempt to steal her powers? At that moment I realized that I didn't know Nicolas nearly as well as I thought I did. After all, I'd only known him for a short time. I was letting the sexual chemistry between us cloud my judgment.

Nicolas and Liam followed me up the grand steps toward the large black front door. Maybe they wanted to walk behind me so they could catch me if I decided to run away. But I was the leader now. I could run away if I wanted to, although I wasn't sure what would happen to Nicolas then. In a way, I had to save him.

To my left was the parlor and on the right was a room that looked to be used as a library. It was dark in there, but I caught a glimpse of books on the shelves and a couple dark wingback chairs. Turning to the left, I followed the coven members into the ostentatious parlor of the home. The dimmed crystal chandelier was almost too big for the room and looked more suited for a banquet room. Candles flickered in the corner, casting a spooky glow across the coven members' frowning faces. I wasn't sure if I was there for a meeting or a séance. The room was decorated as if it should be in a magazine in shades of blue and white. The fine furnishings and high ceilings cast the impression of opulence, but I knew that darkness hid just beyond the edge of that room, watching and waiting to rear its ugly head.

Jacobson motioned toward a plush velvet armchair. "Please have a seat."

For a moment, I hesitated. All eyes were still on me. Finally, I walked over and eased down into the chair. Why did it feel as if he was in charge of this meeting? Sure, he was the leader of the coven, but they'd called me to settle this situation. I didn't like his bossy attitude. I'd find out what he wanted, then we'd be out of there. And none too soon either. Jacobson sat in the chair next to me while Nicolas and Liam sat across from us on the sofa. The other members stood around the room as if on guard. This environment was more than a little hostile.

I looked at each woman in the room. Was the woman who had accused Nicolas of stealing her powers and turning her in the room with us? Everyone was staring at me, as if they were waiting for me to start this meeting. It finally struck me that this was the meeting—nothing special or grand. I supposed it was time for me to stumble my way through this whole thing. I'd do my best to pretend that I knew what I was doing.

I sat up straighter in the chair, then folded my hands in my lap. It was my best professional business like posture. "I've been called here because there's a problem. When does the meeting start?"

Jacobson stared for a beat with a sly smile on his face, then finally said, "Yes, there is a problem. This is the meeting."

Just as I'd suspected—this really was the meeting. I figured there would be some big elaborate production.

This was just a bunch of people sitting around in a living room.

"I'm glad you brought the accused with you."

He looked at Nicolas with a slight sneer. Of course Jacobson's reaction to Nicolas made me dislike Jacobson even more. Jacobson was assuming Nicolas was guilty right away. There was no way I would rush to judgment like that. This guy was really rubbing me the wrong way and I'd only known him a few minutes. Enough of the chitchat, I wanted to get straight to the point.

"Why don't you just tell me what's going on so we can get this settled." I glanced at my watch.

"Do you have somewhere else to be?" he asked with disdain.

As if that was any of his business. I looked him in the eye. "As a matter of fact, I do. I'd like to be in bed right now. It's late and I'm tired. It's been a long day."

He smiled. "Yes, I heard. You fought off Mara. That is very impressive."

I wasn't sure how impressive it was, but at the moment I didn't care. Mara was the last thing I wanted to think about.

She was the witch who had killed Nicolas' mother, her own sister. Mara had wanted to be the leader of the Underworld and she'd come after the Book of Mystics... and me. With Nicolas and Liam's help, I had banished her and her demon friend Isabeau to hell. And I hoped that was where they stayed.

"Anyway, back to the reason why you've called me here tonight." I was determined not to allow Jacobson to lead the conversation.

He leaned back in his chair, all casual and relaxed-looking. "I'm sure you can understand that the charges against Nicolas Marcos are quite serious." He glanced at Nicolas again, then back to me. "We just can't allow this kind of thing to happen. He's very dangerous."

A smile crossed his face as he said that, as if he got great pleasure from the words as they rolled off his tongue.

"With all due respect, Mr. Stratford, I don't think Nicolas is dangerous at all." I cast a quick glance at Nicolas.

His expression was still blank, almost catatonic. Was he in shock? This was no time for him to freak out. If I could hold it together and feel my way through this leader thing, then he could help me out by not zoning out into some zombie-like state. I wanted to snap my fingers and bring him out of the trance. Liam looked like he was ready to kick Jacobson's ass.

"How long have you known Mr. Marcos?" he asked with a smug smile.

Oh, well played, Mr. Coven Member, well played.

"Well, I haven't known him long, but I am a good judge of character and I feel he is a decent man," I said, folding my arms across my chest.

Okay, even I knew that sounded ridiculous. Nicolas gave a half-hearted smile. At least I'd gotten some reaction out of him, which was more than I'd had in the past hour.

"Let's get right down to the charges, shall we?" Jacobson folded his hands in his lap.

Well, that was what I'd wanted about ten minutes ago. It was about time.

"Please. I'd love to," I said, drily.

"I'm not sure if you're aware, but my sister Sabrina was attacked by Mr. Marcos," he said.

I bit my tongue. The overwhelming need to defend Nicolas came over me, but I had to listen to what this man had to say before I dismissed him. It was only fair that I got to the truth about what really happened.

Holding my composure, I said, "I was filled in on what happened from Mr. Marcos. With all due respect to your sister, he has a different version of the story."

He chuckled. "I'm sure he does. That doesn't make it true."

16

"You're right, but that doesn't make what your sister says true either." I stared him straight in the eyes.

He glowered. "Are you calling my sister a liar?"

I had to remain strong. "No, that is not what I'm implying at all. But I need to know the facts behind the whole situation. Is your sister here? I need to speak with her."

"She is too upset to speak." He cut me a sharp look as if daring me to argue.

This conversation was going nowhere.

"I can't just take your word for it, Mr. Stratford." I looked at Nicolas again. "Or Mr. Marcos' either, for that matter."

"The fact of the matter is she is a vampire now. There is no denying that. Mr. Marcos is even admitting to biting her." Jacobson gestured wildly in Nicolas' direction.

He had me there. Nicolas had admitted to that much.

"As I've been made aware, she asked him to turn her as a last resort over death. Mr. Marcos felt he had little choice and was only trying to do what was right. Aren't you grateful that he saved your sister's life?" I returned the annoyed gleam in his eyes with an angry glare of my own.

He focused his attention on Nicolas. "There was nothing to save her from. It was an unprovoked attack."

Nicolas shifted in his seat. I felt his tension. I knew he wanted to say something, but in order for this not to turn into an all-out war, it was best if I did all the talking. Even Liam was letting me handle the situation. Was I really stepping right into my role as leader? Sure, I had no idea what I was doing, but I was giving it my best shot. The local Coven wouldn't believe it. I used to screw up witches' spells for miles around and now people were coming to me to solve their problems.

"A demon beast attacked her. Nicolas was saving her," I said with too much panic in my voice.

It was funny how quickly things could change because I suddenly felt as if I was losing control of this situation fast. The Coven members laughed, a cacophony of humiliation.

"That is an absurd story. There was no such beast. Why would this demon run away simply because Mr. Marcos approached? Wouldn't the beast just attack both of them?" Jacobson looked at me with an unflinching glare.

"I can assure you that I am no expert on this matter, so how can I answer that question?" I cut him a warning look, letting him know that I would be a fierce enemy if crossed.

"You can say that again," a woman scoffed from across the room.

I glared at the women. I was *so* going to get her name and write her up. Was there some kind of ticket system? Could I fine her for being a jerk? Probably not. If that were the case I would have been fined for my crappy magic ages ago.

"Have you not noticed that Mr. Marcos' skills have greatly improved?" Jacobson flashed a smug smile.

He had me again. The facts were not going in Nicolas' favor at the moment. There had to be a way to prove his innocence, but at the moment I had no idea how that was going to happen.

I stood from the chair. "I think it's time for us to go."

"Aren't you going to take care of this?" Jacobson demanded.

I scoffed. "Am I going to take care of this tonight? No. Without looking into the facts and getting the truth? No."

He glared at me.

"What did you expect, Mr. Stratford? For me to find Mr. Marcos guilty tonight based on your version of the incident? That is not going to happen." I wouldn't allow him to have the upper hand.

"You are the leader now. This is your job to take care of this." He pointed.

"I will take care of it, but not tonight." I stepped closer to him. "And if you don't like it, well, then that is just tough." My finger was so close to his face it almost touched his nose.

Who did this guy think he was anyway? I wasn't a member of his Coven and I didn't have to answer to him. What would he do? Call my mommy? I wouldn't lie and say that my adrenaline wasn't pumping because of this confrontation, but it had to be done. I would not let him boss me around.

The group neared the door and I feared we would soon have a fight on our hands if we didn't get out of there. We were being surrounded. Did my leader of the Underworld status mean nothing? Apparently they didn't care. What had I gotten myself into? I wasn't sure I wanted this gig. One hour in and it was already a headache.

Nicolas and Liam followed me to the door. The energy changed in the room. It was thick like walking through a bag full of cotton balls. Was someone trying to cast a spell? I hoped they weren't trying any funny business.

"The allegations against me are false and you know it, Jacobson. Just because I'm a…" Nicolas stopped before finishing the sentence as if someone had stuffed a sock in his mouth.

"I should have known better than to allow vampires into the coven." Jacobson turned his lips up in a sneer.

Liam whipped around. "You didn't have a choice in allowing us to join."

Underneath the fabric of Liam's long-sleeved shirt, the muscles of his strong forearm tightened when I grabbed him. I pulled him toward me before the venom-laced words turned into a physical confrontation. Liam had said Jacobson hadn't had a choice in allowing *them* to join the coven, but only Nicolas was a vampire, right? There wasn't time to think about that now. We needed to abandon the meeting right away.

"Come on, guys. It's time to go." I motioned for the men to hurry.

As we walked out the door and down the porch steps toward the car, I felt the presence of the others right behind us. Magic flew across the night sky with silent stealth.

When I turned around, Jacobson's face at turned red and his eyes slits of rage. Within seconds, Jacobson slammed his fist into Nicolas' face. Nicolas grabbed Jacobson, throwing him to the ground. Jacobson hit the pebbled driveway with a groan. The men struggled, pounding each other while the rest of the group gathered in a circle and watched the fight unfold.

If I didn't act quickly, this could turn deadly. The men broke free for a second, but they stood in a showdown ready to pounce again. During a momentary lapse in judgment, I ran over and shoved my fist into Jacobson's stomach. His stomach muscles were harder than I had anticipated. In hindsight, I should have handled the situation in a more professional manner. But that Jacobson really set my temper on fire.

I shook off the pain in my hand as Nicolas rushed forward again. Thankfully, Liam jumped into action and pulled Nicolas off Jacobson. My other hand was spared the pain. I would have thrown another punch to the gut if needed.

Once the men had stopped throwing punches, they stood in a stare down. I was pretty sure I was supposed to say something at this point. But what?

"I want this to stop right now. If you touch him again, I'll have you arrested." I poked Jacobson in the chest.

Reflecting back on the situation at hand, my statement hadn't sounded very authoritative, but what was a newly appointed leader of the Underworld to do? Winging it through this was not the best way to go.

From out of the darkness, a figure emerged. The silhouette had come from around the side of the house.

This night couldn't get any stranger. One minute I'd been fighting off a demon and a crazy witch, and now it appeared I'd be fighting off a whole mess of crazy witches. But what was this thing walking out of the darkness?

As I watched with apprehension, the figure moved closer, appearing under the glowing lights from the plantation. The lights highlighted the features of this mysterious creature. Only it wasn't a *thing*, but a woman.

The woman was tall, with deep brown eyes and ebony hair that fell in waves just below her shoulders. She wasn't dressed as casually as the others. The dark-haired woman wore a long white gauzy dress. Her good looks didn't disguise the hatred shooting out from her eyes though. She looked from Nicolas, to Liam, and then fixed her stare squarely on me. I got the distinct impression that she didn't like me. But she didn't know me. What was her problem?

The woman walked by, not once taking her gaze off me. Finally, she stood beside Jacobson.

"This is my sister Sabrina," Jacobson said with a smirk.

Was I supposed to be impressed? So this was the woman whom Nicolas had turned. I eyed her up and down. She crossed her arms in front of her chest as she returned my scrutiny. A strange vibe danced around her and came off in waves. Was it magic? Did it have something to do with the fact that she was a vampire now too? I didn't know what this feeling was, but I wanted to get away from her as soon as possible.

"I need to question you about what happened." I directed my comment to Sabrina.

Jacobson stepped in front of his sister as a shield. "Like I told you, she's too upset to talk about it right now."

"She has to talk to me soon. There is no avoiding it," I said.

Sabrina's creepy silence was weird. All I wanted to do was curl up under the covers in my bed and sleep. I hoped every day as the leader didn't go like the first day had.

There had to be some job perks somewhere, but so far I didn't see a single benefit.

"I hope that monster is happy with what he did to her," Jacobson said.

"Like I told you before, I don't know what happened yet. Rest assured though, I will get to the bottom of it and let you know," I said through gritted teeth.

I couldn't make my statement any plainer for him. Jacobson Stratford was good at bullying, I'd quickly discovered. I'd dealt with my share of bullies though and he was no different from the others. As far as I was concerned, this meeting was officially over. I needed to get away from there and figure out what I was going to do next.

"I assume I will hear from you in the morning?" Jacobson's lips puckered with annoyance.

"You'll hear from me when you hear from me," I said as I climbed into the front seat of Liam's car and shut the door.

"Aren't you just the badass witch now," Liam said as he slipped behind the wheel.

Heat rushed to my cheeks. Never mind that my stomach was a giant tangled knot and I couldn't guarantee that I wouldn't be sick very soon.

"Hallie, I am sorry I put you through this. I had no idea that it would come to this," Nicolas said from the back seat.

Without turning around to face him, I said, "You had no way of knowing that I would be the leader of the Underworld and that this would happen."

Well, technically I guessed he had known if I possessed the Book of Mystics that I'd be the leader, but that was neither here nor there now.

It was nice of him to say that, but I was just surprised that he was actually speaking. His glazed-over eyes had been freaking me out the whole time we'd been in the home. It was dark in the car and I couldn't see his eyes now, but I hoped that he'd lost that strange look.

CHAPTER THREE

"That was one of the strangest conversations I've ever had. And I've had some weird ones lately." I leaned my head back against the headrest and released a deep breath.

"Jacobson Stratford has always been odd and his sister is right up there with him. Hell, the whole family is strange." Liam looked straight ahead at the dark road ahead of us.

"There are more of them? That's a scary thought," I said.

"Yes, there's another sister. Parents, cousins—like I said, they're all wacky," Liam said.

I massaged my temples. "I really don't know why we even came here tonight. It seems pointless. Couldn't they just have emailed me the details and let me get to the bottom of it?"

Liam chuckled. "They're not really the email type. Besides, I think they just wanted to meet you and intimidate you."

"And you brought me so they could do that? You acted as if they were going to hang Nicolas tonight." I couldn't hide the uncertainty in my eyes.

Liam had pulled me away from a passionate embrace with Nicolas earlier in the evening. I wasn't sure where things had been headed with Nicolas, but I knew that it had been the best kiss I'd ever experienced.

"Did they intimidate you?" Liam asked.

I contemplated his question. It wasn't an easy answer. "Did I act intimidated?" I passed the question back to him. Maybe I could come up with my own answer in the meantime.

He paused, then said, "As a matter of fact, you didn't seem intimidated at all. Remind me never to mess with you." He winked.

I bit back a smile. "Yeah, and don't forget it."

I might have acted unfazed by the whole thing, but on the inside I was freaked out. Who wouldn't be? Anyone would be lying if they said it didn't. Right now I just wanted to rest.

"You say that Jacobson has always acted weird. Do you care to give me an example?" I asked.

When I glanced in the mirror on the visor, Nicolas appeared to be sleeping, although he might have just closed his eyes.

"He is offended at every single thing, so I guess you can see that what happened to his sister is cause for a beheading," Liam said.

"Hmm. In his mind, I guess I can see that." I glanced back at Nicolas who still had his eyes closed. "To be honest, I don't know what to think. I don't know how I would feel if I was turned."

"The problem is whether Nicolas did it on purpose or not," Liam whispered.

I released a heavy sigh. I didn't want to continue the subject with Nicolas in the backseat. My heart told me that Nicolas' account was the truth, but my head told me to get all the facts first.

We traveled the dark and winding road in silence, each of us lost in our own thoughts, although it appeared that

Nicolas was sleeping. I must have drifted off to sleep for a brief time too because the next thing I knew we'd pulled up in front of LaVeau Manor.

LaVeau Manor had a long pebble driveway with an iron gate securing the entrance. The veranda spanned the width of the manor with large columns on each side of the outside staircase. Trees surrounded the perimeter of the property. LaVeau Manor was tucked away in a little world of its own.

The house didn't seem nearly as creepy when I was exhausted. When I got inside, I'd collapse into bed and worry about this mess in the morning when I could think clearly... well, when my thoughts were slightly less muddled.

The first drops of rain began to fall as we climbed out from the car and headed toward the front door. A slight breeze carried the scent of damp earth and fallen leaves. Nicolas stopped and stared up at the sky, as if he was looking for something.

"Are you okay?" I touched his arm and drew his attention away from the dark sky.

He stared for a beat, then said, "I'm fine."

"It's raining. Let's get inside," I said, grabbing his hand.

Okay, Nicolas was still acting out of it, but maybe he was just exhausted. Nevertheless, my heart ached seeing him like this. In the morning we'd have to talk—a serious one-on-one conversation.

Memories of when Nicolas had kissed me flooded my mind—his fangs grazing the soft delicate skin on my neck. I'd been vulnerable, and either I hadn't cared, or I'd been unaware of just how susceptible I had been. Nicolas had had plenty of opportunities to bite me, but he'd never done it. Whether he'd wanted to or not was something I couldn't answer, but he'd never acted on the urge if he had.

The inside of LaVeau Manor was just as imposing as the outside. Every room was trimmed with rich wood and intricate moldings. A large staircase swooped down as if it wanted to grab you and force you up to the other floors. Hardwood floors echoed each step through the house. Tall windows adorned each room except for the library. It was a dark space with wood shelves loaded with books. Even with several lamps in the room it was hard to read the books.

As we entered the foyer, Nicolas grabbed my hand and pulled me aside. His actions took me off guard, considering this was the first sign for the entire ride back that he was not just an empty shell.

He brushed my cheek with his finger. "How can I prove this to you?"

I wasn't sure what to say. This wasn't the type of thing that could be settled in an hour. "You did nothing wrong. We'll find a way to prove it."

My voice probably hadn't sounded convincing, but I'd given it my best shot.

Nicolas placed his full lips on mine and my heart sped up. I wasn't even sure if Liam had gone upstairs or into the kitchen, but why was I worried about where Liam was at this moment anyway? There was an unexpected hunger in Nicolas' kiss as he eagerly moved his mouth across mine. At least he was acting more like himself now. He gently sucked on my bottom lip.

Just as I'd erased the jumbled thoughts from my mind and given in to the pleasure of his kiss, we were interrupted by a loud rap on the door. Nicolas and I froze, both turning to gawk at the door. Who could it be? Not another bed-and-breakfast guest, right? I prayed it wasn't someone looking to take the Book of Mystics away. I'd hoped that I'd put that all behind me now. It seemed like ages ago that Nicolas and Liam had shown up at my door on that dark and stormy night. Well, actually Liam had shown up the next morning in the sunshine, but I digress. Nevertheless, it had been a scene right out of some silly vampire movie. As it turned out, Nicolas really was a vampire. How ironic was that?

There was only one way to find out who was on the other side of the door— answer it. I moved over to the door and peeked out. The rain was coming down steadily now. A man and woman huddled close to the door. They were exceptionally good-looking, like they'd stepped off the set of a soap opera. The woman had dark hair and the man had a thick head full of gray hair. Both were dressed in dark suits as if they'd just stepped out from a board meeting. They stared straight ahead as if they saw right through the wood and knew I was staring at them.

"Who is it?" Nicolas asked from over my shoulder.

"I don't know. A man and woman," I answered.

My best friend Annabelle Preston would freak out when she found out I had more guests. She was terrified of LaVeau Manor. It wasn't just LaVeau Manor that gave her the heebie-jeebies, all paranormal stuff really creeped her out. I couldn't say that I blamed her, although this Underworld stuff was turning out to be good for business. It was bad for my sanity, but perfect for filling up the empty bed-and-breakfast rooms.

One thing was for certain, I knew it was no coincidence that this couple had shown up on my doorstep. LaVeau Manor wasn't the must-see travel destination. I'd bet the last bit of cash in my purse that they were here because of the Underworld. I supposed I'd have to open up the door and find out what exactly they wanted. Couldn't they have waited until the morning? Didn't these paranormal people ever sleep?

"Is someone at the door?" Liam asked from over my shoulder as he stepped into the foyer.

Apparently, he had been in the kitchen after all.

Nicolas stepped around me and placed his hand on the doorknob. He wasn't going to give Liam a chance to handle the situation. Liam moved next to Nicolas, leaving me standing in the background. Hello. Who was running the bed-and-breakfast here? Nicolas peeked through the peephole for a second, then looked back at Liam and nodded. What was that supposed to mean? Was it some kind of secret code?

Nicolas opened the door and stepped to the side, giving space for the couple to enter. Maybe I didn't want them to enter. Had they ever thought of that?

"Good evening." The woman brushed the wet hair from her forehead and flashed a forced smile my way.

Good evening? That was easy for her to say. By the smiles and nods exchanged, I knew that this wasn't their first meeting. I just wished they'd hurry up and include me in their little club. Or did I? I was probably better off not knowing what this was about.

"We're sorry to drop in so late, but we figured we'd better get to Ms. LaVeau before something happened." The man looked at me and smiled, then winked at Liam and Nicolas.

Get to me? What did they want to do to me? Okay, enough was enough. I had to know what this was about.

"Hold on a minute. It seems everyone knows each other except for me. Maybe you'd care to introduce yourself?" I said, folding my arms in front of my chest.

"I'm sorry. My name is Miles Shepard and this is Nina Watson." He motioned toward the woman standing next to him. "We are members of the Underworld Committee. And on behalf of the Committee, we'd like to welcome you as the leader of the Underworld."

"It's a pleasure to meet you," Nina said, stretching out her delicate hand toward me.

A welcoming committee? How nice. What was next? A fruit basket?

I reluctantly stretched my hand toward Nina, then Miles. "It's nice to meet. Um, thank you for the welcome, I guess."

In spite of being tired and fantasizing about being in my comfortable bed, I decided to be a gracious hostess and invite the pair into LaVeau Manor. By the way they were looking around, it looked as if that was exactly what they wanted.

"Would you like to come into the parlor?" I gestured toward the room.

They both smiled widely.

"We'd love to," Nina said.

They seemed nice enough. So far they gave no indication that they wanted to kill me. Their attitudes were far from the way Jacobson had behaved. I wondered if they were witches, vampires, or some other paranormal beings. It didn't matter right now though. I'd save the small talk for another day. I still didn't know whether there was an actual Underworld or that was just what they called it. And they thought I was suitable to be their new leader? What a joke. I definitely questioned their method of choosing me as the one in charge. In my opinion, it was a flawed system.

When we stepped into the room, I motioned toward the sofa. "Please have a seat. Can I get you anything to drink?"

My mama hadn't raised a rude hostess. At least the caterers had cleaned up the mess from the Halloween Ball. It seemed like ages since that had happened instead of just hours ago.

Nina waved her hand. "No, thank you. We know it's late, so we won't take up too much of your time."

Smart woman.

"We just wanted to speak with you about the Underworld before you are called to look into any broken laws or other urgent matters." The corners of her mouth lifted into a wide smile.

"It's too late for that," I said matter-of-factly.

Nina's smile quickly faded. The room fell silent. Only the amplified tick-tock of the grandfather clock remained. Nina and Miles looked at Liam, then to Nicolas with wide eyes. Obviously my answer had taken them by surprise.

"She knows?" Miles asked Liam.

Odd looks were exchanged around the room. Was there something they hadn't told me?

CHAPTER FOUR

"If you're talking about what Nicolas did to the witch, then yes, I already know. We went to New Orleans tonight," I said.

The pair remained silent for a minute.

Nina stammered, then said, "Well, what happened?"

"As expected, Jacobson isn't happy." Liam folded his arms in front of his chest.

"Do you plan to consult the book for this?" Miles asked with curiosity.

I shifted in my chair. "I haven't really had a chance to read the book from cover to cover, but yes, I plan on it."

This book better have a whole lot of details because I needed them… like yesterday.

"So you do have the book with you?" Nina asked while scanning the room.

"Yes, it's in a safe place," I said.

It seemed as if they didn't trust me with the book. I'd been through a lot to hold on to it, I wasn't about to lose it now.

"We know this seems overwhelming right now, but we're sure you'll settle right into your new role," Miles said with a critical expression.

He didn't appear too confident about his statement. "Thank you," I said.

Miles cleared his throat and then said, "There is one other matter. In light of recent events, we feel it's best that you have protection right now."

I looked around the room at the faces staring back at me. "What do you mean protection?"

"Just like with the last leader, Liam would be assigned to protect you," Nina said.

"Why would I need protection?" I asked in a louder tone than I'd intended.

They wanted Liam to protect me? That meant that he would be around all the time. As I glanced at Liam's sexy face, his gaze locked with mine. This would not be good. Breaking free from his stare, I looked to Nicolas. He had that same far-off look in his eyes. It was as if he hadn't even heard what they'd said.

"Nicolas, are you okay?" I asked.

As if an alarm had gone off in Nicolas' head, he jumped up from his seat. "That won't be necessary. I'm capable of watching over Hallie."

Nina and Miles stared at Nicolas as if he'd just said he could fly. And not with a magical broom either.

"Nicolas, I can understand your concern for Ms. LaVeau, but Liam has a job to do," Miles said with a hint of challenge in his tone.

This was an awkward situation. Liam had been in charge of protecting Nicolas' mother when she'd been murdered. Nicolas' posture tensed and his arms remained still by his sides. I understood Nicolas' apprehension, but if I was reading his body language correctly, he didn't want Liam around me period. I had to admit I had my doubts too... about Liam protecting me of course. After all, the last person he was protecting was no longer here.

"You're not employed with the Underworld in that department. You'd have to be authorized first. That could take months and we don't have that kind of time," Nina said with a wave of her delicate hand.

"You don't want Ms. LaVeau to be harmed, do you?" Miles quirked a gray eyebrow at Nicolas.

Nicolas shook his head, then walked out of the room. I was sure the memories of his mother were flooding his mind. Should I run after him? No. He needed his space and a moment to collect his thoughts. Liam was staring out the window. He knew what we were all thinking—we were questioning his ability to protect me.

Nina and Miles stood.

"You'll let us know if we can be of any assistance?" Nina said as she shook my hand.

I nodded. "You'll be the first to know."

That wasn't true. I was too stubborn to ask for help. It was definitely a personality flaw of mine.

"Thank you again for accepting the job." Miles shook my hand again.

They hadn't left me much choice, right? I'd found the Book of Mystics, so the job was mine for the taking. But for all I knew, there were hundreds of highly qualified candidates for the position.

"Yes, it was a pleasure to meet you, Ms. LaVeau." Nina smiled.

"It was a pleasure meeting you as well. Thanks for stopping by so late," I said.

See, I really was trying to be polite.

After walking Nina and Miles to the front door, I released a heavy sigh and leaned back against the wood frame. Liam had stayed in the parlor, so I was alone in the foyer. The silence was only interrupted by the sound of the clock. Would it stay that way for long? Where had Nicolas disappeared to? I peered up at the stairs. Maybe he'd gone to bed. I needed to talk with Nicolas and Liam too.

When I returned to the parlor, Liam was still standing in front of the window. Something must have been very interesting since he'd been staring at it for so long.

I reached out and touched his arm. "Are you all right?"

He nodded, but didn't look at me. "I know you are concerned about whether I can protect you, but I promise you I won't let anything happen to you."

"I didn't think you couldn't protect me…"

Footsteps sounded from the foyer and I wondered if Nicolas had been listening. As much as I wanted to comfort Liam, I knew that Nicolas needed me more at the moment.

"We'll talk about this tomorrow," I whispered.

He turned to me and smiled softly. "Good night."

Liam walked out of the room without looking back. When I thought he'd had time to head up the stairs, I made my way to the foyer.

Nicolas flashed his gorgeous smile at me. "I thought maybe you'd gone to bed."

Maybe my mind was playing tricks on me, but had the blank look in his eyes disappeared? Why was his odd behavior coming and going?

"Without saying good night to you first? Never." He wrapped his strong hand around mine. "You know, we didn't finish our dance."

"No, I suppose we didn't," I said.

Nicolas led me into the parlor to the same spot where we'd shared the kiss earlier.

"I hope we're not interrupted this time," I said as Nicolas circled my waist with his hands.

Nicolas pulled me close and placed a soft kiss on my lips. "Me"—he kissed me softly again—"too."

This time the kiss wasn't light, but full of passion as his lips moved with urgency across mine. Whatever had been affecting him earlier in the evening apparently had passed and I hoped that it never returned.

I wasn't sure if he'd just freaked out from the stress of the situation or if something more sinister had been at work. I wished the night had ended this way. That it had never taken that bizarre turn. If only I could turn back time. But how far would I have turned it back? All the way before finding the book? Before Nicolas and Liam? Life had been simpler then, but then I wouldn't have met Nicolas and Liam. In spite of everything, I didn't think I would have changed a thing. Well, maybe I would have wished for only the good parts of the last few days—unfortunately that was never an option.

Breaking free from the kiss, he gently held me in his arms and said, "Thank you for being wonderful tonight."

I shook my head. "I don't think much of what I did was wonderful."

Nicolas placed his iPhone on the table next to us. After a couple of seconds, soft music drifted across the room. "May I have this dance?"

Nicolas and I swayed back and forth to the music. His hands skimmed down my back before coming to rest on my hips. As he held me tight in his arms, I tried to let my mind relax and be carried away by the moment, but my thoughts weighed heavy on my mind. We continued moving in sync to the music, back and forth to the rhythm. Nicolas' strong arms around me were comforting, but something was nagging at the back of my mind. I tried to ignore it, but I knew it was everything that had happened through the night.

I had to prove that he was innocent. Nicolas must have sensed my tension. He paused and searched my eyes.

"Is everything okay?" he asked.

I plastered a smile on my face and nodded. "Everything is perfect."

What a big fat lie. He probably knew it too. I was a lousy actress. He embraced me again and we continued dancing. As I rested my head on his chest, I inhaled and caught his warm masculine scent. The aroma was almost hypnotizing.

The first song had ended and another beautiful melody spilled from the tiny speakers. Unfortunately, just as I'd allowed myself to relax, my phone rang, breaking me away from the moment.

"Don't answer it," Nicolas whispered.

I thought about ignoring the incessant ringing, but if it was Annabelle or my mother they'd just call right back, thinking that something terrible had happened to me. I had to answer it.

"I'll be right back," I said, stepping away and grabbing my phone from the nearby table.

Nicolas groaned as I walked away. When I looked down at the phone, I saw Annabelle's number. She'd called several times. I knew this would be her last before she picked up her gigantic purse and hauled her butt over to the manor. She hated coming to LaVeau Manor, so I wanted to spare her that agony. But I had a lot of explaining to do about the night's latest events. I'd fill her in as quickly as possible on the key moments, then give the full details tomorrow. It was getting late and I really needed to get some rest. I stepped out into the foyer so that Nicolas wouldn't have to relive the events of the evening via my phone conversation with Annabelle.

"Hey, I tried to call you, but didn't get an answer. Is everything okay?" Annabelle asked suspiciously.

Annabelle claimed to have zero paranormal ability, but I wasn't convinced that was completely true. She had a bit of a sixth sense about stuff. She sensed things about the people she cared for. How would I begin to tell her what had happened?

"There was a bit of an issue after you left," I whispered.

"Why are you whispering?" Without taking a break for me to answer, she continued, "Did the demons come back? I knew it. I shouldn't have left you."

What did she think she could have done if she hadn't left? The demons were nothing to mess around with. I wanted to stay as far away from them as possible and she'd be wise to do the same.

"The demons didn't come back, but Liam did."

She sucked in a sharp breath. I heard the sound loud and clear through the phone. "Oh, dear. Did they fight?"

"No."

"So what happened then?" she asked.

"Nicolas has been accused of stealing another witch's powers and we drove to New Orleans so I could formally hear the charges against him."

"Get out. Tell me everything." Her voice echoed loudly through the phone.

After I explained what had happened, there was a long pause.

"So what are you going to do now?" she asked.

"Check back with me tomorrow and I may or may not have an answer for that." I chuckled nervously.

"Just please be careful." Annabelle's tone had turned serious.

I assured her I would, but that didn't necessarily mean much. It was kind of out of my control.

After hanging up, I rushed back to the parlor. When I stepped back into the room, Nicolas wasn't there. I looked over my shoulder to see if I'd possibly missed him, but he wasn't there either. Maybe he'd gone into the kitchen for a snack. There was still food left over from the Halloween Bash and none of us had eaten much. I was starved myself. If it hadn't been so late, I'd whip up a batch of cupcakes. I'd recently mastered a cupcake spell that produced drool-worthy sweet treats.

Nicolas' phone still sat on the table where he'd placed it, so I knew he couldn't have gone far.

"Nicolas?" I whispered. "Where are you?"

It was like playing a game of hide-and-seek, although I didn't think he was hiding on purpose. Had he overheard my conversation with Annabelle? I hadn't thought I'd said anything to upset him, but just the mention of what had happened might have been enough. When he didn't answer, I decided to check out the kitchen. I tiptoed across the room and to the kitchen door.

When I stepped into the room, Nicolas wasn't there either. Why did I have a surge of panic? That nagging feeling at the back of my mind was pushing its way to the front. I told myself that I was just tired. It had been a long night and I needed rest. Heck, it would be daylight before long. I stepped from the kitchen over to the dining room thinking that maybe he was in there eating. But once again the room was empty.

"Nicolas?" I whispered again.

Why was I whispering anyway? It wasn't as if anyone was in the room. Did I think he was hiding or something? Next thing I'd be checking under the tables. I'd look in all the rest of the rooms. If he wasn't downstairs, then he must have gone to his room. Maybe I'd been so consumed in my conversation with Annabelle that I hadn't noticed Nicolas slip up the stairs. He'd probably thought that our dancing time had ended when I'd spent so much time on the phone. In my defense, it had been hard to stop Annabelle from asking a million questions.

After searching everywhere downstairs, I made my way up to the second floor. Unless he was in my bedroom waiting for me, then I couldn't imagine why he would be on the second floor. When I opened my bedroom door, I was slightly disappointed to find that he wasn't waiting on the bed for me, but I digress.

I headed up to the third floor thinking that Nicolas was for sure already in his room. He was probably already fast asleep, exactly where I should be. When I noticed that his room door was open, I got a sinking feeling in my stomach again. This was really odd. I stepped into the space, but the room was empty.

I decided to check downstairs one more time. Maybe he'd gone outside for some fresh air. If he wasn't downstairs this time, I'd just go to bed. He probably needed time alone to think about everything that had happened. I couldn't say that I blamed him.

As I rounded the corner of the landing to head back downstairs, a noise sounded from down the hallway. Much to my chagrin, I knew it had come from that creepy attic. There was always some kind of creak or bang coming from that room. No wonder people had claimed a body was hidden in there.

When I stepped up to the little attic door, memories came flooding back—confusing memories of when I'd found the Book of Mystics. The book had been hidden in the attic along with a map leading me on a weird paranormal scavenger hunt. Did I mention that my Great-Aunt Maddy had been eccentric? The Book of Mystics was written in an unknown language. I still hadn't been told what it all meant. Maybe someday someone would be nice enough to clue me in.

I really didn't want to check the attic again, but since I'd looked everywhere else, I knew I might as well look there too. What harm could it do?

I opened the door just a little and peeked in. So far I didn't see anyone, but it was dark, so someone could be hiding in there for all I knew. I'd found Liam looking for the book in there one night so I wouldn't be surprised by anything I found in the attic. With some hesitation, I finally stepped into the room, but after looking around I saw nothing.

A musty smell hung in the air and cobwebs decorated the corners. A few boxes lined the wall to my left and a couple of brown vintage suitcases set to the right. An old wingback chair with a bureau pushed up next to it took up space at the back of the room. I didn't want to waste any time stepping farther into the space. If there was another ghost in there, well, they'd just have to stay there. I didn't want to know about it. I closed the door and headed back down the stairs.

When I reached the bottom of the stairs, Nicolas was standing in the parlor where I'd left him.

"Oh, you're here," I said with shock. How had I missed him? "Were you outside?"

He looked at me blankly. I stepped closer and studied his expression. Something seemed different again. That blank expression had returned, but that wasn't all— it was something else. I studied his face as he smiled slightly. Even his smile seemed different. When I looked down, I noticed a necklace around his neck. He hadn't been wearing it earlier. I definitely would have noticed something that gold and shiny. That was odd. I looked up at his face again, but he remained silent.

"I'm really tired. I think I'll just head off to bed." I gestured over my shoulder.

He nodded. "I understand. It's been a long day. I'll walk you to your room."

His voice even sounded different. This was not the Nicolas that I knew, but I followed him across the room anyway.

"Oh, wait. I left the spell book in the kitchen. I'll be right back." I held up my index finger indicating I needed a second.

Nicolas nodded. His silence was eerie. Once in the kitchen, I grabbed the book and hurried back across the house. When I stepped into the foyer, Nicolas wasn't there. Had he already gone upstairs? He'd said he'd walk me to my room, but had he changed his mind? I looked up to the second floor landing, but didn't see him there either. As I made my way up the staircase, a sound caught my attention. When I looked up, I spotted what I thought was a woman. What the hell? Who was in the house?

I rushed up the steep and winding stairs, trying not to trip and kill myself. The first thought that came to mind was that I had another ghost in the manor. Word had probably spread within the graveyards that I could reanimate the dead. How had the ghost gotten into the house though? I'd cast a spell to protect LaVeau Manor, although there was no guarantee that it had worked.

When I reached the second floor landing, I caught a glimpse of the figure again. The only thing visible was the back of her long off-white dress as she continued up to the third floor. Her gown reached all the way to the floor. I had to warn Nicolas that a ghost was coming his way, but she would probably reach him before I did.

"Stop," I called out.

Would Liam hear me and come running? I didn't want to startle him over something as simple as a ghost. The only harm she could cause was if I brought her back to life, right? And I had zero plans of doing that. It had caused nothing but problems when I'd done it accidentally. I sure wasn't going to do it on purpose.

The ghost didn't stop when I called out to her, but I hadn't anticipated that she would. It had been worth a shot though. I rushed around the landing, down the hall, and up the third flight of stairs. My day had been strenuous already, and now I had even more cardio. I would need an oxygen tank by the time this day was over. When I finally reached the third floor landing, I stopped in my tracks. There was no female ghost in sight. In fact, there was no ghost at all. However, Nicolas was standing at his door. His back was facing me.

"Nicolas, are you all right?" I asked.

At the sound of my voice, he turned around. That same blank look filled his eyes. Something was definitely wrong with him. This wasn't normal behavior.

He smiled that dazzling smile as if nothing was wrong, but that strange look in his eyes remained. He couldn't hide that no matter how hard he tried. "I'm fine. Just thought I'd get some rest. You should do the same."

"Did you see someone else up here just now?" I asked as I looked down the hallway.

He shook his head. "No, it's just me."

The ghost must have disappeared into another room. I'd have to check the empty rooms for her, but what if she'd gone into Liam's room? I'd have to warn him that a ghost might be lurking in the manor.

"I thought I saw a woman in an ivory-colored dress come upstairs. I'm almost sure of it." I sighed. "There may be another ghost in the house."

As soon as I found her I'd order her to leave. Or better yet, first thing in the morning I'd find a spell to force her out of the house. She couldn't hide out in here forever. I'd banished a demon; surely I could banish a ghost too.

"You're tired. Maybe you were just seeing things." He brushed my cheek with the back of his hand.

He was right of course. I was tired, but there was no way I'd imagined that, right?

Nicolas leaned down and placed his lips lightly against mine. The nagging feeling that something was wrong wouldn't go away. Even his kiss didn't feel the same. It didn't feel as if Nicolas was there. It was like I was kissing a stranger. I stepped back and stared Nicolas directly in his eyes.

"I need to go to bed now," I said, trying to act as if I didn't suspect anything was wrong. "I'll see you in the morning."

He smiled, then stepped into his room and closed the door. I'd have to talk to Liam about Nicolas' behavior and the strange look in his eyes. But first I'd check the empty rooms for the ghost, although she had probably disappeared to wherever ghosts go when they weren't making themselves visible. They retreated to some kind of in-between world, I supposed.

Once at the end of the hallway, I opened the doors to the other rooms and poked my head inside. The ghost wasn't there just as I'd suspected. The only other place left was in Liam's room. As tempted as I was to peek in there, I'd have to wait until morning to talk to him about Nicolas and what I'd seen.

After placing the Book of Mystics in my room, and finding no ghost, I headed downstairs to search for her. Now I was playing a game of hide-and-seek with a ghost. When I reached the bottom of the stairs, Liam was just stepping out from the parlor. A glimmer sparked in his eyes and he looked genuinely surprised to see me.

The air seemed thicker in the room. It didn't feel like only magic—there was something more. "I thought you were in bed already," I said.

"I couldn't sleep, but you need to get some rest." He ran his hand through his thick dark hair.

Had the ghost kept him awake?

"I need to talk to you about a couple things." I pointed toward the parlor. "Let's go back and have a seat."

He frowned. "Is everything okay?"

I looked over my shoulder toward the staircase. "I'm not sure."

Liam followed me back into the parlor. I sat on the large red velvet chair in front of the stone fireplace. He eased down onto the matching chair across from me. The only light came from the kitchen, so the room was dim. Since the parlor was massive in size, I'd placed two chairs in front of the fireplace to create a more cozy setting. I'd tried to make the parlor more casual, a place where I could hang out and watch TV. LaVeau Manor was so big though, it was hard not to feel as every room was part of a museum.

Liam shifted in his chair. "If this is about me being your bodyguard… I can see if they can find someone else for the job."

What was making him so anxious?

"No, no. It's not that. I want you to have the job. I trust you." I tried to reassure him with my eyes.

Had I just officially agreed to allow Liam to be around me all the time?

"What is it then?" His posture straightened and his muscles tensed.

"Did you notice anything strange about Nicolas tonight?" I searched his face for a reaction.

"More strange than usual?" he asked with a grin.

"I'm serious. Did you notice his eyes?" I waited for Liam's answer, but as I searched his eyes, I noticed he looked a bit odd as well.

What was happening? For a split second it felt as if I was frozen, as if held captive by his gaze. Liam's eyes glowed silver, then returned to bright blue. My lack of sleep was obviously catching up to me.

When Liam didn't answer, I continued, "Nicolas' behavior seems to have gotten worse as the night went on. There is a black, blank look in his eyes. I mean, he was quiet as soon as we left for New Orleans, but I think it got worse when we left the plantation."

"I hadn't really noticed, but I guess I wasn't paying attention." He frowned.

"Do you think it had something to do with the trip to New Orleans? Could Jacobson have placed a spell on Nicolas?" I asked.

Liam leaned forward and squeezed my hand. I sucked in a sharp breath. He must have noticed my reaction because he immediately released my hand.

Liam pushed to his feet and stood beside the fireplace. "It's definitely possible that Jacobson did something. I wouldn't put it past him, but we have no way of knowing what kind of spell he would have placed on Nicolas."

"I can't believe he would do something like that." I leaned my head back against the chair; I was beyond exhausted.

He shook his head. "I told you he has a screw loose."

I raised an eyebrow. "Then why is he the leader of the New Orleans Coven?"

He threw his hands up. "People love him. I guess he convinced them to look past his eccentricities."

"Well, I'm not going to look past them."

After a few moments of silence, Liam said, "I was close to Gina too. After my mother died, I lived with her sister, then after a time my father came for me. His new wife Gina, Nicolas' mother, was like a mother to me as well." Liam looked down at his black shoes.

"I had no idea," I said softly.

Why had I been so stupid? The realization hit me that something didn't add up.

"Witches live longer lives, but you've been around just as long as Nicolas." My heart rate increased. There was only one explanation for what I was about to ask. "You're a vampire too, aren't you?"

For a moment he didn't look up at me, then finally he met my stare. Fangs peeked out over his bottom lip. He nodded shyly.

"What the hell? Why didn't you tell me? This is how you tell me by exposing your fangs?"

"I came downstairs because I was hungry." He turned his head so I wouldn't stare at his fangs.

"You came down to get blood," I said.

"I thought you were in bed. I can only hide my fangs for so long. Sometimes they have a mind of their own."

I snorted. "I just bet they do. So that's why your eyes turned a different color just a second ago. I thought I was imagining things. Why do you both continue to be so evasive and not just tell me the truth?" I demanded.

I was more than a little frustrated with both of them.

"I didn't keep this from you on purpose. There was never the right time to tell you." Tenderness had slipped into his voice.

"Nicolas found the right time. You've been here as long as he has." I waved my hand through the air.

"I realize that," he said.

I ran my hand through my hair. "So that was what Jacobson meant when he said he shouldn't have allowed vampires into the Coven."

"Nicolas and I were both born witches before we were vampires. We have every right to be a part of the Coven." Liam paced in front of the fireplace.

"Were you turned by the same vampires as Nicolas and Gina?" I asked.

He nodded. "Yes… but Nicolas killed the leader of the vampire clan soon after it happened."

There was so much I didn't know about both of them. I wasn't positive that I wanted to know everything. For now, I'd let the subject go, but what other secrets were they keeping from me?

"Well, if Jacobson did something to Nicolas, he'll be sorry." I gestured wildly with my hand. "Wait. What can I do to him?"

Liam chuckled. "You're the leader now. That's something you'll have to decide." He held his hands up. "I have nothing to do with that."

"How the heck am I supposed to know what to do?" I asked.

"That's what the book is for. You need to consult the book." He leaned against the mantel.

I released a slow breath. "Yes, the book. I need to read the book. But who has time when they're fighting demons, demon witches, and traveling to New Orleans at all hours of the night?"

"So what else is wrong? You said the first problem was Nicolas. Is there another problem?" He crossed his arms in front of his chest.

I looked out across the room again. "Yes, I think there's another ghost in the house."

His mouth dipped into a frown. "Again? Did you put up a welcome sign out front?"

I scoffed. "Funny. No. I have no idea how she got in the manor."

"She?" Liam quirked his eyebrow questioningly.

"Yes, a woman wearing a long ivory dress with big puffy sleeves. I didn't see her face, just the dress as she made her way up the stairs. I thought she was following Nicolas. It was as if she was walking right after him. When I got to the third floor, Nicolas was standing at his door."

"What did you do then?" Liam asked.

"I asked Nicolas if he'd seen the ghost, but he said he hadn't. I checked the other rooms, but no one was there. You may want to be on the lookout for a female ghost. I plan on doing a spell in the morning to get rid of her." That was my plan all right, but I was more uncertain about my spell casting than ever.

"Just be careful." His expression grew serious.

What? He doubted my witchcraft skills still? I couldn't win. How would I ever prove myself to everyone?

CHAPTER FIVE

When the loud thud woke me, I rubbed my eyes and rolled over on my side. The clock beside my bed read four a.m. I sat up in bed. Looking around the room, I half expected to see another ghost. The other ghost that I'd reanimated had appeared in my room in the middle of the night. I figured it was a ghost thing.

The only thing visible in the room at the moment was Pluto's glowing green eyes. His black fur blended in with the darkness of the room. "Did you hear something?" I whispered to Pluto. He meowed as if answering yes. If he hadn't been on the bed with me, I would have blamed him for the sound. He had a way of protesting in the middle of the night when he was unhappy about something. Most of the time, he purposely waited until I was fast asleep before running laps through the manor.

Pluto meowed loudly again as if he had read my mind. I hadn't paid enough attention to him lately. His favorite fish treats would probably make him forgive me though.

Another loud bang sounded and I knew that it had come from downstairs. I contemplated ignoring the noise and covering my head with the pillow. Maybe whatever it was would go away.

But I had to know what was going on downstairs. After Nicolas' weird behavior and seeing what I thought had been another ghost, ignoring the loud thud wasn't an option. Slipping out of bed, I shoved my feet into my pink slippers and I headed down the staircase. It was probably nothing to worry about, right?

Once at the bottom of the staircase, I paused, listening for more noise. The rhythmic sound of that darn grandfather clock clicked in the background again. With a house that big it was no surprise that the slightest noise echoed off every wall. Just when I was ready to give up and go back to bed, the sound of footsteps caught my attention. Someone was walking in the library.

I tiptoed through the parlor and into the library. The woman in the ivory dress stood next to the tall bookshelves. I had hoped to see Nicolas or Liam, but no— it was the ghost. There was no denying that she was there. Her figure was translucent and a ring of white glowed around her. She had her back facing me. Was she perusing the many books lining the shelves? Her lace-covered dress looked like it was straight out of *Gone with the Wind* with a big hoop skirt underneath. Her dark brown hair was pulled up with rings of curls falling down on each side of her head. She didn't turn to look at me as I moved across the floor. I didn't think she'd even heard me. What would I say to her? Politely ask her to leave? Or demand that she get lost right away?

Who was I kidding? I knew I'd go with being polite. I really needed to toughen up and not be such a pushover.

"Who are you?" I asked.

It was the best happy-medium question that came to mind. To the point, but not too rude. Why was I worried about being rude to someone who had entered my home uninvited? I had issues.

Slowly the woman turned around. Thank goodness she hadn't been some hideous monster. I would have run out of the house like Annabelle. The beautiful woman appeared to be in her fifties with big brown eyes and round cheeks. She didn't seem startled by my appearance as she stared straight at me.

"Please forgive me for intruding, Ms. LaVeau." She clasped her hands together and flashed a warm smile.

Whoa. She knew my name. That hardly seemed fair.

"I'd feel more comfortable about your intrusion if you'd tell me who you are." A flicker of apprehension coursed through me.

She glided closer toward me and I contemplated running. You'd think I'd be used to ghosts by now, but I never knew when one of them would be a bad one. After dealing with Isabeau recently, I'd become more wary. She had been totally bad… as in *a demon* bad.

"My name is Gina Rochester. I need you to reanimate me."

Wait. I'd heard her name before, but where? After a couple seconds, it came flooding back to me. This was Nicolas' mother. She had been the leader before me. My stomach flipped. She'd probably come back to tell me what a terrible job I was doing.

"You're Nicolas' mother. I didn't expect for you to be dressed that way," I said.

She smiled softly. "This was always my favorite dress."

"Oh—" Was that all I could say? I sounded stupid.

"We don't have a lot of time. Listen closely. I've come here to help him. Normally, I wouldn't ask you to bring me back because there can be bad consequences, but in this situation I need to help him. He's in danger."

I knew the charges against Nicolas were serious, but I was the leader now. As far as I was concerned, he wasn't in danger. There was no way I would allow anything bad to happen to him. She didn't know me though, so she probably didn't trust me.

"You want me to use the spell book to bring you back?" Why was I repeating what she'd just said? Of course that was what she wanted. The fact of the matter was I didn't want to bring anyone back.

"My energy is fading, so I need you to do this soon. Since I'm newly passed, I'll have to be here in spirit in order for this to work," she said.

I wasn't sure bringing her back was such a good idea... but this was Nicolas' mother. Did I really want her haunting LaVeau Manor? I'd better just do as she asked. Besides, having her back to show me the ropes wouldn't be such a bad thing, right? What if she took her position as the leader back? I wasn't sure how I felt about that.

"My magic isn't that great. Well, it's improved a lot since I found the Book of Mystics. I can't guarantee that it'll work though," I said.

"I'm sure you'll be fine. The leader always performs the spells flawlessly. No matter how bad your magic used to be, I'm sure that is a thing of the past now." She managed a small, tentative smile.

She had no idea. That was a bet I wasn't willing to take. But what other options did I have? I had to try to bring her back.

"Why are you dressed like that?" I asked, looking her up and down.

"I told you, this is the way I looked when I was turned. This was my favorite period of clothing, so why not spend eternity in what you love, right? Now you have to hurry." She was clearly losing her patience with me.

I'd forgotten that Nicolas said they had been turned in the 1800s. According to what Nicolas had told me, the whole family had been turned. Nicolas' father had died before this horrific attack had occurred. Liam's mother had died when he was just a baby. A year later his father had married Nicolas' mother, and the following year Nicolas had been born. They were only a couple of years apart in age. I'd never realized that Liam had been turned at the same time. I'd assumed Liam would have told me if that had been the case, but I'd assumed wrong.

"I'll have to get the book," I said.

"Hurry, dear. I don't have much time," she pleaded.

She was right. Her time was obviously limited because her outline became more transparent as she spoke. After staring at her in disbelief for another couple seconds, I turned and rushed up the stairs to retrieve the Book of Mystics. The book had the spell which allowed me to reanimate the dead.

Once I reached my bedroom, I thought about waking Nicolas so that he could see his mother, but there wasn't time. She was fading fast and I had to perform the spell. With the book tucked securely under my arm, I rushed back downstairs to the library.

Gina was gone. My heart sank. I looked over my shoulder and around the room, but she had vanished.

My legs gave way and I fell to the floor. What would I do now? I'd let Nicolas and his mother down. How would I explain that I'd had a chance to bring his mother back but let it slip through my fingers? He would be so disappointed. Not to mention I had no idea what she'd meant when she said he was in danger.

Tears formed in the corners of my eyes as I sat in the middle of the floor. Crying wouldn't help me. I needed to suck it up and find a way to fix the situation—but sometimes tears cleared the way to reasoned thoughts. Letting all the emotion out paved the way for logic and plans. At least that was what I kept telling myself.

As I wiped the tears from my cheeks, the wind stirred. Softly the wind blew at first, but then it came stronger. Stronger the wind grew until my hair was whipping wildly around me. The pages of the Book of Mystics flipped rapidly. When the wind finally died down, the pages stopped, coming to rest at a spot in the middle of the book. The same thing had happened to me before with this book, and that was what had gotten me into this whole 'Leader of the Underworld' mess in the first place. So I doubted anyone would hold it against me if I said I was apprehensive about even looking at the spell on the pages in front of me.

Taking in a deep breath, I leaned over and looked down at the page. It was the same spell that I'd performed when I'd brought back the last ghost. That had been a disaster, but would this time be different? It was worth a shot to try it again, right? What was the worst that could happen? Hmm. I'd asked myself that question before and it had never ended well. What made me think this time would be any different? But just maybe I could still bring back Nicolas' mother.

Before I lost my nerve, I picked the book up from the floor and headed into the kitchen to gather the items I'd need for the spell. With any luck, I wouldn't mess up any other witches' spells. I'd caused many a spell to backfire over the years. That feat had earned me the Worst Witch title many times.

Stepping into the kitchen felt like entering my safe haven. Not that I could cook or anything, but there was something about all the spices and herbs that gave me hope... hope that one day I would be as good at witchcraft as my great-aunt. The kitchen was all shades of white with a large island in the middle. Apothecary jars lined every shelf to my left.

I placed the book on the counter, careful not to lose my spot. On one wall of the kitchen was a large stone fireplace. A big black cauldron sat in the middle of the fireplace. After filling the cauldron with water, I lit the fire underneath. As soon as the water began to bubble, it would be time to cast the spell. I had to be quiet so that I wouldn't wake Nicolas or Liam. I didn't want either of them to know what I was doing.

With any luck, within a few minutes, I would have brought Nicolas' mother back. He would be so happy. Maybe it would relieve some of the guilt from Liam too.

Rushing around the room, I grabbed all the spices that I needed. Once the water had come to a steady boil, I sprinkled the items into the cauldron. With each drop into the water, I intoned the words written in the spell book: "Bring the magic to me. Protection from all negativity surrounds me. Harm threefold to thee who sends destruction my way. All hateful actions directed toward me will be inflicted upon thee."

They were the words I'd used when I'd brought back the other ghost. But this time there were more words visible to the spell. Why had the extra words appeared this time? Perhaps that was why the spell had gone wrong the first time. All the necessary words hadn't been there.

I tossed in the last of the spices. "Bring the spirit near, it should not cause fear. From death I give life. Come forward from beyond. So mote it be."

Colorful lights swirled skyward from the cauldron, but after reciting the words, I realized this simply wasn't enough for me. There was no room for a mistake this time. I wanted to add my own words to the spell. Calling to the elements had helped me use the magic to my full potential before, and I needed all the help I could get for this important spell.

"Element of Earth, I call to you to allow the spirit to rise again. Element of Air, I call to you to push the spirit back to the manor. Element of Fire, I call to you for warmth and protection. Help me have the knowledge. Element of Water, I call to you for force and tranquility. Give the spirit the power to return."

The lights circled around me and my hair whipped around my face as a fiery wind blew through the kitchen. Smoke billowed up from the cauldron as the water bubbled, almost overflowing over the top. The smell of earth circled me, consuming the room. In a flash, the wind disappeared, the lights vanished and the earthy smell faded.

Releasing a deep breath, I looked around the room. It was the calm after the storm. Had the spell worked though? As if on cue, footsteps sounded in the library again. My heart beat faster and sweat beaded on my forehead. With any luck, the spell had worked and Nicolas' mother had now returned from the dead.

Not wasting another second, I rushed out of the kitchen and toward the library. When I reached the library door, I stopped so quickly that I almost fell flat on my face.

A woman stood beside the desk in front of the tall windows. She had one of the thick red velvet curtains pulled to the side as she peered out the window. It was too dark for her to see anything. The woman wasn't Nicolas' mother though. And she wasn't see-through either. She looked to be from the same era, maybe the late 1800s. The woman wore her hair in the same up-style as Gina with ringlets falling gently against the side of her face. Her hoopskirt dress was a beautiful shade of emerald green and black lace decorated the bodice. My stomach sank. I knew I was in trouble now. What had I done this time?

"Who the heck are you?" I asked, letting my politeness fly right out the window.

"You called me here to help, my dear." A huge smile spread across her face.

CHAPTER SIX

"No, I didn't call you here." I looked around the room. "I called Gina Rochester here. I don't even know you. What is your name?" I asked.

"My name is Catherin Butterfield." The sweetest of smiles curved her lips again.

"Well, it's nice to meet you, Catherin, but I don't know why you're here." I crossed my arms in front of my chest.

"I came here to help you. You called for someone to help you, right?" She waved her hands through the air. "So here I am."

Kind of like a fairy godmother, huh? Where had I gone wrong with the spell this time and where had Nicolas' mother gone?

"Yes, here you are indeed." I shook my head.

Of all the darn luck. I'd managed to mess up a spell again. But how? Nicolas' mother said I'd be fantastic with my magic now that I was the leader. Obviously, she hadn't known who she was talking to when she said that. But I'd gotten rid of a demon with my new magic. What had changed in such a small amount of time?

"Listen, you have to get out of here. You can't stay." I motioned toward the front door.

She shook her head. "No, I can't do that. I'm here to stay as long as you need help. And that could be a very long time."

"How did you know I needed help?" I asked.

"I am your great-great-great-aunt. My grave site is right outside." She pointed in the direction of the back yard.

In the rear of LaVeau Manor sat a small family graveyard where previous members of the LaVeau family were buried. My Great-Aunt Maddy was there too.

"I was the sister of your great-great-great grandfather… the famed alchemist. He built this home, you know? I lived here."

I looked her up and down suspiciously. Something didn't add up and I smelled a rat. Of course, maybe I was overly sensitive because the last ghost I'd brought back had really been a demon. Lightning probably wouldn't strike twice though, so I needed to just calm down. A clear head would help me work through this problem, I reminded myself.

She looked around the room. "So, where will I be staying?"

I released a heavy sigh and motioned for her to follow me. "Come on. I'll show you to your room."

There was no use fighting this and I supposed she was family. Plus, apparently this place had been hers originally. She was being very polite about this under the circumstances. Maybe she hadn't even wanted to come back and I'd forced her with my screwed-up magical ways. But it seemed as if I was no longer running a bed-and-breakfast for living, paying guests. In reality I was running a bed-and-breakfast for dead ghosts who didn't have two nickels to rub together. How would I pay the utility bill around this place with no income? Did they pay the leader of the Underworld a salary? Hmm. I'd have to look into that.

What would I do with this woman? It was more than a little embarrassing to ask Liam or Nicolas for advice considering I was the leader now and should know what to do. I'd show this ghost to a room, then find a spell to get rid of her. Well, in theory that was the way it would work.

"The home has changed quite a bit since we first built it... what with the new inventions and all." She looked up at the chandelier.

How did she even know about new inventions? But I imagined that it would be quite a shock to see the house after that many years.

As I ascended the stairs with Catherin following closely behind me, I asked. "What did the home look like back then? Are there a lot of other changes?"

"No, no, not that I notice." She didn't sound entirely convinced.

She hadn't even looked around when she said it. Now that I thought about it, why hadn't she asked to walk through the house and take a look around? I knew if I had built this place and hadn't been in it for years, I'd probably want to take a peek around.

But regardless of my uneasy feelings, I had to get her into different clothing. If anyone saw her they'd think I was putting on a Civil War reenactment. But most importantly, I wanted to keep her true identity a secret from Liam and Nicolas. Like I said, they didn't need to know just how much of a failure the new leader was.

Once at the end of the hallway, I turned toward the bedroom directly across from mine. It was the room where Isabeau had stayed and it was the perfect room to put former ghosts whom I wanted to watch.

"I hope you like what we've done with this room," I said as I opened the door.

I motioned for Catherin to enter first.

She smiled graciously and stepped across the threshold. The fabric from her long dress made a swooshing sound with her movements. "Thank you, dear. I'm sure I will love it."

"I just need to change the linens on the bed." I pulled clean sheets from the bureau.

"Please, allow me. It's no problem at all. I know you must be tired from your long day." She reached out and took the sheets from my arms.

I stopped in my tracks. "How did you know I had a long day?"

Her lips formed a thin line as if she was appalled that I'd asked her such a question. "You have bags under your eyes. It looks as if you haven't slept, so I assumed."

I stared for a beat, then said, "Oh, well, I'm sorry. I guess I've just been on edge lately."

She patted my arm. "It's understandable. You must have been through a lot."

"By the way, I think we should keep the little mishap that brought you here a secret. Okay? We'll just tell my two other guests that you're a paying guest, okay?" I nodded, hoping she'd go along with my story.

She looked down at her dress. "I think this will be a dead giveaway, no?" Her mouth twisted at the sides at her presumably unintended pun.

I motioned over my shoulder. "I'll see what I can find for you to wear."

When I reached the door, I paused with my hand on the knob. Now that I thought about it, Catherin hadn't even mentioned my name. Had she really known who I was, or was she a complete fake? My paranoia really had reached extreme levels.

"How did you even know who I was? I mean, I could have been anyone. You just assumed I was Halloween LaVeau. How did you know you are my aunt?" I asked.

She chuckled. "You are a suspicious one. But I understand your trepidation. I'm not around just because I was a ghost. We can come and go as we please."

"So you've been in the house before?" I asked.

"Why yes, of course," she said sweetly.

"You just said you couldn't believe how things had changed in the house." I crossed my arms in front of my chest, waiting for her to get out of that one.

"That isn't a lie. I couldn't believe the changes. That doesn't mean I hadn't seen them before." A forced smile crossed her lips.

Well, she had me there. That was a good explanation. Maybe I was being too hard on her. She probably was there just to help. After all, I was the one who'd messed up and brought her here.

"I'm sorry for being so suspicious. Please forgive me," I said.

She focused her attention to the bed linens and looked away. "You're forgiven. Think nothing of it."

"If you need anything else, I'll just be right across the hall." I gestured.

She nodded. "Thank you, dear."

I closed the door and leaned against the wood, releasing a deep breath. This was an absolute disaster. There was no way I'd get back to sleep after all that had happened. Besides, it would be time to make breakfast in just a couple hours. I hurried across the hall to my room and grabbed my cell phone. Annabelle would be upset with me for calling her at this hour, but she should be used to the craziness from me by now.

My bedroom had a large mahogany bed in the middle of the room placed against the far wall. The walls were a cream color. To the left of the door was a floor-to-ceiling bookshelf where I displayed my small collection of witch figurines along with my large book collection. I'd taken a gorgeous deep purple velvet chaise from one of the other bedrooms and placed it by the window in my room.

The white down comforter on the bed called my name. I sat on the bed and hit redial. Just when I thought Annabelle wouldn't pick up, she answered with a groan.

"Oh, Annabelle. You're not going to believe this," I said.

"Are you kidding me, Hallie? I would believe anything out of you at this point. The most important question right now is are you okay?" Worry colored her words.

"Yeah, I'm fine. Well, I think I'm okay… but something else happened." I rushed my words.

"What happened this time?" The excitement in her voice increased.

After explaining about seeing the ghost of Nicolas' mother, casting the spell, and then the wrong ghost showing up, there was silence at the end of the line. I couldn't believe it, but I'd finally left Annabelle speechless.

"Talk to me, Annabelle. What do you think? Should I trust her?" I asked.

"You truly are a magnet for trouble," she said.

"Don't remind me. Are you coming over for breakfast?" No doubt I would need help dealing with Catherin.

"I have to tell you, Hallie, all these ghosts really are freaking me out. I mean, I knew the place was creepy before, but now…" Fear crept in to her voice.

"What? No, the house is fine. Really. Besides, I guess Catherin seems innocent enough. She's kind of like a sweet fairy godmother come to help me solve my problems, now that I think of it," I said, trying to sound casual.

She snorted. "Yeah, right. She's your evil fairy godmother maybe." Annabelle sighed. "I'll be over soon. But I'm just coming into the kitchen. Maybe the dining room, but that's as far as I go, okay?"

"Okay, it's a deal. I'll see you soon," I said.

I really needed to work on Annabelle's phobia. Maybe there was a spell for that. No, I didn't want to jeopardize my friendship. If I messed up a spell on Annabelle, she'd never forgive me.

As I made my way downstairs to prep for breakfast, a thought popped into my head. Catherin had said she was buried in the back yard. Her grave would be there. If her name wasn't on one of the tombstones, I'd know right away that she was lying to me.

Once I made it to the kitchen, I stepped out under the canopy of the darkened sky and headed toward the old graveyard located at the edge of the property. Tall moss-covered oaks ringed the cemetery, shading the graves and making the grounds even spookier. The sun hadn't popped up yet, so I had to watch my step as I trailed through the grass—had I mentioned how spooky it was out there? No wonder Annabelle found even the outside of LaVeau Manor scary. Spooky movies could be filmed on location at LaVeau and they wouldn't have to change a thing.

The sensation of being watched followed me everywhere I went. I hoped a ghost or other creature didn't step out of the shadows and come after me. The sound of water lapping against the edge of the earth carried across the air.

It was hard to believe that a short time ago I'd been fighting for my life in that water. Mara had wanted the Book of Mystics so she could be the leader of the Underworld. We'd battled in the backyard, and when I'd run out of places to run, I had been forced to jump in the water. I'd been known to use a water noodle as recently as last summer, so that had been no easy decision on my part.

I'd seen my Great-Aunt Maddy in the old graveyard too. She'd reminded me of my new powers of the elements. If it hadn't been for her, I probably would have drowned. Would she appear to me now? I could really use more advice right about now.

A black wrought-iron fence surrounded the graveyard. I pushed my way through a curtain of Spanish moss and stepped through the little gate and looked around at the aged tombstones. The names and dates had faded on most of them. Where would I even begin to find Catherin's stone? I'd have to look at each and every one. The sun had yet to pop up, so my visibility was low. I pulled my phone out of my pocket and clicked on the flashlight.

As I stepped through the graveyard, navigating the uneven terrain, I stopped at each stone, holding up the flashlight to read the names etched in the stone. Most of the markers ended with the last name LaVeau. But there were a few other names that I didn't recognize. I wished I'd taken more of an interest in my ancestry now. I'd always planned on researching the graves sometime in the future, but I hadn't gotten around to it yet.

With each passing grave, my apprehension grew. What would I do if Catherin's name wasn't on one of these stones? I'd have to find a spell right away and try to get rid of her. Maybe I'd have to break down and ask for help from Liam and Nicolas. But Nicolas didn't appear to be in any shape to help. Asking for help was one of the things I liked doing the least. I wanted to be able to handle all of this on my own.

I reached the last row of graves and had almost given up hope on finding her tombstone, when I saw it. On the stone was the name Catherin Butterfield. Born 1813 and died 1865. The epitaph read: *We shall meet again.* A huge weight of relief had just been lifted from my shoulders. I'd found her grave site, but it was creepy nonetheless.

A cold breeze blew across my skin like a whisper from the dead. Dizziness overwhelmed me and then there was blackness.

CHAPTER SEVEN

The sound of my name being called out caught my attention. When I looked around I realized I was lying on the ground next to the grave. How the heck had that happened? Had I blacked out? The last thing I remembered was looking at Catherin's grave. The sun had just begun its rise, illuminating my surroundings. I'd probably been out for at least thirty minutes. How could I have missing time?

Maybe I'd fallen asleep. Was that possible? After climbing to my feet, I brushed the dirt from my clothing and hurried out the old iron gate and toward the house. Annabelle was standing on the back steps waiting for me. Her blonde hair glistened in the sunlight.

She rushed over to me. "Where the hell have you been?"

I brushed more dirt from my arms, then gestured over my shoulder. "I was in the graveyard."

"What? Buried in the graveyard?" She looked me up and down.

I glanced down at my hands and clothing. It looked as if I'd tried to dig up a grave with my hands. "Maybe I fell and hit my head."

"What happened?" She grabbed my arm and led me to the house.

After stepping inside the kitchen, I sat on one of the stools next to the center island. "I decided to look in the graveyard for the new ghost's headstone."

"And what happened?" Annabelle asked, handing me a towel, and then sitting next to me.

I ran my hand through my hair and pulled out a dead leaf. "It was still dark when I went out there. I had my phone as a flashlight." I felt my pocket. To my relief, my phone was still inside. "Anyway, I looked though the whole cemetery."

"But you didn't find her grave?" Annabelle asked with widened eyes.

I shook my head. "No, I found it at the back. But just as I found it... I blacked out, I guess."

Annabelle frowned. "What do you mean, you must have blacked out?"

"I don't remember anything after looking at her grave. The next thing I knew, the sun was up and I heard you calling for me. It must have been about thirty minutes." I attempted to run my hand through my tangled hair.

"So you think you hit your head?" she asked, touching my head.

"Well, I don't remember hitting my head, but what other reason would there be for me blacking out? I don't remember being dizzy. And there was a low-hanging branch," I said.

"Maybe you should go lie down?" She furrowed her brow.

I shook my head. "No way. I need to take a shower, then make breakfast."

She scrunched her nose. "You go shower and I'll make breakfast."

Annabelle never hid the fact that my cooking abilities were lacking. Since my magic had improved, I'd resorted to cooking via magic spells. Sure, it was cheating, but that was better than eating burnt pancakes. Annabelle slipped a ruffled floral apron over her T-shirt and jeans and motioned for me to go away.

Nicolas and Liam were obviously still sleeping since I hadn't heard any movement coming from the third floor. My bigger concern at the moment though was Catherin Butterfield. All I wanted to do was get to rid of her as soon as possible. Right after breakfast I was definitely casting a spell to send her back to the grave.

While in the shower, I thought back on what had happened in the cemetery. It was very disturbing to think that I'd been out there in the middle of the graveyard passed out like I'd crawled home from an all-night college party. Since I had no other explanation, I had to assume that I'd either fallen asleep and not remembered, or bumped my head. Either way, I hoped it never happened again.

All this magic and running around was cutting into my routine. Dirty laundry overflowed from my hamper and my cupboards were bare. After finally finding a half-decent clean pair of jeans and a blue sweater that I hadn't worn since senior year of college, I slipped on the clothing.

Next, I needed to find something for Catherin. I sifted through my closet, but there was nothing that looked remotely like something she'd wear. She would have to settle for modern clothing. I decided against the sweats with *Juicy* written on the butt though. Something told me she wouldn't appreciate that. I pulled a pair of brown slacks and a cream-colored silk blouse from their hangers and headed out the bedroom door.

The faster Ms. Butterfield came out of her room, the sooner I could cast a spell and push her into the afterlife permanently. I knocked softly on the door, but before I'd even lowered my fist, the door swung open.

"Hello, dear," Catherin said with a wide smile.

She was awfully bright and cheerful for so early in the morning. A morning person. Ugh.

I held out the clothing to her. "This won't be a style you're used to, but it was all I have. I've missed laundry day for a while."

"I'm sure it'll be fine. I wouldn't want to embarrass you with my old-fashioned clothing," she said, gesturing toward her dress.

"Oh no, you're not embarrassing me at all. I just want you to be comfortable." And to hide the fact that she was a ghost from Liam and Nicolas, but I left that part out. But who was I kidding? The truth would slip out and it probably wouldn't take long either. "Please come down for breakfast when you're ready. My friend is here and she's preparing food for us."

"Isn't that lovely. You must be starving from your walk," she said while studying the blouse I'd brought her.

I froze on the spot. "How did you know I'd been outside?"

She smiled sweetly. "I looked out the window and saw you, dear."

"Oh yes, right. Well, whenever you're ready," I said, still not convinced.

As I turned to leave, a crash rang out from downstairs. I dashed away from the door and down the hallway. I hoped that Annabelle was all right. The sound of running footsteps sounded from above me, then Liam bounded around the corner, almost smashing right into me.

His eyes were wide. "Are you okay?"

"I'm fine. The sound came from downstairs. Annabelle is down there," I said breathlessly.

Liam rushed around me and down the stairs. I must have been slower than I thought because as I ran down the stairs, Nicolas caught up with me. It was good to see that he was awake, but the guilty feeling of knowing I had allowed his mother to slip away came flooding back.

"Are you okay? What happened?" he asked.

He sounded like Nicolas, but when I looked into his eyes, they had that now-familiar blank stare.

"Annabelle is downstairs. She must have knocked something over," I said, searching his eyes for answers.

Before he answered, another loud crash rang out. When we reached the bottom step, I noticed the front door was wide open. Nicolas and I ran over and out onto the veranda. Liam stood on the front driveway, but he wasn't alone. Jacobson Stratford was there and he had his arm around Annabelle's throat. She was trying to scream, but he was cutting off her airway.

"Let her go now, Jacobson," Liam demanded.

"I'll let her go when you turn over Mr. Marcos." He yanked Annabelle tighter as she tried to escape.

This had gotten totally out of hand. What would I do now? I was the leader and I had to think of something. Pronto.

"Jacobson, I demand that you release her right now, or I'll be forced to strip you of your witchcraft powers. You'll no longer be the leader of the New Orleans Coven." I shot daggers at him with my eyes.

Where had that statement come from? I wasn't even sure I could do that. But the words had just popped into my head and it sounded like the right thing to say at the time. Annabelle's terror-filled face was killing me. I knew she hated the paranormal stuff anyway. She'd tolerated it because we were best friends, but that friendship was in serious jeopardy at the moment.

The magic's energy was waiting to be unleashed. The power zinged through the air. Who would be the first to cast a spell? I was scanning spells in my head, trying to think of one that would work the best to get Jacobson to release Annabelle.

"This is your last warning!" I pointed and a furious wind blew around Jacobson, almost knocking him to his feet.

I couldn't believe that had actually worked. For a nanosecond I glanced at my finger in shock. Why hadn't my magic worked when I'd cast the spell to bring back

Nicolas' mother? Maybe it was the rush of adrenaline that coursed through me at the moment. With the way I felt, I could've probably lifted a truck off someone right now.

As if he'd lost control over his actions, Jacobson released Annabelle. She stumbled up and ran over to the veranda where I stood. I wouldn't have blamed her if she'd jumped in her car and driven away.

I grabbed her arm. "Are you all right?"

"Yeah, that lunatic just popped up in the kitchen and snatched me from behind." Annabelle rubbed her neck.

Annabelle was safe at the moment, but now I had another problem on my hands. Liam and Jacobson tumbled to the ground. Liam smashed his fist into Jacobson's face. Jacobson viciously swung his right arm, but Liam easily ducked the blow. I clearly had no idea what being a leader of the Underworld meant. Things had spiraled out of control.

By the time I rushed over, Jacobson had managed to slip away from Liam. He rushed over to his car, spewing a few colorful words on his way.

"Jacobson, as your leader I demand that you leave the premises right away." I pointed at his car. "I'm calling an emergency meeting with your Coven. I'll be at your home this afternoon at three."

He actually looked stunned that I'd called him out like that. Having the meeting this afternoon would give me time to consult the Book of Mystics for the proper procedure on a situation such as this.

After a long tense pause, he turned on his heel and climbed into his black Ford sedan. Jacobson didn't look up as he turned the ignition and sped down the driveway. A disaster had been averted. The situation was under control for the moment, but how long would that last?

Liam and Nicolas stood together, talking in a hushed tone. I'd never seen the men that quiet in any discussion they'd had since I'd met them. Were they discussing their next move against Jacobson? Whatever. I needed to check on Annabelle. She sat on the veranda step, rubbing her neck where Jacobson had had her in a chokehold.

"Who was that?" Annabelle asked.

"Jacobson Stratford is the head of the New Orleans Coven. His sister is the one who accused Nicolas of turning her into a vampire and he's not too happy about it," I said matter-of-factly.

She nodded. "Well, that makes sense."

It was good to see that she hadn't lost her sense of humor after I'd almost gotten her killed. "I'm really sorry about what happened. I had no idea he would show up. How did he get into the house?" I asked.

"I guess I left the kitchen door open. He grabbed me from behind," she said softly.

"Well, it won't happen again. You have my promise." I squeezed her in a big hug.

After making sure that Annabelle was still okay, I left her sitting on the step and approached Nicolas and Liam.

I ran my hand through my hair and let out a deep breath. "That man is clearly unstable. What am I going to do?"

"You did exactly what you should have done. Since he grabbed her from behind he probably thought Annabelle was you," Liam said.

I brushed a strand of hair off my face and exhaled. "I hadn't thought of that, but I guess you're right. This takes it to a whole new level."

"I'm assuming you'll consult the books before the meeting that you just called?" Liam studied my face for a reaction.

Yeah, yeah, the book. Apparently everything I needed to know was in the book. That had better be the truth or I was in deep trouble.

I changed the subject and asked, "What have you two been talking about?"

Liam shrugged his shoulders. "Not much. Maybe I'd better let the two of you talk."

I looked from Liam to Nicolas. Something was going on and I knew I was getting ready to find out what. From the grim expression on their faces, I had a feeling I wasn't going to like the news.

Once Liam had stepped away, I touched Nicolas' arm. "Are you okay?"

That seemed like the question of the morning. Nicolas had moments when he seemed normal, then he'd zone back out again. I had to get to the bottom of this behavior. I had a strong suspicion that it had everything to do with Jacobson. As far as I was concerned, his magic days were over. I'd find a way to stop him from hurting others with his powers.

"I am so sorry for what happened, Hallie." Nicolas looked down, avoiding my stare.

"It wasn't your fault. You didn't know he would come here." I grabbed his strong hand.

"I had an idea that Jacobson would try something crazy. I shouldn't have allowed this to happen." He touched my cheek. "I have to leave. Jacobson will only cause more problems for you and Annabelle."

CHAPTER EIGHT

My mouth opened in shock. "What? That isn't the way to handle this. You just need to let me figure everything out. Okay?" I asked.

"It would be easier if I took off. I'll get things settled and come back. You'll be fine here with Liam." Nicolas ran his hand through his hair.

Okay, this was bizarre. There was no way Nicolas would say that. What was going on with him? Maybe he really had forgiven Liam for not protecting his mother, but something still seemed off.

"You guys were at each other's throats and now you trust me here with him?" I asked.

"Like I said, Jacobson will just come back for me. If I'm here, that won't be good for you," he said.

"Do you keep forgetting that I'm the leader now? You should have faith in my abilities to control the situation," I said.

I searched his eyes. He appeared to be staring at me, but I just wasn't sure.

Finally, he nodded. "You're right. But if he comes back, I'll have to leave."

"I'll be the judge of that," I said. "Come on. Annabelle was making breakfast. I'll finish it up and we can sit down and discuss our next move."

I grabbed Nicolas' hand and led him back toward the veranda. A new problem had popped up. Catherin had Annabelle and Liam's undivided attention. Had she revealed my little secret? How long would I be able to keep this secret from Nicolas and Liam? They weren't the only ones keeping secrets.

"I see you've met my new guest," I said, as I stepped up onto the porch.

Annabelle and Liam smiled. I couldn't read their expressions though. It wasn't clear if she'd told them about what I'd done. As soon as breakfast was over, I would pull out the spell book and banish her back to the great beyond.

Catherin's lips curved into a big smile revealing little dimples on each cheek. Looking at her sweet face made me feel guilty that the thought had crossed my mind. It was like kicking your grandmother out on the street.

"Mrs. Butterfield was just telling us about her famous blueberry pancakes." Liam rubbed his hands together. "I can't wait to taste them."

"I didn't get a chance to make the breakfast," Annabelle offered.

"Well, it's understandable after what happened to you." Catherin winked at me. "I told them that I'd make breakfast this morning. You all have been through so much."

Had Catherin witnessed the attack by Jacobson? In the midst of the action, I'd forgotten about Catherin and what she must have thought.

"I can't let you make breakfast. You're a guest," I said with a forced smile.

"Nonsense. Think nothing of it. I wouldn't have it any other way," she said with a wave of her hand.

Annabelle grabbed Catherin's arm and led her into the house. "I'm starving."

Liam walked closely behind them, so I held Nicolas' hand and led him into the house. This was odd. Apparently Catherin had charmed Liam and Annabelle. No matter. Catherin still had to go.

"I'll just go shower and be back down in a few for breakfast," Nicolas said with a sweet smile.

I nodded. At least his speech and behavior was better.

As Nicolas disappeared up the stairs, Liam approached. "So, how did everything go?"

"Did you know he intended to leave?" I whispered.

Liam shook his head. "He asked me to watch over you."

I stared for a beat, then said, "So that's what you all were talking about. What did you tell him?"

"I told him I would," he said.

"Don't you think that's my decision?" I asked.

"Of course it is, but what could I say? I figure he's a grown man and can make his own decisions."

"Well, yeah, but this is a little more complicated than that. Jacobson has it in for him. Don't you think we owe it to Nicolas to protect him from this?"

Liam let out a slow breath. "Of course we do."

My thoughts were a tangled mess. Nicolas had been acting weird and I had to figure out what had happened the night he turned Sabrina. Maybe the way he was acting now was nothing new. He could have been out of it when he attacked Sabrina.

"Nicolas still isn't right. Don't you think we should find out what Jacobson did?" I asked.

Liam nodded. "Yes, I do."

"And aren't you concerned about him?" I asked.

Nicolas was his brother, for heaven's sake.

"I'll do everything I can to help you figure out what's going on," Liam said.

Without answering, I turned around and headed for the kitchen. Liam followed closely behind me, but he didn't say another word. He had to sense my frustration.

When I reached the kitchen, Catherin was carrying plates stacked high with the most scrumptious-looking pancakes I'd ever seen. Blueberries filled the tops of the pancakes and were scattered around the plates. Blueberry syrup oozed down the sides of the cakes, coming to rest in a pool of sweet blue liquid. My mouth watered just looking at them.

Catherin smiled widely when she saw us. "You're just in time. Would you like orange juice?"

My gaze honed in on the pancakes again with a laser-like focus. It was as if Catherin had the carrot and I was the horse. I was practically drooling; I had to have those pancakes. I followed her into the dining room.

As we sat around the large wood dining room table, I momentarily forgot about my current dilemmas as I inhaled the pancakes. With each bite I slipped into my own little heavenly world. When my fork scraped the plate, I knew that the end had come.

I stared at the empty plate sadly, then finally realized what was going on. Catherin had probably used magic to make the pancakes so scrumptious. Catherin was trying to trick me into allowing her to stay. She probably suspected that I was ready to send her away.

"So where are you from, Catherin?" Liam asked as he shoved a forkful of pancake into his mouth.

Uh-oh. I grimaced. I wanted to keep them from talking to each other. Annabelle frowned when she noticed my expression. She was probably under Catherin's spell as well. This little grandmother had swooped in and mesmerized everyone. It would take more than delicious blueberry pancakes to get to me though.

"I'm from Biloxi, Mississippi." The words rolled off her tongue.

She was really good at the lying thing.

"Where are you traveling to?" Liam asked, then took a drink of juice.

"I'm just visiting the grandchildren in Enchantment Pointe," she said in a sweet grandmotherly voice.

When Liam and Annabelle weren't watching her, she winked at me.

She was sneaky, but I'd give her bonus points for not spilling my little secret. Maybe I'd let her stay for an extra hour.

Annabelle pushed to her feet. "Hallie, can I speak to you for just a moment?"

I looked at her suspiciously, then said, "Sure."

I followed Annabelle out into the kitchen. What did she want? Was she angry about what Jacobson did?

"Hallie, I know the look in your eyes," Annabelle said

"What are you talking about?" I asked.

"You can't get rid of her. She's a doll. What could she possibly do that is bad?" Annabelle asked.

"You've let her sweet-talk you." I pointed.

Annabelle shook her head. "That's not it at all. Just let her stay and if something happens, then you can get rid of her."

"It might be too late to get rid of her if she does something really bad," I said.

"I just have a feeling on this." Annabelle pleaded with her eyes.

"According to you, you never have a feeling about anything, so what makes now different?" I studied her face.

"Well, I do have feelings about things. What about that time I had a feeling about the lottery numbers? I won, didn't I?" She placed her hands on her hips.

I sighed and nodded. "Yes, you were right about that, but it only paid five dollars."

"But I was right," Annabelle pushed.

"I'm just sayin'." I shrugged.

"What do you say? Let her stay. She can help out around here. And you need help right now," Annabelle said.

She definitely had a point there. I wondered if Catherin knew how to work a washing machine?

I shook off the thought. "I can't ask her to help me around here. That would be rude."

"I'd love to help you," Catherin said from over my shoulder.

I whipped around to find Catherin standing behind us.

"How long have you been standing there?" I asked.

"Long enough to know that you need my help." She wiggled her finger. "I told you I could help you."

Catherin had told me that, but I didn't think she'd meant with my day-to-day tasks. Did she have magic in mind? And speaking of magic, where was Nicolas? It had been more than enough time for him to shower and dress. My stomach turned. Had something happened to him?

"I need to check on Nicolas," I said, rushing down the hall.

Hurrying through the massive rooms of the manor, I finally made it to the staircase. Footsteps sounded behind me, but I knew Annabelle wouldn't come upstairs with me. It still creeped her out up there. She liked the idea of being close enough to an exit door so she could run when needed.

I climbed the stairs as fast as I could. Just when I thought the long trip up the stairs was over, the third flight came into view. Why had they needed to add a third floor anyway? I sucked in a deep breath and huffed my way up the remaining stairs. Nicolas' door was open when I reached it and my heart sank. I had a feeling that he wouldn't be in there. There was only one way to find out. I rushed into the room and looked around. His bags were gone, but there was a note on the bed. He'd even taken the time to make the bed.

I picked up the paper from the comforter. The note read:

Hallie, I'm so sorry for the problems I've caused you. I'll be back when I've righted my wrong.

What was he thinking? He wasn't making my job any easier. Now I had to worry about what he was doing. Would he go to New Orleans? I had to tell Liam. As I turned around to head downstairs, I bumped into Liam's chest and sucked in a breath.

"Nicolas left a note," I said breathlessly.

He took the note from my outstretched hand and read.

"Where do you think he went? Would he go to New Orleans?" I asked.

Liam's mouth set in a grim line as he nodded. "Yes, I think that might be where he'd head to first."

"We need to go there," I said.

And I'd thought I'd have time to look over the Book of Mystics for answers. I'd have to wing it yet again. Maybe now was the time to tell Liam about seeing Nicolas' mother? There wasn't time though. I'd tell him in the car on the way back to New Orleans.

"You're coming with me, aren't you?" I asked.

"I'm your bodyguard, aren't I?" Liam grabbed my hand.

"So I've been told," I said.

When Liam and I returned downstairs, Annabelle and Catherin were standing in the foyer talking. Annabelle was nervously twisting a strand of her hair around her index finger.

I handed the note to Annabelle. "Nicolas left. We think he went to New Orleans."

"What are you going to do now?" Annabelle asked, peering down at the paper.

"Liam and I are going there. We'll get to the bottom of this problem once and for all. I can't put it off any longer," I said.

"I'm coming with you," she said, handing the note back to me.

I stared in disbelief. "What? You can't. It wouldn't be safe. Jacobson already attacked you once."

"You all need someone else to drive. You need to keep all your strength," she offered.

"She does have a point," Catherin added.

"It may be best if she does come with us," Liam said. "After what happened, I can't guarantee that Jacobson or one of the other Coven members won't come after Annabelle again just to get to you."

Okay, now they were ganging up on me. But Liam had a point and I didn't want Annabelle in any more danger. I hated leaving Catherin here alone though. I still didn't trust her.

Catherin must have read my mind because she said, "I should come on the drive with you."

Liam frowned. "I don't think that's such a good idea."

"I think it's a great idea," Annabelle said with a smile.

"We're wasting time talking about this. We need to be on the road," I said.

Without looking back, I locked the front door and we all hopped into Annabelle's car and took off down the driveway. This was one sad-looking group going to defend Nicolas. I was pretty sure that Liam hadn't signed on to be the bodyguard for all of us. I'd left him with little choice though. I had no idea what was in store for us, but it probably involved a fight or ten.

CHAPTER NINE

Tension hung in the air as we drove the same stretch of highway as the night before. It was slightly less spooky in the daylight... but only slightly. The temperature had turned cooler, but that was fall in Louisiana. One morning it might be forty-five and the next it might be eighty. I rolled the window down a little to enjoy the crisp fresh air. Usually I wore a t-shirt under my sweater so that I could peel it off when the sun started blazing down. Thoughts of what was in store for us flooded my mind. I couldn't believe that I was going to confront one of the largest covens. And I was dragging a little old lady and my best friend along with me to do it.

My phone rang so I pulled it out from my purse. I'd used my cell phone number on all the bed-and-breakfast advertising, so I never knew how to answer the phone—a simple hello, or LaVeau Manor? I went with "Hello?" this time.

"Is this Halloween LaVeau?" the soft female voice asked.

As much as I wanted a normal guest at the moment, I also didn't want to bring someone into the weird stuff that

I had going on around me. I'd have to tell this woman that I didn't have a vacancy.

"Yes, may I help you?" I asked.

"I was told that you're the new leader of the Underworld." Her voice wavered.

Wow. How had she gotten my number? Was it listed already? I wasn't sure how to answer. Was this a trick question? Was Jacobson responsible for this call?

"May I ask who is calling?" I tried to keep up the professional tone.

I figured I'd get her information before answering her question.

"My name is Ginny Love. I own a bar in the French Quarter." She paused. "Anyway, I have some information about the recent event involving Nicolas Marcos."

Well this was a turn of events that I hadn't expected. What could she possibly have to tell me?

"Yes? What information?" I asked with curiosity.

"I need to speak with you in person." Her voice faltered again.

What did I say to that? No? I had to know what she was talking about. What if she knew something that would keep Nicolas out of danger?

"Can you give me your address?" I reached down and pulled a pen and paper from my purse, then scribbled down the address.

"How soon can you be here?" Her voice lowered.

"Is he in danger?" I asked.

"He could be, but I just need to speak with you in person," she said.

Something about this conversation was making me very uneasy. But I had Liam with me, so he could help if I got into a dangerous situation, right?

"I'll be there as soon as possible," I said.

"Please hurry." The phone went dead.

"That was an interesting call," I said as I clicked off the call.

Liam glanced over at me. "What's going on? Who was that?"

"Do you know a woman named Ginny Love?" I asked.

"I've heard of the name, but no, I'm not sure that I know of her," he said.

"She was very cryptic. All she would tell me was that she has information about Nicolas and that she needs to see me in person."

He glanced over and frowned. "You told her we would come there?"

"I don't think I have any other choice." I let out a deep breath.

"No, I don't think you do have any other choice. You should definitely go." Catherin seemed to have an answer for everything.

She'd obviously been listening to my conversation from the front seat and had her own opinion.

"She's right." Annabelle nodded. "You have to find out what she wants."

It looked as if I would be going whether I wanted to or not. Good thing I wanted to.

"Where is this place?" Liam asked.

"A bar in the French Quarter called The Graveyard."

"A vampire bar—." Dread lingered in Liam's tone.

***

After another thirty minutes, we'd made it to the French Quarter. Historic buildings with iron balconies lined the streets. People walked up and down the sidewalks. A man played his saxophone in front of a little café. Enchantment Pointe never had this much activity.

"Have you ever been to this place?" I asked as we drove through the streets of the French Quarter.

"Yes, I think I've been in there once. Like I said, a lot of vampires hang out there. The wilder vampires like to go there," Liam said.

He'd waited until we were almost there to tell me this? Why hadn't he mentioned this earlier? That would explain a little bit of why this woman had information about Nicolas. But was this just a setup by Sabrina? After all, she was a vampire now too.

After finally finding the street, Liam found a spot up front and pulled along the curb.

Liam shoved the car in park. "Maybe you should let me go in first. I can check things out and make sure it's safe."

I shrugged. "Okay. Whatever you think is best."

Liam jumped out of the car, but only took a few steps before he turned around and motioned for me to get out of the car. "On second thought, I don't want to leave you all alone in the car. You all have to come in with me."

This woman was really going to think I had a bizarre security detail—a handsome guy, a pretty blonde best friend, and a grandmother. We were an odd match.

The place was dark and a shock to the eyes after coming in from the bright daylight. When I finally adjusted my vision, I spotted a woman behind the bar, wiping off the counter. She looked up when we approached. The smell of stale beer permeated the air. Shelves of liquor lined the wall behind the bar. Mirrors behind the shelving reflected the varying bottles, making the space appear much larger than it actually was.

"We're here to see Ginny Love." I looked around the bar.

She gestured with a tilt of her head. "She's in the back room. You can go on back there if you'd like."

We moved into the back section of the bar. Liam led the way with Catherin being the caboose in our odd little train. The room was filled with small loveseats in the corners and tables with wooden chairs in the middle of the room. At the back of the room was a small stage. I supposed this was where they had the live bands that the sign out front had advertised performed five nights a week.

At first, I hadn't noticed anyone in the room, but then I happened to catch a glimpse of a dark-haired woman sitting at the back in one of the booths. She wore dark blue jeans and a white blouse. When she spotted us, she jumped up and headed our way.

As she hurried over, I stood with my hand out. "You must be Ginny Love? I'm Halloween LaVeau."

The woman took my hand in hers and shook rapidly. "It's such an honor to meet you."

Before now no one had ever been this excited to meet me. Now everyone was being polite and nice to me. Well, everyone but Jacobson and his Coven. Just because I'd found some stupid book too. Why hadn't they been polite before? All of a sudden now I was special? That was far from the truth.

"It's nice to meet you too." I spoke the words, but until she told me what she knew about Nicolas I wasn't sure if it really was nice to meet her.

"This is my… my…" I looked at Liam and scowled. What should I call him?

He stuck out his hand. "I'm Ms. LaVeau's security."

That was awkward. I'd just thought of Liam as a friend. But I guessed there was no room for friendship right now.

"And these are my friends, Annabelle and Catherin." I gestured at the women.

How else would I introduce Catherin? *Oh, this is a ghost I accidentally brought back and now she's stuck following me around to strange places with vampires and witches.*

"Please, let's have a seat." Ginny pointed at the table closest to us.

"We really don't have long," I said, as I pulled out a chair and sat down.

Liam, Annabelle and Catherin all pulled out chairs and sat around the table. Ginny paced around the table and twisted her hands.

"So, can you tell me why you invited me here?" I asked.

Ginny looked over her shoulder. "Nicolas Marcos was here last night." Her voice was barely above a whisper.

"Are you sure you saw him?" I exchanged a look with Liam.

She nodded. "He was here last night. He sat in the front at a table with another man and woman."

I shook my head. "You must be mistaken. It must have been someone who looked like him. He couldn't have been here yesterday. He was an hour away at my place all day."

She twisted her hands again. "No, no. I heard them call him by name."

"What did they say?" Liam asked.

"I don't know what the conversation was with Mr. Marcos. I couldn't hear that part. It's what happened before he left that has me upset."

"What happened before he left?" I asked, leaning forward in my chair.

Her hands and legs were shaking. I knew this wasn't normal behavior and she was acting fidgety. For what must have been the hundredth time she glanced over her shoulder. Who was she looking for? Her heels clicked loudly against the floor as she paced back and forth. I glanced at the others. Annabelle frowned and Liam shrugged his shoulders.

"Ask her what's wrong," Liam mouthed.

I supposed it was my job to get to the bottom of things. She paused when she turned around, realizing that we were all watching her.

I met her stare. "Are you there's nothing else you need to tell us?"

She opened her mouth as if she was about to speak, but then she stopped and turned around again. She paced the length of the floor. How long would this pattern continue? I was about to get up and leave, but I thought I'd give her one more chance. To my relief, she finally turned around and marched toward us. She pushed her shoulders back and stood straight. After releasing a deep breath, she stepped closer.

"There's something I need to tell you." Her voice was low and she looked over her shoulder again.

"Yes." I pleaded for her to continue with my eyes.

"I didn't want to get him in trouble," she said with disappointment in her voice.

"Who didn't you want to get in trouble?" I asked.

Liam leaned forward in his seat, clearly interested in what she had to say.

"Nicolas," she said, looking down at the floor.

"Nicolas?" I asked with surprise. "Why would you be getting him in trouble?"

"Because of what he did," she whispered, avoiding eye contact with me.

"We don't know that he turned that woman," I said defensively.

"No." She shook her head. "Not that. It was something else."

My stomach turned. I wasn't sure I wanted to hear anything else.

"What else?" I asked cautiously.

She looked from me to the other faces staring at her, then met my gaze again. "He turned someone else this morning," she whispered.

CHAPTER TEN

I grabbed the table to brace myself against the dizziness. Liam jumped up from his seat.

"What are you talking about?" My voice shot up.

Her face turned white. "One of the waitresses was helping their table and he just jumped up and bit her neck. After he was finished, he dropped her and walked out the door."

"You mean not everyone working here is a vampire?" I looked over my shoulder.

She shook her head. "No, and it hasn't been a problem until now."

"What happened after that?" Liam asked.

I was still in shock and had apparently momentarily at a loss for words. I was pretty sure the leader of the Underworld was supposed to keep it together, but what could I say? I hadn't expected this turn of events.

"Like I said, he left. We grabbed her up and brought her to the back room." Ginny gestured toward a little hallway on the left.

No wonder she'd kept looking over her shoulder.

"How is she?" I finally found my voice.

Ginny shrugged. "She's doing okay, I guess. I'll know more later today on how she's handling it."

"I'm really sorry that this happened," I said.

Why was I apologizing? As the new leader of the Underworld I guess I thought it was my responsibility to make sure everyone behaved.

"Can you take me to her?" I asked.

She hesitated, then said, "Sure, she's in the back room."

"Are you sure you want to see her?" Liam asked.

I nodded. "I'm sure."

"She'll probably be out of it. She was resting the last time I looked in on her. I gave her blood, but she didn't want it," Ginny said.

I swallowed hard. "I want to see her."

Ginny turned and motioned over her shoulder for us to follow.

"We'll just stay here," Annabelle said with trepidation.

I nodded. That was probably for the best.

Liam and I followed Ginny down the long hallway. The walls were covered with photographs of patrons and employees enjoying different events at the bar. There were a lot of photos from Mardi Gras, some photos from Halloween, and other photos from ladies' night events.

The dimly lit hallway seemed to drag out forever, like an endless tunnel.

"It's the last room down this hall. I put her in my office," Ginny said.

"What do newly turned vampires do?" I whispered to Liam as we headed down the hall.

"Well, no two vampires will handle it the same way," he said.

I knew Ginny was trying not to listen, but with her right in front of us it was impossible.

"Some people just want to sleep for days. Those are the easy ones. But others just want blood and they can't get enough. They can be difficult. It's like feeding a baby every twenty minutes. Only the newly turned vampire isn't cute like a baby."

I nodded. "I can see your point."

We made it to the end of the hall and Ginny paused with her hand on the doorknob. "Are you ready to go in?" she asked.

Okay, she was making me nervous. It was like she was about to open a lion's cage. Should I be prepared to run?

I inhaled a deep breath. "I'm ready."

She eased the door open and my adrenaline level spiked. The room was dark except for the glow from a little lamp that sat on a table in the corner. A desk was against the far wall with a chair in front of it, and a leather sofa was up against the wall to the right. The woman was lying on the sofa with her eyes closed. It looked as if she was sleeping, but how could I be sure? For all I knew, if I got close enough, she would attack me. Maybe she would blame me for Nicolas' actions. Remnants of dried blood covered her neck and the puncture wounds stood out as reminders of the violent attack. This was all too real now. There was no denying that she had been attacked and apparently everyone had seen Nicolas commit the act. Maybe I hadn't known Nicolas at all.

The victim's brown hair reached to her shoulders and she looked to be around twenty-two or three years old. But I always had been terrible at guessing ages. I wondered if she was one of the quiet ones. If she had been in there sleeping for hours, then it sounded like she matched the description of a quiet one. But I needed to talk to her. I needed to hear the words from her mouth. Had Nicolas really attacked her?

"She was a very sweet girl. I just hope this doesn't change her."

I glanced over at Ginny. "You mean this could change her personality?"

Liam scowled. "No, she'll be fine. Don't put ideas in her head." He scolded Ginny. "If she was sweet before then she'll be sweet afterward."

Ginny shrugged. "If you say so."

She didn't sound convinced. Maybe she was just being dramatic though. I chose to believe Liam. What he said sounded like a much better scenario.

"Is it okay if I speak with her?" I asked.

"If you think you can get her to answer. Go right ahead." Ginny motioned for me to move closer. Why did I feel the need to find a big stick and poke this woman from a safe distance? Okay, if I was going to be the leader then I needed to toughen up.

"What's her name?" I asked.

"Marisa Hanley," Ginny answered.

I stepped closer, but the woman didn't move. "Excuse me, Marisa," I said weakly.

I didn't want to poke her, but it didn't look as if she was going to come around if I didn't.

I reached out and shook her shoulder, then immediately snatched my hand back before she had a chance to bite it. Liam snorted and I scowled at him. Her eyes remained closed. When I reached out to shake her again, her eyelids popped open. She glared at me and jumped up to a seated position, backing up on the sofa. She looked as if she wanted to get far away from me.

I held my hands up in surrender. "I'm not trying to hurt you. I just have a couple of questions about what happened."

Her complexion was pale and her eyes were wide as she stared at us.

"Who are you?" Marisa finally asked.

Ginny answered for me. "This is Halloween LaVeau. She's the leader of the Underworld. She takes care of problems with the paranormals."

Marisa looked at me strangely for a moment. "Well, she'd better take care of that beast who attacked me," she spat.

"That's what I'm trying to do," I said.

"He should be locked up," Marisa said.

"Can you tell me what happened?" I asked trying to sound as sympathetic as possible.

"There's not much to tell. I went over to leave the bill for their drinks and he jumped up and attacked me. I didn't have time to get away or anything." She ran a hand through her hair. "I've worked here for a long time and never had a problem until now."

"So I hear," I said, letting out a deep breath. "So everyone saw him do this to you?" I asked.

Marisa scowled. "Of course they did."

I nodded.

"Look, I was attacked and it was totally unprovoked. So what are you going to do to him?" she asked, looking me right in the eyes.

Talk about pressure. I had no idea how to answer that question.

"First I'll have to find him," I said.

"Well, you'd better hurry before he does this to someone else." She rubbed her wounded throat.

She was right about that. If everything she said was true, then I had to stop Nicolas. As much as it would hurt, I had to save another innocent person from being attacked by him.

"Are you going to take care of him?" she asked.

I nodded. "I'll take care of it."

It was a good thing she hadn't realized that I was just telling her what she wanted to hear. Of course I would try to take care of it, but I couldn't make any guarantees.

"Thank you for talking to me, and again I'm sorry about what happened."

Her expression softened a little. "Thanks. Now who is going to give me some blood?" Marisa's softened appearance changed instantly as she looked around the room with a wild-eyed expression.

Uh-oh. I felt the need to cover my neck. It sure wasn't going to be me.

"I'll take care of her," Ginny said with exasperation. "Just give me two seconds." Ginny shook her head. "She's a very demanding one. She was always so quiet before."

Ginny looked at Liam as if to say, *I told you so.*

"We'll see ourselves out. Thank you," I said.

I couldn't get out of there fast enough. Every time I looked at that woman I envisioned Nicolas on some wild rampage attacking everyone in sight. That certainly wasn't the Nicolas I'd known.

Liam and I stepped out into the hallway and I glanced over my shoulder. To my relief, Marisa wasn't following me.

"What do you think?" I asked Liam as we walked back down the hallway toward Annabelle and Catherin.

He shook his head. "None of this makes sense. If you're asking me if I think Nicolas did this, then I'll say no, but it looks as if he did."

"Maybe it wasn't unprovoked. I know she said it was, but how do we know any of these people are telling the truth? Heck, they could be lying about Nicolas even being here," I said.

Liam glanced over at me. After a second, he said, "That's true. I'd never thought of that."

"As far as I'm concerned, Nicolas is innocent until proven guilty. But we need to find him so we can ask him for the truth," I said.

"It isn't like him to run away or abandon a situation. He's a stand-up guy. Nicolas always takes care of his responsibilities, so that's the opposite of what they're saying about him," Liam said as we moved down the hall.

"That's why I said I didn't think he did this," I said.

When we stepped out into the larger room again, Annabelle and Catherin were still sitting at the round table.

Annabelle noticed that we'd returned and gave me a pleading look. Catherin was talking and it looked as if she'd been chatting nonstop since we'd left. Annabelle clearly needed to be rescued.

"Ms. LaVeau?" Ginny hurried toward us.

By her expression it didn't look as if she was about to deliver good news. I wasn't sure I could handle more bad news right now.

"There was one more important thing," she said when she approached.

"Yes?" I asked, dreading what she was about to say.

"The woman who was at the table with Nicolas?" Ginny said.

I nodded.

"Once Nicolas had left, she said that they had to get rid of Nicolas… and you." Ginny pointed at me.

My stomach turned. I immediately thought of Sabrina and Jacobson. But it couldn't have been them because they hated Nicolas. They would have just taken him out right there and then instead of sharing a few beers with him. Besides, Nicolas would never meet and talk with Jacobson and Sabrina.

But the strangest part about this whole scenario was how Nicolas had been here last night when I knew for a fact that he had been at LaVeau Manor. That was when it hit me. A glamor spell. Someone was obviously pretending to be Nicolas. Alas, this opened up the unfortunate possibility that it was *my* Nicolas who was fake, and the real Nicolas was the murderous psychopath.

I'd even done it myself once. It was a long story, but I'd wanted to discover the truth about Liam and Nicolas, so I'd taken on Nicolas' appearance in order to get Liam to talk to me. It hadn't turned out as planned, but who would be pretending to be Nicolas and why? Especially when the man and woman he'd been talking to wanted to kill him. This was all so confusing.

"You have no idea who this man and woman are?" Liam asked.

His expression had taken a serious turn, which didn't help my anxiety. Annabelle looked as if she might be sick at any moment. Oddly, Catherin seemed cool and calm.

Ginny frowned. "I'm not sure."

She didn't sound convinced about her last statement.

"Are you a witch, Ginny Love?" I asked.

I hadn't sensed any magic when I came into the bar, so my guess was no. I hated to pull out the fact that I was the leader now to her, but she needed to confess. I hated using titles and ranks. It seemed weird.

She frowned. "No, I'm a vampire."

"You know you need to tell me the whole truth? If I find out you're lying or withholding important information, then I'd be forced to take some kind of legal action," I said.

Ginny scrunched her brow. Yeah, she probably knew that I was totally making all this up as I went along. But she couldn't prove it, so that was to my advantage.

Finally, she said, "They were witches. I heard them mention the New Orleans Coven. But that's all I know, I promise." She held her hand up as if under oath. "I mean, would I have called you if I didn't want to help?"

"I've learned to assume nothing," I said.

"Thank you for the information, Ginny. I appreciate it and you did the right thing." I offered a small smile.

"You won't tell anyone that I told you, will you?" she asked with wide eyes.

I shook my head. "I won't say a word."

We made our way out into the main part of the bar again. As I neared the door, a woman touched my arm, stopping me. She had the same nervous expression on her face as Ginny. The woman wore the bar's blue logoed t-shirt and jeans. A hint of a gold necklace peeked out from under her collar. Her brown hair was pulled back in a ponytail.

"Are you the new leader?" she whispered, looking around the bar.

I looked her up and down. "Yes, I'm Hallie."

Liam stepped between us.

"I don't mean to interrupt, but I had to tell you." She glanced around again. "I had to tell you about the man and woman."

I eyed her suspiciously. "The man and woman who were here talking to Nicolas Marcos?"

She twisted the end of her ponytail around her index finger. "Yes, I overheard them talking."

"Thank you, but Ginny just told me about it." I smiled warmly.

"Did she tell you who the woman was?" she whispered as she looked around again.

I stared at her for a moment. "No, she said she didn't know."

The woman nodded. "Ginny probably doesn't remember who she is, but I take care of a lot of tables here in the bar and I remember a lot of people."

"Wait. So you know who this woman is?" I asked, looking over my shoulder.

This woman had me paranoid now.

She leaned against the table. "Her name is Janet Brock. She's a witch who lives just across town. It's an old house next to a swamp. I don't know the address, but I could draw you a map."

"Yes, please. That would be wonderful," I said.

Liam grabbed my arm. "I'm not sure we should go there. We don't know how many people are there."

The woman waved her hand. "Oh, no. She lives there alone."

"How do you know her?" Liam asked.

"She's been in the bar before. It was a couple times and I waited on her both times. She was kind of talkative. Anyway, she told me that she lived alone."

"So how do you know where she lives?" Liam pushed.

She shifted from foot to foot. "I'm not proud of this, but she told me that I could have some of her witch's blood. I wanted to see if it worked and she said she needed the money."

Apparently witches' blood gave vampires witchcraft power. Not as much as a witch possessed, but something was better than nothing.

"So you went to her house?" I asked.

She nodded. "Yeah, but when I got there she had changed her mind, which was just as well because she made me nervous."

"Why did she make you nervous?" Annabelle asked in a shaky voice from over my shoulder.

She shrugged. "It was just a vibe I got. You know how sometimes people just don't seem on the up and up?"

I nodded. I knew that feeling all too well.

"Did she speak to you when she was in here last night?" Liam asked.

"No. She acted as if she didn't know me. That was fine with me though. You know, she'd been in here alone before. That's why I was a little surprised to see her speaking with the man and then Nicolas," she said.

"But she was definitely talking with Mr. Marcos and another man?" Liam asked.

She grabbed a napkin from the bar and pulled the pen from behind her ear. "I'm one hundred percent positive. I'll draw a map for you. Sorry I can't remember the name of the street."

"Do you have any idea why she was talking with Nicolas?" I asked.

After drawing out a sketch, she handed me the napkin. "I heard the same thing as Ginny. Janet and the man said they wanted Nicolas and you dead."

I looked at her. "Why are you telling me this?"

Her expression darkened. "I thought it was the right thing to do."

I nodded. "Well, thank you."

"Please be careful," she called out over my shoulder.

As we walked toward the door, Annabelle asked, "How do we know she's not setting you up?"

"She's right. We could be going right into their trap," Liam said.

"Well, that's the chance I have to take. What if she has information about Nicolas?" I threw my hand up. "Heck, what if she has Nicolas there?"

Liam stared for a second. "All right. But I go check it out first. I'll leave my gun with you. If anyone approaches and tries anything to harm you, you'll have to use it."

CHAPTER ELEVEN

We made our way out of the bar and into the bright sunlight. I shielded my eyes until they had a chance to adjust.

"You still haven't explained how vampires can go out into the sunlight," I said as we hurried toward the car.

"We take a pill," Liam said without glancing over at me.

"You take a pill?" I asked suspiciously.

"We don't really have time to go into the basics. Annabelle, I can drive if you'd like," Liam said.

"Gladly," Annabelle said, handing over the keys.

"The least you can do is explain to me what kind of pill. Do all vampires take it?" I asked.

"Leave it to you to be interested in how this works now," Liam said.

I chuckled. "Hey, I need something to keep my mind off what may happen when we get to this house."

He paused, then nodded. "You're right. Okay, well, vampires discovered quite some time ago that there was something in beets that allowed us to go into the sun."

I snorted. "Beets?"

"I know it's not glamorous, but it is what it is," Liam said.

"So how does this translate to a pill?" I asked biting my lip to fend off a giggle.

"They made the beet extract in pill form," Liam responded quickly.

"Of course." I shook my head.

"Does that explain enough?" He avoided my puzzled stare.

"Enough for now, I guess. Anyway, about Nicolas, I think it was a glamor spell that was used," I said as we approached the car.

"That makes sense, but who is pretending to be Nicolas?" Liam asked.

"The better question is why are they using the spell to pretend to be him?" I opened the car door.

"Oh, a glamor spell. I remember those." Catherin waved her hand.

She'd been quiet since we stepped out of the bar.

I looked at her and frowned, as if to say, *Not now.*

Had I been crazy for bringing her along? To answer my own question: Yes, I had been completely bonkers. She kept pushing her grandmotherly charm on us.

Catherin gave a little smile, but didn't say anything else.

"We need to go to this house right now to find out," I said, climbing into the passenger seat.

"All of this is making me nervous," Annabelle said from the back seat.

"Oh, don't worry, dear. Halloween is the leader now, I'm sure she has everything under control," Catherin said with a wink.

Now I felt like she was just mocking me. She wouldn't do that though, right?

I gave Liam step-by-step directions according to the sketch the woman had drawn out on the cocktail napkin. When we reached a winding ribbon of dusty road with no traffic and no visible homes, I felt Annabelle's tension from the backseat of the car. She frowned.

"We'll be fine," I said with a smile.

I knew I had to say that whether I believed it or not. But what was the worst that could happen? I'd already fought a demon and Jacobson. Could it get any worse? Trees lined both sides of the road. The sketch had us turning on the next right.

Up ahead I spotted a turn-off. "That must be it," I said, pointing straight ahead.

When we reached the turn-off, I realized it was nothing more than a gravel drive lined with thick brush. I prayed that we didn't run into an alligator when we got out of the car. I'd rather fight a bad witch than wrestle an alligator. I wasn't sure that I had magic to compete with that beast.

The shade of the trees around the house made it appear almost night time. The setting was spooky and hauntingly lovely at the same time. I couldn't deny the knot I felt in the pit of my stomach. After inching down the gravel drive, we finally came into a clearing. A small white house with a wraparound porch sat in front of us. There was no car or any signs of life. Liam pulled the car up in front of the house and cut the engine.

Liam handed me the small silver gun. "Okay, I'm going in. I'll check it out and motion when it's safe. Have you ever used one of these before?"

I stared down at the object, then looked up at him. "No. Why can't I use magic if someone tries to attack me?"

He shook his head. "The gun is loaded with silver bullets." He pointed at the gun in my hand. "Point it at your attacker and pull the trigger."

"That's it? That's all you're going to tell me?" I asked.

"Sorry, but there's no time for a detailed lesson. Besides, I'm sure you won't have to use it. Just don't accidentally shoot yourself in the foot." He pointed at my foot.

I quirked a brow. "Yeah, I'll try not to do that."

We watched in silence as Liam walked around the car and up the steps of the house. Once on the porch and in front of the door, he knocked and waited for someone to answer. After several more knocks and no one opening the door, he tried the knob. The door inched open.

Liam turned around and looked our way. He held up his finger, indicating to give him one minute. Why was I waiting? I was supposed to be the leader now. Sure, he was assigned to be my bodyguard, but wasn't I supposed to be tough now? A tough person wouldn't sit in the car and wait for someone else to check things out, would they? Then I thought about Annabelle. My poor best friend that I'd dragged into this mess. I couldn't leave her alone out there, and I certainly wouldn't take her inside the house without knowing it was safe. Besides, if no one was home, then there was no reason for us to go inside anyway.

Just then the back door of the car opened. I whipped around and saw Catherin climbing out of the car.

"Where the hell do you think you're going?" I yelled.

"What is she doing?" Annabelle asked with panic in her voice.

"I have no idea, but we have to stop her. Come on," I said, jumping out of the car with the gun tightly clutched in my hand.

Annabelle hurried out of the back seat, although she looked like she'd rather jump behind the wheel of the car and take off. Catherin ran up the steps and through the front door of the house. We trailed her, running up the rickety front steps and across the unstable floorboards on the porch. Annabelle and I rushed through the open door into the darkened front room of the house.

Catherin stood in the middle of the room looking around. No one else was in sight. Not the owner of the house, Nicolas, or Liam. I was beginning to think that my apprehension was rising to Annabelle's level.

Just then Liam ran down the hall toward us. "What's going on? I thought you were staying in the car. Did something happen?"

"Catherin ran out of the car and into the house." I pointed at Catherin. "What the hell is wrong with you?"

"I couldn't leave him alone in here. He needed help and you shouldn't have allowed him to come in here by himself." She waved her finger in my direction.

That was it. This woman was crazy too. I was back to finding a spell to get rid of her. As the thought of getting rid of her crossed my mind, she offered a warm smile. Her warm smile reminded me of chocolate-chip cookies straight out of the oven and giant hugs—just like Grandma. Again I was forced to consider how it would feel if I banished this sweet grandmotherly woman to the other side. I frowned at Catherin then looked at Liam.

"Did you find anything?" I asked, handing Liam the gun. I wanted to get rid of the thing before I really did shoot myself in the foot.

Liam shrugged his shoulders.

"What does that mean?" I asked, my apprehension growing by the minute.

"Well, there's something back here maybe you should see." Liam motioned for me to follow him down the hallway.

"Do you think we should be in here without someone being home?" Annabelle looked over her shoulder.

"I'm not sure anyone lives here, Annabelle," I said, pointing around the room.

Peach-colored floral wallpaper peeled back from the walls and an old torn upholstered chair sat in the corner of the space. Across the way a small wood table and one broken chair that had been tipped over on its side sat on the floor. Dust covered the floor and the furniture. Outside the trees surrounded the house and shaded every room into darkness. It didn't look as if anyone had been in this place for a long time. I didn't want to scare Annabelle any more than she already was, but I was almost positive that the woman at the bar had set us up. Were we sitting ducks just waiting for the witches to attack? I should have known and listened to Annabelle's warning. She had more psychic intuition than she realized.

I followed Liam down the small hallway, trailing him like a shadow. There were two open doors on the right and one door on the left. Each room was empty, devoid of furniture or even curtains on the windows. We turned into a small room on the left.

Dust floated in the air as I stepped through the door. I stopped when I saw the wall across the room of us. Words and an odd painting covered the wall in front of us like prehistoric cave drawings. I couldn't read the words, but I knew instantly that it was the same language as in the Book of Mystics. The painting had sketches of witches with other creatures that certainly looked demonic to me.

"What does all of this mean?" I pointed toward the wall.

"I'm not quite sure," Liam whispered. "But I know it's not good. We should get out of here."

I'd never seen this look of distress on Liam's face before. If he felt the need to get out of there, then I was right there with him in his thoughts. We headed out the door and back down the hallway. When we reached the front door, Annabelle approached.

"Look what I found," she said, stretching her hand out toward us.

I looked down and saw a wallet in her hand. "What is it?"

"It's Nicolas' wallet," she said.

CHAPTER TWELVE

I hurriedly grabbed the wallet from her outstretched hand. When I opened the brown leather wallet, I saw a picture of Nicolas looking back at me. It was definitely his driver's license. My head was spinning. I handed Liam the wallet. How could it have gotten here? If Liam had been there this morning, then we'd just missed him.

"So someone pretended to be Nicolas and that person was somehow connected to this house. And now we figure out that Nicolas has been here too?" I asked.

Liam ran a hand through his hair. "It appears that way. We need to find out who owns this place." He looked around. "Or if it's just abandoned."

"It looks like no one has lived here for years. Maybe we should go back to the bar and speak with that woman who sent us here. She has a lot to answer for," I said.

"Anything to get out of this place." Annabelle shivered.

"You okay?" I asked Annabelle.

She nodded. "Yeah, I'm fine. I just want to know what the hell is going on. That woman who sent us here is going to answer to me."

Annabelle stomped out of the house. She might be a scaredy cat when it came to the paranormal—but when someone made her mad, look out!

"Oh, dear. I've certainly been pulled into a strange situation." Catherin shook her head as she followed Annabelle down the stairs.

I felt terrible about dragging both of them into this mess. The more involved this situation got, the more I realized I had no idea what I was doing. I needed backup.

"After we speak with the woman at the bar, we have to go to the New Orleans Coven right away. Maybe we should call for more security. You know, so Annabelle and Catherin don't have to come with us. They could go home and maybe someone else could watch over them." I gestured toward the back seat with a tilt of my head.

"No way. I'm here to help you, Hallie. I can't let you handle this alone." Annabelle leaned forward from the back seat.

"If she stays, then I stay." Catherin folded her arms in front of her ample chest.

I looked at Annabelle. "Are you sure?"

She quirked a brow. "Don't I look sure?"

Okay, I knew there would be no talking her out of it.

Liam backed the car up and pulled out onto the road again. We headed back to the bar for answers. I didn't know what kind of game that woman was playing with us, but I intended on getting to the bottom of it.

After retracing our trip back to the bar, we pulled up to the curb in the same spot. The French Quarter was growing more crowded, so we weaved our way through a group of people on the sidewalk and headed back into the bar. A few patrons had arrived by now, but the place was still quiet. The same woman was behind the bar and looked up at us as we approached. Again I was reminded of what an odd group we must have seemed. We looked more like tourists than a group involved in a paranormal investigation.

I hurried over to the bar with determination in my eyes. Maybe if I looked the part someone would fall for it and think I knew what I was doing.

"You're sexy when you're on a mission," Liam whispered.

I bit back a smile. This was no time for flirting.

The woman frowned when she saw that I was walking her way. "I didn't expect for you to be back so soon," she said.

"I didn't expect to be back so soon either," I said.

"We're looking for the woman we spoke with earlier." Liam cast a stern look her way.

"You mean Ginny?" She gestured toward the back of the bar toward the room we'd been in earlier.

"No, I mean the woman we spoke with over there by the door on our way out." I pointed.

A scowl covered the bartender's face. "I don't know who you're talking about."

I exchanged a glance with Liam. Annabelle scoffed and Catherin was looking out the window as if she didn't have a care in the world.

"The woman who works here. She stopped us on our way out." I pointed again.

She shrugged. "I can get the owner for you."

I nodded. "Yes, please."

"Someone is playing games with us," I whispered when she walked away.

Liam frowned. "I wish I could disagree with you, but it seems that way."

I moved over to Annabelle. "We'll get out of here soon. Are you doing okay?"

She stood a little straighter. "I'm fine, just pissed that they are playing games with us."

"Language," Catherin warned with a wave of her finger.

"Sorry," Annabelle said quietly.

After a couple seconds, Ginny appeared from the back room. She looked shocked when she saw us.

"Is everything okay?" She frowned.

"I'm not sure." I studied her face. "I'm looking for the woman who works here who gave us false information."

She looked from me to Liam and back. "I don't know who that is. What did she look like?"

"She had brown hair pulled back in a ponytail. She wore the t-shirt with the bar's logo on the chest and jeans," I said.

Ginny shook her head. "Elaine and I are the only employees here right now. Other than Marisa in my office. That's the way it's been all day. I don't have anyone who works here who fits that description."

I didn't know what to say. How did I know she wasn't lying to me? Someone was lying because I knew we'd talked to someone.

I pulled the napkin from my pocket. "She drew these directions for me."

Ginny looked over at the napkin. "Wait a minute. I heard about this place." She took the napkin and studied it. "There was rumor that a group of witches were performing black magic there."

"That would explain the drawings on the walls," Liam said.

I took the napkin back. "Do you know who these people are?" I asked.

She shook her head. "No, I don't remember. It's a while back."

Annabelle stepped forward and crossed her arms in front of her chest. "So you can't tell us who this person was who gave us this address?"

"I'm sorry. I just don't know," Ginny offered with a frown.

"It must have been another glamor spell," Liam said.

I didn't know who was real any more. I couldn't trust anyone. I looked at Liam, Annabelle and Catherin. Were they real or someone else pretending to be them? Catherin smiled sweetly as if she'd read my mind. Where had she come from? I knew who she claimed to be, but could I really trust her?

I focused my attention back to Ginny. "Thank you again for your help."

"It's not a problem. Let me know if you need anything else." Ginny waved.

We made our way back to the front door, but this time no mysterious woman stopped us.

"We need to get to the New Orleans Coven right away. I'm going to demand answers," I said.

Liam held the door for us as we ushered out and back toward the car. We all piled in and pulled out onto the street.

"What do you think is going on, Hallie?" Annabelle asked from the back seat.

"I think someone sent us to that location for a reason, but I don't know why. Was it to find Nicolas' wallet? That doesn't make sense," I said.

"Maybe they thought we'd find Nicolas?" Annabelle said.

Liam navigated the busy street. "I don't think that's it. Nicolas wouldn't go there. He would have no reason to be there."

"Then why was his wallet there?" I asked.

He shook his head. "That I can't answer."

After making our way through the busy streets and around the traffic we made it to the outskirts of town. We pulled into the tree-lined driveway of the plantation. It looked different in the daylight. Not quite as spooky, but still haunting. Day or night, the place was beautiful.

My apprehension mounted. I wasn't sure I was ready for a battle with Jacobson again. I knew he could be volatile by the way he'd grabbed Annabelle and I didn't want a repeat of that situation. No cars were in front of the place just as the last time, but that did little to ease my nerves. After Liam came to a stop in front of the plantation, we sat in silence for a moment and soaked in its beauty.

"Let's go," I said, trying to sound brave.

Maybe if I played the part I could convince myself.

We walked up the grand stairs of the massive porch and approached the front door. I knocked, then realized there was a doorbell, so I pushed the button. A loud ring echoed on the other side for a ridiculously long time. We waited and I listened for any sound of movement. When no one came to the door, I rang the annoying doorbell again. After a few more seconds and still no answer, I placed my hand on the doorknob. The door inched open.

"It's open," I said, looking at Liam. "Just like the other place."

He frowned. "That's odd. Let me go first."

I stepped to the side and allowed him to enter the house. Once he was inside, we followed closely behind. The place was quiet. The only sound was our footsteps across the polished hardwood floor.

"Hello?" Liam called out.

No one answered. We stepped into the parlor and looked around. A few half-full wine glasses dotted the top of the table in the parlor. A couple of the glasses had lipstick rings. It looked as if someone had stepped out in the middle of a party.

Annabelle rubbed her arms. "This place gives me the creeps."

I couldn't disagree with that assessment. It gave me the creeps too. Even the paintings of what I assumed were Jacobson's ancestors seemed to watch our every move. It was as if the eyes followed us.

"Where do you think everyone went?" I asked Liam.

Liam shook his head. "I don't know. But something isn't right."

"Why don't we just go back to LaVeau Manor so that I can consult the book and figure out what the heck I

110

should be doing? We're getting nowhere like this." I made my way toward the door.

"I like the sound of that," Annabelle answered as she stared at one of the paintings.

"Yeah, I guess that's the best idea," Liam said as he looked out the side window, distracted.

We hurried out into the hall and Annabelle paused by the entrance to the other parlor.

"I think there's something you might want to see in here." She pointed toward the room.

We hurried toward the room. "Excuse me," Catherin said in a sweet voice as she grabbed my arm.

I frowned. "Yes?"

"You don't want to go in there. This place is spooky. Let's get out of here." She rubbed her arms as if fending off a chill.

I quirked an eyebrow. "I think we'll just check out the room real quick, okay?"

She scowled, but didn't argue.

On the farthest wall was another large mural. It took up most of the space, and it had the same writing and depictions that we'd seen at the little house by the swamp. My stomach flipped and it felt like the air had been sucked out of my lungs.

"How did you find this?" I asked Annabelle.

"I just walked over here and saw it," she said.

"Why do you keep finding things?" I stared at her.

She looked at me and shrugged. "Well, I keep my eyes open and look for things."

I wasn't sure what was going on, but I knew I needed the Book of Mystics to help me. I had to get back to LaVeau Manor as soon as possible.

"Never mind that now. Let's just get out of here." I gestured.

"I'm right behind you," Catherin said with that same overly sweet voice.

Where were these clues leading us? In the right direction, I hoped.

CHAPTER THIRTEEN

As soon as we returned to LaVeau Manor I headed straight for the Book of Mystics. If it didn't contain some kind of directions on how to fix this mess, I was totally screwed. I'd have to call for some kind of special meeting with the members of the surrounding covens. I supposed I would have to include the Enchantment Pointe Coven members, even though they'd snubbed me for years. I wouldn't stoop to their level though. I'd show them I was a bigger person than that.

After grabbing the book, I rushed back downstairs. Annabelle had said she'd wait for me in the kitchen. I couldn't keep her hostage forever. Sure, she said she wanted to stay and help me, but I had no idea how long this thing was going to drag out. It could take days, weeks, or heaven forbid, months. She couldn't put her life on hold because I'd dragged her into this. And then there was the little matter of Catherin. I knew that Annabelle had taken an instant liking to Catherin's sweet grandmotherly ways, but she just couldn't stay forever. I didn't want to be the witch who messed with bringing back the dead. I might have done it a couple times, but that didn't mean I wanted to continue to do it forever.

From almost the first moment Nicolas and Liam had arrived at LaVeau Manor, I'd hidden the book. It wasn't that I didn't trust them now, but I didn't trust other people within the Underworld. If one person had wanted it, then that meant there had to be other people who wanted it as well. Why other people wanted to be the leader was beyond me. It wasn't all that it had cracked up to be. Over and over in my mind I contemplated why I'd accepted the job as leader. The only answer I came up with was only because I felt Nicolas' mother would have wanted me to. Even though I didn't know her, she had been friends with my Great-Aunt Maddy and that meant something. Plus, my mother was thrilled with my new status as leader. I'd disappointed her in the witchcraft department for so long. I felt like I owed her this one. So I'd continue to hide the book. Maybe I needed to look into getting a safe.

When I reached the kitchen, Annabelle wasn't there. With the book clutched to my chest, I ran down the little hallway and into the dining room. To my relief, Annabelle and Liam were sitting at the table eating sandwiches.

"Whew. I was worried that Jacobson had returned," I said.

Annabelle chewed, then finally said, "Nope. Peanut butter sandwiches."

Liam laughed. "She'll be okay as long as I'm here." He held up a plate with a sandwich. "I made you a peanut butter sandwich too. You didn't have a wide selection of options."

How sweet was that? He'd thought to make me a sandwich too. So what if it was only peanut butter on bread. He'd cut it down the middle just like I liked it.

"Yeah, I'm a little behind on my grocery shopping." I smiled.

Liam winked at me and my stomach flipped. I loved Liam's crooked smile. The way his lip twisted to one side made my insides flutter.

Liam patted the seat beside him. "Come and eat."

If only I didn't need to do the spell first. "I'll be back in just a minute, okay?"

He smiled softly. "Don't keep us waiting too long."

Forcing myself out of the room, I headed back to the kitchen to collect the ingredients for the spell that would send Catherin back to where she came from. Sending her back would be the first step, then I could figure out what the mysterious writing and paintings meant.

I placed the spell book on the counter and ran down the list with my index finger. Luckily, everything I needed was right there on the shelves where my Great-Aunt Maddy had left it. She had an extensive collection of spell-casting ingredients.

With any luck, Liam wouldn't hear the magic in progress. I didn't want to tell him that Catherin had been a ghost. If I got rid of her, I could just say that she'd checked out and gone home. That wouldn't be a lie. Well, not completely a lie. I'd been a screw-up with magic for so long. Now that I was the leader, I wanted to try my best to do the job right. Bringing back random ghosts was not the way to achieve that goal.

Since I was in a hurry, I didn't have time to wait for the water in the cauldron to reach a boil. So I helped it along with a little spell that I'd read up on in the book.

"Bring heat my way, but without harm. The water will bubble like a charm."

With a wave of my hand the water began to boil. This spell was only to be used in emergencies, but I felt this was one of those occasions.

Once the water was boiling, I placed the spices and herbs into the cauldron. Then I recited the words from the book that would with any luck take Catherin back.

"Element of Earth, I call to you to allow the spirit to enter earth again. Element of Air, I call to you to push the spirit away from to the living. Element of Fire, I call to you for knowledge and protection. Element of Water, I call to you for force and tranquility. Give the spirit the power to move to the next dimension."

The wind whipped my hair wildly and the air around me was full of electricity. Dazzling lights flickered through the air and sparkled up from the water. After a minute, the wind died down and the lights flickered away. I released a deep breath. A weight had been lifted from my shoulders. I really felt as if I'd done things right this time.

Before returning to the dining room, I thought I'd try Nicolas' cell phone. It was probably pointless, but I had to give it a shot. After ringing many times, I figured it would go to his voice mail. When he answered, it caught me off guard.

"Um, I just wanted to make sure you're okay," I said.

"I'm in New Orleans." His voice was barely audible.

Uh-oh.

"I hope you're not thinking of doing something stupid. Don't try to confront Jacobson," I said.

"What makes you think I'd do something stupid?" he asked.

The reception on the phone was spotty and his voice was going in and out, so I assumed that was what he had said.

"You need to let me take care of this without violence." My voice probably showcased my insecurity.

There was no answer.

"Hello?" I said.

Still there was silence on his end. I looked at the phone and saw that the call had been dropped. It figured that he'd lost service just when I needed the cell phone coverage the most.

I dialed his phone again, but this time it went straight to voicemail. What could I do? I left a message warning him again not to confront Jacobson. My warning would probably fall on deaf ears though. I hadn't even gotten a chance to ask him about the wallet or if he'd really bitten that woman's neck.

After the call, I turned around and spotted a single red rose on top of the counter. It hadn't been there a second ago. There was no way I would have missed it. I picked up the beautiful fragrant flower and sniffed. It reminded me of the red roses Nicolas had sent to me when he'd first come to LaVeau Manor. I pulled a vase from the shelf, filled it with water, and placed the rose inside. Had I somehow conjured a rose while casting the spell? Maybe my subconscious had made it appear.

After staring at the rose for a few seconds, I returned to the dining room. I hoped I didn't have guilt written all over my face. Liam and Annabelle had finished their sandwiches, but were discussing the various restaurants and shops in Enchantment Pointe. Liam scrunched his brow together when he looked up at me. I was so busted. He knew I'd been performing magic. What had made me think I could hide it from him? I was just surprised that he hadn't figured out that Catherin was a spell gone wrong. I tried to avoid his stare and slipped into the chair at the end of the table.

He placed my sandwich in front of me. "You'd better eat. You must be starving after all that work."

Ugh. He was just taunting me now. I took a bite from my sandwich, but still didn't look up at him.

"Is everything okay?" Annabelle frowned.

I smiled. "Yes, everything is fine."

After a couple seconds of my chewing in silence, Annabelle asked, "Where is Catherin, by the way? I haven't seen her since we returned to the manor."

Now that she mentioned it, I hadn't seen or heard from Catherin even before I'd performed the spell to get rid of her. That was a bit strange. She had wanted to be involved in all the conversations before. But I wasn't going to complain. She was gone now and I could focus on finding Nicolas. Getting rid of Catherin had been for the best. She would just cause more problems and I didn't need that at the moment.

"Maybe she went to bed for a nap," I said.

Why did I feel so guilty for lying? It had been the right thing to do.

Annabelle jumped up from the table. "I'll go check on her."

She bounced out of the room. Oh great. She wouldn't find her. Plus, that would leave me alone with Liam. He would want to know what magic I had been performing. Not that I had to tell him, but with that sexy stare, it was hard to say no to anything he asked. Extremely hard.

I felt Liam's eyes focused on me, but I continued to look down at my plate.

"You want to tell me what's going on and why you're being so secretive?" He fixed his eyes on me.

I placed my half-eaten sandwich down. "Do I want to? No."

"Come on. You know you'll tell me eventually. You might as well save the energy and tell me now." He winked.

Why did he have to look at me like that? I bit my lip, stifling a smile. He was right though. Eventually I wouldn't be able to stand it and I'd tell him about what I'd done. But right now was not that time. I figured I should take this opportunity to tell Liam about my recent conversation with Nicolas.

Finally, I admitted, "I dialed Nicolas' number."

Liam froze. "What happened?"

"He answered." I studied his face for a reaction.

"You're kidding. What did he say?"

I sighed. "He said he was in New Orleans."

"What did he say about the wallet or the attack?" Liam asked.

"I didn't get a chance to ask. The phone went dead. But I have to say, he didn't sound like Nicolas." Uneasiness sounded in my voice.

"I'll try to call him again." Liam pulled out his cell phone and looked down at the screen. "I guess I'll have to wait. There's no service here."

Annabelle returned with a frown splashed across her face. She stood with her hands on her hips.

"I can't find Catherin anywhere," she said with her brow scrunched up.

Would I be able to continue to lie? Oh, what a tangled web we weave. I should have just told everyone the truth about Catherin from the beginning. But once you tell one lie, you have to tell another, then another. I hated lying to Annabelle.

"Maybe she checked out and went home. Would you blame her?" I asked.

"No, I guess not. But she seemed as if she wanted to help," Annabelle said.

"I think she was just being polite. We probably scared her to death." I took a bite of my sandwich and chewed.

Oh, that was a bad pun. Good thing no one knew how bad it truly was.

After taking another bite, I said, "I wouldn't be surprised if she didn't call the police on me. At the very least, she will give me the worst bed-and-breakfast review ever."

Annabelle shook her head. "Oh my gosh. I can't believe I almost forgot. You have another guest outside in the foyer. I was so distracted by looking for Catherin that I forgot to tell you."

I jumped up. "What? I have a guest?"

Annabelle nodded. "Yeah. A man is standing out in the foyer. I asked him if he wanted a room and he said yes."

Annabelle seemed awfully calm about this. After what had happened with Jacobson, I figured Annabelle wanted to keep her distance from strangers when at LaVeau Manor. I brushed past her and out the door and down the hallway. Liam rushed past me, stopping me from walking into the library.

"What are you doing?" I asked.

"You don't know who this person is. I need to go first and check them out. I'm your bodyguard, remember?" He crossed his arms in front of his chest.

Hmm. I guessed I had forgotten about why Liam was there. I wasn't used to having a person following me around.

I released a heavy sigh and reluctantly shook my head. "Okay. But be polite in case it really is a guest."

His mouth twisted to one side. He looked as if he wanted to laugh.

I scowled. "What? I could have a real guest. Maybe. Well, one of these days it's bound to happen."

Wait. If he thought this wasn't a real guest, had he known that Catherin wasn't a real guest too? Maybe I had just thought I'd been fooling him all this time.

Annabelle and I followed Liam through the library and into the foyer. Just as Annabelle had said, a man stood in the foyer. His back was to us as he looked into the other room. At least he wasn't wearing clothing from another century. His chestnut-brown hair was cut short and he wore a dark blue suit.

"May I help you?" Liam asked in his best tough-guy voice, which wasn't hard for him, by the way.

"I was called here," the man said a professional clipped tone.

Uh oh. I'd heard that statement before. My stomach flipped and I thought I might be sick. He didn't have to tell me. I knew already that I'd done it again. This man had to have been brought back by me. I had brought him back from the dead.

"What do you mean you were called here?" Liam asked.

I had a feeling Liam already knew the answer to that question. And right about now he was probably figuring out what magic I'd been performing.

"By the magic, of course." The man smiled. "I have to say I am elated to be here too. So whoever did it, thank you."

Liam looked at me.

"I guess I should explain from the beginning what happened," I said.

Liam nodded. "It would probably help, yes."

"Do you mind if I come in?" The man stared at Annabelle as he spoke.

Something about his eyes gave me the creeps. Then again, a lot gave me the creeps lately.

CHAPTER FOURTEEN

I hesitated, but eventually stepped to the side and allowed the man to enter the parlor.

"Would you like to have a seat?" I was becoming a regular hostess to mysterious strangers. Only I had a feeling there wasn't much of a mystery as to where this man came from. I'd brought him back from the dead instead of sending Catherin away.

"Well, first of all, I'd like for someone to tell me where I am. I mean, I realize I'm not dead anymore. For that I am thankful, by the way. I was really tired of the haunting thing." He plopped down on the sofa.

Annabelle let out a little gasp. "Another one," she whispered.

She didn't know the half of it.

I held my hand up. "Um. I'm the one responsible for bringing you here."

Liam was staring me. I shrugged. What else could I do?

"Okay, but where am I?" he asked.

"This is LaVeau Manor. I own this place and run it as a bed-and-breakfast." I waved my arm through the air.

"How quaint," he said drily.

Great—another sarcastic ghost. I hadn't dealt with enough of those lately.

I sat down opposite the man. "Where are you from?"

He eyed me up and down, then finally said, "I'm from New Orleans."

I looked at Liam, then back at the man.

"Do you mind telling us your name?" I asked.

"Of course not. Why would I mind?" His tone held a mocking bite. It sounded as if he really did mind. "My name is Claude Hammond. I suppose you want to know more than that about me, huh?" He looked at all of us.

This had to be weird for Claude—three strangers standing around gawking at him. He'd been called here by me. It wasn't as if he'd asked to be here. I really needed to stop casting the spell that was bringing the spirits back. Obviously, I lacked the skills needed to make it work.

"Well…" He waved his hand through the air. "I died in a tragic automobile accident ten years ago. I worked at a law firm. No wife and no children. That about sums it up."

Didn't he have some kind of connection to LaVeau Manor? Why him? It couldn't have been a random selection.

"Do you have family in Enchantment Point?" I quirked a brow.

"No, not that I'm aware of," he answered breezily.

Hmm. "And you've never been to LaVeau Manor?" I asked.

"Not until you brought me here." His face split into a wide grin.

Liam and I exchanged a glance. He had to be thinking the same thing as me. This would be another mystery. Why had he been brought back? Was it something about the spell?

"Well, I'm sorry about bringing you here. I can help you get back," I said.

He frowned. "Get back to where? New Orleans? That would be great. Thank you."

"No, I could help you get back to the other side." I gestured toward the front door as if that was the portal to the other side.

He scowled. "What the hell? Why would I want to go back there, for heaven's sake? Look at this ugly suit they dressed me in. Would you want to spend eternity in this thing?"

I looked at his clothing and shrugged. As a matter of fact, no, I wouldn't want to spend eternity in that, but that was neither here nor there. But he had to go back. As I said before, I didn't want to be the one who brought these people back. That was not going to be my thing.

"Well, I can offer you a place to stay until you can get back to New Orleans. I'm not planning a trip there this evening," I said.

Liam scowled. It might not seem like it, but I had a plan. I had a plan to make this darn spell thing work and send all these ghosts out of here. I prayed that the ghosts that had been stalking me outside didn't return. They had been lurking around outside since I'd discovered I could reanimate the dead. I hadn't seen them since for a while now, but I was positive they would be back. My collection of ghosts kept growing.

"So are you going to tell me who you are?" he asked with a smile.

"Oh, where are my manners?" I'd been a terrible hostess to my latest ghost guest. "My name is Hallie LaVeau. This is Liam Rankin. And my friend Annabelle Preston." I gestured across the room.

"Pleased to meet you," he said.

Annabelle and Liam returned the greeting with less than exuberant jubilee. I stood and gestured for Claude to follow me.

"I'll be right back," I said to Liam and Annabelle.

They were staring at me as if I'd lost my mind. I wanted to get Claude out of the room so that I could perform another spell and get rid of him. With the help of

Liam, I'd be able to perform it correctly this time, right? I was obviously doing something wrong. Liam would be able to spot my mistake and point it out. Yeah, that was what I was telling myself.

"Come on, Claude. I can show you to your room. Would you like something to eat?" I asked.

"I'd love something. Do you have cupcakes?" he asked.

I froze with my foot on the bottom step. I spun around and looked at him. "Why do you ask for cupcakes?"

He held his hands up in surrender. "I didn't know it was against the law. It's my favorite. I thought I'd take a shot and ask. I haven't had one in over ten years. Forgive me," he said sarcastically. "Should I have asked for steak?"

I stared for a beat. "It just reminded me of someone else." I looked him up and down as he frowned.

The last ghost had been a huge cupcake fan. Could he be Isabeau in disguise? That would certainly be a connection to LaVeau Manor. Yes, I definitely had to get rid of this man as soon as possible.

I led him to the second floor and down the hallway. Since Catherin was staying in the room across from me, I'd have to put Claude in the last room down the hall. Not that he'd be staying for long if my plan went smoothly.

"You have a great home. Do you live here all alone or was that your husband down there?" he asked.

"Thank you. No, he's not my husband. And yes, I do live here alone," I said.

As I neared Catherin's room, I noticed the door was wide open. When I peeked in, the clothing I'd given her to wear was on the bed. I scanned the room, hoping that I wouldn't catch her walking around wearing no clothing. Technically, I shouldn't be snooping around in the first place. So if I did catch an eyeful it would be my own fault.

The room was empty and the bathroom door was wide open too. Did I dare peek in there too? Where had she gone? I stepped through the room and over to the bathroom door.

"Catherin, are you in here?" I called out.

There was no answer.

"Do you usually snoop on your guests?" Claude asked.

I glanced over my shoulder and frowned. "No."

Okay, I had been snooping on my guests a lot, but only because it had been necessary. It was pure necessity.

Upon closer inspection, I noticed the closet door was open. Where was the dress that Catherin had been wearing when she'd arrived? It wasn't hanging in the closet and I didn't see it anywhere else in the room either.

I let out a sigh. "I guess she stepped out for a while." I tried to give a professional smile. It wasn't easy though.

Had I sent Catherin back and replaced her with Claude? Was that even possible? Now that I thought of it, I knew that it was very much possible. I had a way of making the simplest spells the most complicated. I had created such a tangled web that I'd probably never escape.

After showing Claude to his room, I rushed back downstairs to figure out how to get rid of him. And with any luck, not bring Catherin or any other ghost back in the process.

CHAPTER FIFTEEN

Liam and Annabelle were waiting for me in the parlor and I knew I had some explaining to do.

"What are you going to do with him?" Annabelle whispered when I sat down.

I blew out a breath. "I'm going to do another spell and get him to go back where he came from."

"Don't you think you should figure out what went wrong with your last spell before you try another one?" Liam offered the sweetest of smiles.

"Well, yeah. I had planned on asking for your help." I smiled sweetly.

"What did you have in mind?" He leaned back in the chair.

"I figured I can tell you what I did and you can let me know what I did wrong?" I asked with a quirked eyebrow.

"I don't think that sounds like the best of plans. Perhaps you should consult the book," Liam suggested.

"That's what I did with this last spell and look what happened." I tossed my hands up.

"Are you going to tell me why you were casting the spell in the first place? Not that it's any of my business," he added.

I hesitated, then said, "Catherin was a ghost that I accidentally brought back."

He chuckled. "So you've established a pattern of bringing back the wrong ghosts."

"Certainly not on purpose," I said in my defense.

"The truth is…" I looked at Annabelle and Liam. They watched with wide eyes for what I was about to say.

"Nicolas' mother came back here," I said nonchalantly.

Liam almost fell out of his chair. "She what? She came back here?"

"She was here the morning I told you I saw the ghost in the cream-colored dress. Gina asked for me to bring her back. But by the time I got the book to do the spell, she was gone. But I did the spell anyway. That's when Catherin appeared." I snapped my fingers. "Just like that."

"Where is Catherin?" Annabelle asked, looking around the room.

I shrugged. "I don't know. I think I might have sent her back when I brought Claude from the grave."

The more I talked the worse it sounded.

Annabelle frowned. "She may have been a ghost previously, but I thought Catherin was nice."

"I don't know what to think. Catherin claimed to be my great-great-great aunt. But something seemed off." I couldn't deny the nagging thought that was settled in the back of my mind.

"Something seems off about this whole thing," Liam said.

I had to agree with him on that one. I didn't know who to trust and I didn't know who was real anymore.

We sat in silence for a moment. Liam was probably thinking the worst. The doorbell rang again, disturbing the quiet in the room and sending my stomach into a nose dive. If another ghost was at the door and I'd brought the person back to life, then I'd probably cry.

"Do you think I have to answer that?" I asked.

Liam nodded. "Let me get it."

Once again, Annabelle and I followed Liam to the door. Liam peeked out the hole, then didn't hesitate to open the door. A tall muscular man with blond hair stepped into the foyer.

"How do you do?" he asked with a smile.

Liam shook his hand. Who was this man? At least it looked as if Liam knew him. I glanced over at Annabelle and her gaze was fixed on the good-looking blond. I waved my hand in front of her face. She finally snapped out of the trance.

"Hallie, this is Jon Santos." Liam gestured toward the man.

Jon stuck his hand out toward me. "It's a pleasure to meet you. I'm honored to meet the new leader."

I followed his gaze to Annabelle. Why was I not surprised that another gorgeous guy had shown up? Did all the good-looking men work for the Underworld? I knew he had to be connected in some way. What were the odds that he wasn't involved? Gorgeous men didn't just show up at my door. Sadly, I'd discovered that the hard way.

I shook his strong hand. "It's nice to meet you too." I looked from Liam back to Jon. "Who are you?"

"I was called in for backup." He exchanged a look with Liam.

Annabelle stepped closer and cleared her throat. I took the hint. "This is my best friend Annabelle Preston." I gestured with a tilt of my head.

"It's a pleasure." Annabelle batted her eyelashes.

Jon's eyes sparkled as he placed his lips on Annabelle's hand. Her face turned a deep shade of red. Liam and I might as well have been invisible.

"So you called for backup?" I asked Liam.

"Don't you think I need it? I can't handle both of you, not to mention all the ghosts you keep bringing back to life," Liam said.

Jon finally looked away from Annabelle and quirked his brow at me. Yeah, he'd heard Liam correctly. The new leader was a screw-up. Deal with it, people.

"I figured Jon can escort Annabelle to her house since I know she doesn't want to stay in your creepy manor, as she calls it." Liam winked at Annabelle.

"Yeah, I guess that's a good idea." I looked Jon up and down. "But you'd better take care of my best friend. Got it?" I poked him in his hard chest with my index finger.

"Yes, ma'am. You have my word on it," Jon said with a little salute.

"I'll just get my bag," Annabelle said as she ran across the room.

It looked as if there would be little chance of me convincing her to stay. Oh well, it was better if she wasn't around this craziness anyway.

I hugged Annabelle. "I'll call you later."

Annabelle and Jon were chatting as they walked down the front steps and to his car. He opened the door and she climbed in, giggling the whole time. He must have told a very funny joke because Annabelle rarely giggled. Annabelle flipped her hand up in a little wave, then focused her attention back to the conversation with Jon.

"Well, it looks like they're going to get along just fine," Liam said.

"It appears that way." I turned to Liam. "Why didn't you tell me that you'd called for backup?"

Liam folded his arms in front of his chest. "You were too busy bringing ghosts back and didn't give me a chance."

"When are you going to let me live that down?" I asked.

"Probably not for a while." Dimples appeared on his cheeks.

It was strange being alone with Liam. Well, besides the former ghost that was upstairs and the other one who was missing. My thoughts shifted to Nicolas. Where was he?

Most importantly, was he okay? Liam must have read my thoughts.

He stepped closer and placed his hands on my arms. "We'll get all of this worked out. Try not to worry about it, okay?"

I nodded. "It's hard not to think about it."

Liam rubbed my arms, sending a chill down my body. He leaned in closer and placed his warm lips against mine. A warm tingly sensation zipped through my body. I didn't resist his kiss. It was hard not to succumb to his chemistry. The room began to spin as his tongue moved across mine. I pressed my body closer to his.

Finally, my thoughts broke through the fog and I pushed him away. "I should check on my guest," I said without looking at Liam.

I dashed up the stairs and didn't look back. When I got to the top of the stairs, I paused to catch my breath and listen. Would Liam come after me? On one hand, I wanted him to, and on the other, I didn't want him to. I couldn't possibly be any more confused. Would Nicolas be angry that I'd kissed Liam? Given their rocky past, I knew the answer to that question. What would be the consequences for Liam and Nicolas' shaky relationship if I was in the middle? There was enough animosity between them without me adding to it.

Without checking on my guest, I retreated to my room. Now more than ever I needed time to be alone and think. Once inside my room, I locked the door out of habit, and pulled out the Book of Mystics. I would read that thing cover to cover if it would just give me the answers I was looking for and the answers I needed.

The next thing I knew, I'd fallen asleep, leaning back against the headboard with the Book of Mystics across my chest. Luckily, the book didn't have my drool on the pages. I really needed to get more rest so that I wouldn't fall asleep while sitting up so often.

After searching through the book, I still didn't have the answers I needed. Sure, it had instructed me on how the covens and vampire clans worked, but it hadn't told me what to do with a problem like the one I was dealing with now.

I needed to ask another witch's advice. The only catch was I didn't really have any witch friends. Since I'd always been the outcast of the coven, most witches avoided me like a burning stake or a broken broom. But there was one witch who would be more than willing to lend me a wand... my mother. She would want to know more about Nicolas and Liam though and that was the problem. If I told her what was going on with them she might freak out. Unfortunately, she was my only option. There was still a little daylight left in the day. Just enough time to catch my mother at her shop before she closed and went home for the day.

I picked up my cell and dialed the number to Bewitching Bath and Potions. "I thought I'd come over for a bit," I said when she answered.

"What's wrong?" she asked with panic in her voice.

"Can't I come see my mother?" I asked in defense.

"Well, you rarely volunteer to come by the store," she replied with frustration in her tone.

I scoffed. "That's because you always put me to work."

"Just get here as quickly as you can," she said around a sigh.

Little did my mother know that I wouldn't show up to her shop as myself.

CHAPTER SIXTEEN

Grabbing the Book of Mystics, I headed downstairs to perform the glamor spell. There was one small problem though. If Liam was down there, I'd have to trick him into leaving me alone for a bit, just enough time for me to cast the spell and slip out of the house.

I had to change my appearance in order to go out of the house without protection. After all, Jacobson and his crazy coven members would be looking for me, not someone else. But who would I change my appearance to? I'd changed my appearance to Nicolas already and that had almost been a catastrophe.

Luckily, this time I had the counter-spell so I wouldn't have to worry about being stuck taking on someone else's appearance. Well, in a perfect witch world that was the way it worked. In my world, there was always some doubt. There was only one person who I felt I would be safe as... Liam Rankin. After all, he was my bodyguard and no one would mess with him. But what if they saw me out and thought that he'd left me home alone? They'd come to LaVeau Manor. It wouldn't matter though. I wouldn't be here.

I tiptoed through the rooms, hoping that I wouldn't hit one of the creaky floorboards and notify the whole house that I was moving around. Where was Liam? I should have checked his room before I'd come down, but I didn't want to accidentally bump into him while in such close proximity to his bedroom.

The house was silent again except for the eerie ticktock of that grandfather clock. I needed to get rid of that thing. The sound was just too creepy. It was as if I was perpetually running out of time. Maybe someone was trying to tell me something.

Fortunately, I'd made it through the house without seeing Liam. Once I reached the kitchen, I hurried and gathered my items—cinnamon, ginger, cloves, and bay leaves. Aunt Maddy's giant cauldron was in the big stone fireplace in the middle of the far wall of the kitchen. I wasn't sure when I'd stop referring to everything as Aunt Maddy's. It was all my stuff now... for better or worse.

After adding water to the cauldron, I swiped a long match against the stone then lit the fire underneath. I dumped the ingredients into the cauldron and waited for the water to boil. Of course we all knew that a watched pot never boiled, so while I waited, I paced.

What would Liam say or do if he found out what I was doing? He'd laughed when I'd changed my appearance to Nicolas, but I knew he wouldn't find this quite as humorous. I was slipping out of the house without him as my protection. If I was killed, it would ruin him. That was kind of selfish of me now that I thought about it. I didn't want to ruin him—far from it. But it was just a risk I was going to have to take. I prayed that everything worked out the way that I intended.

Once the water came to a boil, I recited the words. This time I didn't want to make any mistakes. It was too important.

"For a brief time, make my appearance not mine. Alter my look to that of Liam Rankin and no one's beliefs will falter. So mote it be."

The water bubbled like the angry sea and flashes of light zinged and zapped around the room. Within a matter of seconds, the commotion had died down again and it was just as peaceful and quiet as when I'd started the spell.

Apprehension coursed through my body. Had the spell worked? Of course I was nervous about making the counter-spell work too. Obviously, not nervous enough though because I'd gone through with the glamor spell. I was having spell casting remorse. It was too late to turn back now, right? Or was it? I needed to check the mirror to see if I was still me or if I'd taken on the handsome features of one sexy vampire warlock, Liam Rankin.

I rushed down the hallway into the little bathroom. The reflection in the mirror staring back at me was not my own. I now had a strong jaw, piercing blue eyes, long lashes, full lips and dark hair. Damn. Liam was good-looking. The spell had been a success. Now what? I'd have to hurry out of the house before I was caught.

I grabbed my purse and headed toward the door. Okay, how ridiculous did I look? A guy carrying a giant pink purse? But what was a female witch who'd changed her appearance to do? I needed my purse. It was practically my lifeline. I'd leave it in the car and no one would be the wiser. What would my mother say when she saw me like this? I felt like I was slipping out of the house like when I was sixteen. My mother had always used her magic to catch me though. I prayed that Liam didn't use his magic to catch me.

The ride to my mother's shop was exceedingly long. Perhaps it was because I was anxious and had a million things on my mind. Specialty shops and boutiques made up the bulk of the historic section of town. The main road ran along the river, twisting and turning through Enchantment Pointe. A stone wall surrounded the outer edge of town with cobblestone sidewalks and wrought-iron accents sprinkled around.

After pulling up in front of the building which housed my mother's Bath and Potions Shop in the historic downtown of Enchantment Pointe, I cut the engine and let out a deep breath. I'd started working at my mother's shop years ago, but she still didn't trust me to mix the spells. The full beard on Mrs. Stillwell's face had only lasted a month and it had been a novelty really. In hindsight, she should have thanked me. But because of that and a few other mishaps, I was banned from the cauldron.

Here went nothing. At the very least my mother would be thrilled with my witchcraft skills. Not every witch could change her appearance.

I hopped out from behind the wheel and around to the sidewalk. I looked up and down the street. A few people went in and out of other shops, but no one seemed to notice me. No one knew Liam in Enchantment Pointe though, so I'd probably be safe. Just a regular guy standing on the sidewalk, that was me.

As I pushed through the door of Bewitching Bath and Potions Shop, the bell above the door jangled announcing my presence. Annette LaVeau made all the items right there in her shop. Her merchandise included soaps, lotions, scrubs, and bath salts. She had a special knack for mixing scents—magical oils were her specialty. She was a workaholic when it came to her business: sections of the store were specifically designated for specific items, and you'd better not get them out of place either. Fragrances, oils, powders and herbs on the right. Soaps, shower gels, lotions, shampoos and conditioners on the left.

My mother immediately popped up from behind the counter. People could tell immediately that we were mother and daughter. We were the same small size—five-foot-one—but we packed a powerful punch. My mother had recently cut her blonde hair in a fashionable bob. She wore the store's signature polka-dotted apron over her black T-shirt and black and white Capri pants.

My mother quirked her one eyebrow. My mother had gotten better with drawing on her eyebrows after this many years, but sometimes she forgot and accidentally wiped them off. I'd been responsible for a minor cupcake-related incident involving a partially destroyed kitchen, and my mother had her eyebrows. Other than that, she'd come out unscathed. Never mind that she has to pencil them in to this day, bless her heart. She never had to worry about painful wax treatments though.

"May I help you?" she asked with a giant smile.

As I approached the counter, she scowled. Did she recognize me? Or did she suspect that I was behind the male face?

"Aren't you that witch who corrupted my daughter?" She waved the wand that she'd been using to mix up a potion.

"What?" I asked, my voice coming out only slightly masculine.

I couldn't believe she'd asked me that. It was so tempting to have a little fun with her, but she'd probably never forgive me if I did, so I knew I had to come clean.

CHAPTER SEVENTEEN

My mother frowned. She was a smart woman and she knew something was amiss. And to think I'd actually entertained the thought of playing a prank on her. It would have taken her seconds to figure me out.

"Mother, it's me, Halloween." I waved my hands through the air.

My mother had always called me Halloween and refused to use the nickname Hallie. I'd given up the battle and allowed her to win years ago. It wasn't worth the energy.

She stepped back and looked me up and down. Her mouth dropped open and she wobbled a little for added theatrics. "Why would you do such a thing?" she asked while clutching her chest.

I hurried around the counter and helped her sit on the stool. "I thought you'd be happy with my new talent." I picked up a piece of paper and waved it in front of her as a fan. I believed she had a case of the vapors.

She looked at me again, then said, "Well, I guess I am a little happy." She shook her head. "But no, I still need to know why you did this."

I picked at the invisible lint on my shirt. "It's complicated."

"What isn't complicated with you? I'm your mother, you have to tell me what's going on. Don't keep secrets from me. It's not healthy." She waved her finger at me.

She was making up that last part. There was no evidence that keeping secrets from her wasn't healthy.

"After you left the Halloween Ball, Liam called for me to go to New Orleans," I explained.

"And?" She motioned me to continue.

"Nicolas has been accused of stealing another witch's powers, so now I have to figure out if the charges are true." I rushed my words.

"Oh dear. What are you going to do?" She clutched her chest.

I shrugged. "I'm trying to figure that part out."

"That still doesn't explain why you look like Liam." She pointed at my body, specifically the lower region.

"Oh yeah, that part." I frowned.

I hated sharing the tiny details with her.

"Yes, that part." She placed her hands on her hips.

"There's a guy who isn't very happy because Nicolas turned his sister into a vampire. So the Underworld assigned Liam to protect me." I tested a new shade of pink lipstick on my hand and avoided her stare.

"Nicolas turned a woman?" Her eyes were the size of the large cauldron in front of us.

"Well, he said it wasn't on purpose." I placed my hands on my hips.

She picked up the paper and fanned herself again. "That's not very reassuring. That still doesn't tell me why you are pretending to be Liam."

"I wanted to get out of the house and I knew I couldn't just go out as Halloween LaVeau. That wouldn't be very safe, now would it?" I asked.

"I don't think it's safe no matter what you do. You shouldn't be out without Liam. Not if he is assigned to protect you," she said.

"I figured that no one would mess with me if they thought I was Liam." I flashed a wide grin.

"You have to change back immediately." She grabbed my arms and spun me around to face her. Spinning me around wasn't as easy as she thought considering Liam's muscular frame.

"Why?" I asked, looking her in the eyes.

She averted her gaze and went back to stirring the cauldron.

"Are you going to tell me?" I placed my hands on my hips.

She released a heavy sigh, then said, "The Coven members are on their way and I don't want them to see you like this."

"What do I care what they think of me? I don't have to worry about them and their stupid pamphlets any more. You know that. I'm the leader now. I'm exempt from ridicule." I moved a couple boxes off the counter and onto the shelf behind us.

That was a new rule that I'd just made up. No more making fun of my less-than-stellar skills.

She shuffled papers on the counter and avoided my stare. "Okay, granted they shouldn't have made that pamphlet, but that's all behind us now. You really should try to get along with them if we are going to live in the same town."

I scoffed. "They'd like that now, wouldn't they? I don't have to get along with them. I guess I will tolerate them, but I don't want to be friends with them. What do they want anyway?"

She glanced up. "They want to have a luncheon and they'd like for you to speak. You know, talk about your role as the leader now. That kind of thing."

I shook my head. "No way."

"You need to learn to forgive, Halloween," my mother said as she waved a wand over a bubbling cauldron.

I stepped closer to the big black pot. "What's in there?"

It was probably better if I didn't know. Why had I asked? I tried to remember not to ask what was in my mother's spells. Some things are better left unspoken. I didn't want to know that I was smearing toad's butt on my face. Luckily, my mother had learned a long time ago not to tell people what was really in her potions.

She waved off the question, the bracelets on her wrist jingling with the motion. "Oh, just a few herbs and spices. Nothing too special. It's all in the words."

Just then the bell on the door announced a visitor. Much to my chagrin, it was Misty Middleton. She was the leader of the Enchantment Pointe Coven. We'd gone to high school together. I'd tried to keep my distance ever since. It had been years and I was pretty sure she knew how I felt by now.

Misty was dressed in her usual business attire of dark-colored suit, crisp white shirt and towering heels. She made me feel like an ant. Her eyes met mine and a flicker of flirtation sparkled in her gaze. Uh-oh. Please don't let her start flirting with Liam. That was the last thing I needed this evening.

"Hello," she said coyly, batting her eyelashes.

My mother looked panic-stricken. I knew she didn't want me to divulge my secret, but I wasn't about to endure flirting with Misty Middleton.

But as I opened my mouth to tell the truth, Liam burst through the door.

"Oh dear." My mother swayed on the stool and I righted her.

Misty gasped, then backed up toward the door. "More magic and mirroring images. We don't approve of this type of thing in Enchantment Pointe. What do you have to say about this, Annette?" Misty glared at my mother.

"She has nothing to say about this and neither do you," I said, walking from around the counter.

Liam was ignoring Misty as he glared at me. He was not pleased with me at all. The bulging veins in his forehead were a dead giveaway.

"What do you think you're doing?" he asked.

"Hallie, is that you?" Misty asked, looking at me with wide eyes.

I nodded. "Yes, it's me."

"Why would you do this?" Liam's voice was full of frustration.

"I needed to speak with my mother," I said defiantly.

"You could have done that with me escorting you." Liam's eyebrows slanted in a frown.

"What's going on, Hallie?" Misty asked with her eyes wide.

"There's a situation with the New Orleans Coven," I said in a curt tone.

That was more than I should have told her. She would just run back and tell the Coven the gossip.

She stepped closer. "Really? I saw that Jacobson Stratford over at the Bubbling Cauldron."

That was the local bar for all the witches. I didn't go often because the number of witches singing with the karaoke machine was terrifying.

"What was Jacobson Stratford doing there?" I asked.

She shrugged. "I don't know. He was there with another woman. They were having quite a few beers."

"Was the woman his sister?" Liam asked.

She shrugged. "I honestly have no idea. I don't think I've ever met his sister."

"We need to go to the Bubbling Cauldron right away," I said.

Liam ran his hand through his hair. "I suppose you're right. But you can't go as me. We have to do the counter-spell."

I tapped my fingers against the counter. "You know, I could go as someone else to the bar."

He shook his head. "I don't think you can do more than one mirror spell a day."

I frowned. "How do you know that?"

"It's in the book," he said as if I should have known that little detail.

This was ridiculous. How did he know what was and what wasn't in the book? Half of it was still in a language that I didn't understand. How could he read it? Was this common knowledge for everyone but me? If that was the case I wished they'd clue me in.

"How can I do the counter-spell? I don't have the book," I said with a heavy sigh. Nothing was going as planned.

"We'll have to go and get it," Liam said.

"I'm going with you," my mother said, jumping up from the stool and grabbing her purse.

Liam shook his head. "I don't think that's such a good idea, Ms. LaVeau."

My mother poked Liam in the chest. "Don't push me, young man. And call me Annette. I'm not that old."

"Yes, ma'am." Liam nodded.

My mother scowled.

"I mean Annette," he corrected.

"I was going to the Bubbling Cauldron too. Do you mind if I go with you?" Misty asked.

"Oh no. That's not a good idea." I frowned.

"Actually, that's not such a bad idea," Liam said.

I whipped around and stared at him. "What are you talking about?"

He shrugged. "We could use the extra witchcraft."

Misty waved her hand. "That's true. I'd be happy to help in any way I can."

I couldn't believe that I was currently headed to a bar with Liam, my mother, and Misty Middleton. That karaoke was sounding pretty good at this moment.

CHAPTER EIGHTEEN

Night had fallen over Enchantment Pointe. It was a mild fall evening, not quite cool enough for a sweater, but not so hot that I was sweating buckets. Misty and my mother were sitting in the back seat, Liam drove, and I sat in the passenger seat.

We pulled up in front of the bar. People gathered around in front of the black double entry doors, but at least there wasn't a line to get in. A neon cauldron with bubbles rising up from the top was on a sign above the door with the words *The Bubbling Cauldron*.

"Are you ready?" Liam asked, squeezing my hand.

My insides tingled. "As ready as I'll ever be. Let's go."

We climbed out of the car and made our way down the sidewalk. I wasn't sure what exactly we would say to Jacobson if he was actually in the bar, but he had quite a few questions to answer. Number one: I wanted to know if he'd seen Nicolas. I also wanted to know about the strange markings on the wall at the deserted house and at his plantation. Not that he would tell me, but if he didn't, I knew it would be time to force him to talk. There had to be a way to make that happen.

As soon as we walked through the door, the caterwauling of someone's rendition of *Funkytown* assaulted my ears. That was one way for the bar to sell more liquor. Everyone needed to drink after listening to the singing. People filled every corner of the bar and I didn't see an empty table in sight.

"Do you see him?" my mother asked.

I shook my head. "Not yet. I don't see him, but it's really crowded in here."

I had to raise my voice to be heard over the singing in the background.

"I see a table over in the corner." Liam pointed across the room.

I submerged myself into crowd, swallowed by a sea of writhing bodies. With much effort, we made our way across the bar. In the middle of the dance floor was a huge black cauldron. Fake smoke and bubbles billowed up from the top toward the ceiling. The lights underneath the cauldron changed from red, blue, white, yellow and purple every few seconds. People swayed to the rhythm of the music, grinding their bodies against each other.

As I shimmed through the sea of bodies, I felt a burning stare. Out of the corner of my eye, I noticed a brown-haired woman across the way. When I glanced up, she shifted her gaze and hurriedly walked away. I recognized her from somewhere… but where? Oh yeah, she was the waitress from the bar.

"The waitress who sent us to the house looking for Nicolas was just over there." I yelled into Liam's ear.

Liam whipped around, scanning the crowd. There's no way we'd find her now.

"She's probably gone now," Liam leaned down and whispered in my ear.

He was right. She'd probably left when she spotted me. I scanned the room as we walked toward a table, but I still didn't see any sign of Jacobson or Sabrina. We had probably made a wasted trip. To my surprise, no one seemed to pay attention to us. I had expected that they'd whisper about the new leader. They had probably had so many drinks by now that they didn't even care. Heck, they'd had so much to drink that I thought they were actually enjoying the singing.

Liam pulled out the stools for all of us.

"What a gentleman." My mother beamed.

I offered Liam a little smile. Maybe it was the dim lights obscuring my sight, but I thought for sure Liam blushed.

I sat at on the stool and scanned the room. I still hadn't seen anyone who looked familiar. A waitress approached.

"You need anything to drink?" She pointed at us.

"Bring us four beers?" Liam looked at us for confirmation.

We nodded in agreement. It would look odd if we were just sitting there and not drinking like everyone else. We needed to blend in with the crowd. After a couple minutes, the waitress returned, placing the bottles down on the table. Liam grabbed the bottle and took a drink. As he set the bottle on the table, I spotted Jacobson across the room. Luckily, I didn't think that he'd seen me. My heart rate increased. What was I going to say to him?

"Okay, don't look now, but Jacobson is in the corner of the room." I took a drink of my beer so that it would look as if I hadn't been talking about anything serious.

Everyone turned their heads and began scanning the area.

I grabbed Liam's arm. "I said don't look now. What part of that do you all not understand?"

Liam looked at me. "Sorry. Why don't you tell us where he's at?"

"Okay, but don't look. He's sitting toward the back of the room at a table in the corner. It's to your right," I gestured with a subtle tilt of my head.

No matter how many times I said don't look, they still looked. Luckily, it didn't appear as if Jacobson had noticed us. The room was dim, but I'd recognize Jacobson anywhere. His tall, thin frame and long face didn't stand out in a crowd, but the way he dressed sure was noticeable. Tonight he wore a red silk shirt and black pants. He looked as if he was headed back in time to a disco. Jacobson tilted his head back in laughter. Who was he talking to? I couldn't see who was standing next to him because of the group of people on the dance floor blocking my view.

"I wish those people would get out of the way so I could see who he is talking to," I said.

My mother waved her hands through the air and said, "Lift your feet without missing a beat. You're blocking the view, now move for just a few."

The people standing in front of the table glanced around, confused. They'd obviously sensed the magic, but didn't know where it had come from. I didn't want my mother to get in trouble for disobeying the no-magic policy. I couldn't blame the place for putting that sign out front. With this many witches in one place, the wand-waving could get a little out of hand. Lucky for us, the spell had worked because the two women and the man stepped over to the next table. They probably had no idea why they wanted to move, they just knew that they wanted to move.

But I had a perfect view now thanks to my mother. And I didn't like what I saw.

"I don't think you're supposed to do magic in here, Mother. That's why the sign was outside," I said.

"Desperate times call for desperate measures, right? I think a little magic just this one time won't hurt." She wiggled her penciled-on eyebrows.

I shook my head, but didn't argue. There was no use. She'd already done it now. "Well, just don't do any more while we're here, okay?"

Sabrina Stratford was the person sitting across from her brother. She wasn't such an outlandish dresser as her brother though. Sabrina wore a burgundy-colored wrap dress and matching heels. A little too matching for my taste, but that was neither here nor there right now. She could have been wearing pajamas and bunny slippers and I wouldn't care. I just wanted to get to the bottom of the charges and be done with this.

Sabrina took a sip from her wine glass, then continued chatting with her brother. They still hadn't noticed that we were staring at them. But that soon changed.

Sabrina took another sip, sat the glass down and turned to meet our stare. She looked me dead in the eyes and glared. Her evil stare shot across the room. If power had been behind it, I would have fallen out of my chair and onto the floor.

Jacobson must have sensed the magic too because he looked over at us. He stared for a moment, then set his highball glass down and stood. He was definitely coming our way. I hoped this didn't turn into a fight. I had to find out a way to stop this madness soon.

If only I could figure out what the book said. According to what I'd read so far, I had to unlock the rules of the book one at a time. So if I needed to perform a certain spell to save Nicolas, I sure hadn't discovered it yet. If I could bring Nicolas' mother back, she could tell me what I should do. Heck, she could even have her old job back. I'd go back to being a bad witch just running a bed-and-breakfast. That was all I'd wanted to do in the first place. Who needed this headache?

Jacobson weaved through the crowd, never taking his eyes off our table.

"Oh, he's coming our way," Misty said in a shaky voice.

She'd never dealt with anything like this before. The worst of her problems consisted of what food to serve at the monthly Coven meetings.

"I'll handle him," Liam said as he pushed to his feet.

I grabbed Liam's arm. "Don't let him drag you into a fight."

Jacobson approached the table with a fake smile on his face. "Imagine seeing you here." He looked over at my mother and Misty and nodded.

"I think we can say the same thing to you," Liam said with a cool and clipped tone.

"You're a little far away from home, don't you think?" I asked.

"We were in the area. I've heard a lot of good things about Enchantment Pointe. I thought I'd give it a closer look-see." Jacobson flashed his overly white teeth.

"Cut the crap, Jacobson. What are you doing back in Enchantment Pointe?" Liam asked.

Jacobson shot Liam a dirty look. "I told you why I'm here. There's nothing more to it."

"We stopped by to see you, but no one was home. The door was open though," I said.

Okay, maybe I shouldn't have told him, but I wanted him to know that he wasn't the only sly one. Two could play that game.

"I'm aware that you were in the home. I have cameras set up, you know." He smirked.

"Then you won't mind telling me what you know about the markings on the wall in your place," I said, folding my arms in front of my chest.

"Oh that?" He feigned surprise. "That's just a little part of the witchcraft we practice. Nothing to worry about."

I knew it was fruitless to even ask him what kind of witchcraft. I'd have to figure it out on my own. Whatever they were up to, I knew it wasn't good. Tension hung in the air as he stared at us. Just then, Sabrina sashayed over. She didn't speak as she fixed her stare on me. There was clearly hatred in her eyes. We needed to have a long conversation to get to the bottom of her accusations, but I didn't know whether we should have that confrontation now or get out of there instead. If I knew the Stratfords though, and I was learning their personalities quickly, then

I knew that they were itching for a confrontation. I refused to get into a barroom brawl.

Before I had a chance to mentally debate it any longer, a strange vibe fell over me. I couldn't put my finger on it, but I knew that I'd sensed it before. I looked to my mother and Misty, but they were too busy focusing their attention on Sabrina. Did they feel the strange vibe too? If they did, they didn't mention it.

"What are you doing here?" Sabrina asked as if highly insulted.

It was nice that she'd finally spoken, but I didn't like her first question. How dare she ask me why I was there?

I shot her an evil stare. "Excuse me? I am the leader of the Underworld and I think I can stop in for a drink at the Bubbling Cauldron."

I added the part about being the leader because I knew that would make her angry. I wasn't sure how I knew, I just knew. Probably from the malicious looks she'd been shooting my way. As far as I was concerned being the leader was hardly a perk, more like a burden.

"You do know that witchcraft isn't allowed in the bar," she said in a snippy tone.

"I'm fully aware of the bar policies, thank you," I snapped.

She smirked and was ready to make some pointless comeback when the strange vibe fell over me again. It glided at a steady pace across the room. The sensation wasn't visible, but I felt it. It came toward me in a wave, picking up speed until it finally landed against me with a smash. The wind was sucked from my lungs and I let out a gasp. My mother rushed over and patted me on the back. Liam grabbed my arm.

"Are you okay?" my mother asked.

I nodded as I took a couple quick breaths. Jacobson and Sabrina had sly smiles on their faces. They knew what this was all about. The strange vibe had come from them, but I just didn't know how or why at the moment. I wouldn't stop until I figured out what they were doing. They were into some black magic and I had to prove it.

Just then Sabrina and Jacobson moved a couple steps to the side, opening up a path. Across the bar, I spotted Nicolas. His glassy-eyed stare was fixed on me. The multi-colored lights from the giant bubbling cauldron pulsated behind him, changing from red, then blue to green. What was he doing there? My stomach took a dive. I should be happy to see him, but something didn't feel right. The look in his eyes was the same as when I'd last seen him. Whatever had a hold of him was attached tightly. I had to find out what was wrong with him and get rid of it before it was too late. When Jacobson saw Nicolas, I knew there would be a huge fight.

I glanced over at Liam. He was staring straight at his brother. Liam looked as if he was ready to pounce on Jacobson if he made one move toward Nicolas.

But to my surprise, Nicolas stood right between Jacobson and Sabrina. They smiled at each other as if they were the best of friends. Nicolas looked tired with dark circles ringing his eyes.

"What is going on?" Liam asked.

I couldn't take my eyes off Nicolas' face. "What are you doing here, Nicolas?"

"Hallie. Liam." Nicolas nodded. His greeting was polite, but formal.

"Do you care to explain what is going on?" I asked, looking at Jacobson.

"All is forgiven with Nicolas now. There is no need to go any further with an investigation. He's decided to work closely with the New Orleans Coven. He's the new vampire consultant."

I exchanged a glance with Liam. I didn't believe this for two seconds. No way would Nicolas join Jacobson and Sabrina and try to help them. And there was no way Jacobson would forgive Nicolas for what he'd done.

"Is this true, Nicolas?" I asked.

"Yes, I feel it's for the best. There are no hard feelings between us now. Plus, they need my help." He offered a fake smile.

"Nicolas, can I speak with you in private?" Liam asked, gesturing with a tilt of his head.

Nicolas shook his head. "We were just on our way back to New Orleans. I'll call you soon."

"This isn't something that can wait," Liam said sternly.

"Nicolas, I really think we should speak about this first. I would at least like a chance to close out this investigation." I searched his eyes.

"There are no charges to investigate anymore. Like I said, everything is fine. Right, Sabrina?" Jacobson looked to his sister.

"You can't bring charges and then just decide that it's over. The rules don't work that way," I said.

Sure, I had no idea how the rules really worked, but they didn't know that. Plus, I should be able to make up some of the rules as I went, right?

Jacobson's brow pulled in to an affronted frown. "There is nothing you can do about it."

Well, we'd see about that.

I ignored Jacobson, and said, "Nicolas, we found your wallet in the abandoned house."

He shook his head. "I don't know what you're talking about. I didn't lose my wallet."

Too bad I hadn't brought it with me to prove it to him. He was lying to me now and I knew that wasn't like Nicolas at all.

That was when it hit me. This wasn't Nicolas at all. The person in front of me was the imposter who had been in the New Orleans vampire bar. But why would they have someone pretend to be Nicolas? If this was a fake Nicolas, then where was the real Nicolas?

Sabrina looped her arm through Nicolas'. "Come on, we need to get back to the plantation."

"I'll call you," Nicolas said as he turned around.

I looked for some glimmer of the old Nicolas that I'd known, but I saw nothing in his eyes.

"Stop," I yelled as I watched the three of them walk away.

I hurried around the table with Liam, Misty, and my mother following close behind. There was no way I would let Nicolas walk out of this bar with them. Not without knowing for sure if it was an imposter. Jacobson and Sabrina were up to no good.

The bar had grown even more crowded and it was hard to run through the groups of people and keep up with Nicolas. When I got close enough that I thought I could stop him, I reached for his arm, but didn't make contact. Instead I fell to the ground. Liam rushed over and helped me to my feet. When I looked up, they'd already made their way out the door.

CHAPTER NINETEEN

Without saying a word, I rushed to the door. I wanted answers, and darn it, I was going to get them. Once I made it out into the night air, I looked up and down the sidewalk. The trio had vanished as if a tornado had dropped from the sky and sucked them right up.

"Where did they go?" Misty asked from behind me.

Liam and my mother stood next to me, looking just as frustrated as I felt.

The sound of a cough caught my attention and I whipped around. A man was leaning against the brick building.

He took a puff from his cigarette, then said, "Are you looking for the men and woman?"

"Yes, did you see them?" I asked.

"They used magic and vanished." He snapped his fingers.

"Seriously?" I asked, with my mouth hanging open.

He stared at me for a moment, then said, "No. They jumped in a black car and sped away as if they'd just robbed a bank."

Leave it to me to run into a smart-ass at the most inopportune time. All I wanted was straight answers, not sarcastic remarks.

"Did you see which way they went?" Liam asked. He probably sensed my frustration.

"They went right, away from town." The man pointed, then tossed his cigarette on the ground and stomped on it.

"They're headed to New Orleans, I guess," I said.

The man stared at me with his beady little eyes as he walked past. He disappeared into the Bubbling Cauldron without saying another word. He acted strangely for sure, but I figured he'd had a few too many beers. I wondered though... could he be someone giving us false information? I had no way to know, but enough about him anyway. I had to know what Jacobson and Sabrina had been doing in Enchantment Pointe. And if it was the real Nicolas, then how had they convinced him to tag along with them? Had they used some kind of witchcraft? Why wouldn't Nicolas answer my questions? All good questions without answers.

"I don't think that was the real Nicolas," I said, looking at Liam.

He shook his head. "I think you might be right."

"What makes you think that?" I asked.

"Whoever that was had a necklace around their neck. Nicolas never wears them," he said.

That was something that I hadn't known about Nicolas. I'd have to find out why Nicolas had an aversion to necklaces. I thought back to when Nicolas and I had been dancing. One minute he hadn't been wearing the necklace, then once he returned, he had had one on his neck. Was that when the real Nicolas had disappeared?

After dropping off my mother and Misty, Liam and I headed back to LaVeau Manor. As we drove along, I studied the twinkling stars in the clear night sky.

"I guess you weren't expecting your life to take such a drastic turn," Liam said as he navigated a turn.

I leaned my head back against the seat. "Not exactly, no."

He cast a glance my way and said, "For whatever it's worth, I know you'll figure things out."

"I just wish I had more control." I closed my eyes for a moment.

"You need a good night's sleep. You'll be able to think more clearly in the morning," Liam squeezed my hand.

"I'd better come up with a plan soon," I said.

I realized when we pulled into the driveway of LaVeau Manor that a foreboding feeling fell over me instantly. This time, I didn't have a sense of relief about being home. It was more like trepidation for what might be waiting for me inside. Where had Catherin vanished too and how would I get rid of Claude?

Liam held the door open for me as we stepped inside the massive foyer. He closed the door behind us and turned to me. Pluto rushed over and weaved around my legs. He meowed loudly, letting me know that his food dish was empty and that he wanted the supply replenished immediately.

"Well, I guess I'll turn in for the night," I said.

My heart beat faster as Liam stared at me. His eyes were fixed on my lips. In one fluid movement, he was standing in front of me. My head was swimming as he pressed his body close to mine. I melted into his arms as his lips met mine. As his mouth covered mine hungrily, I was shocked by my own eager response to his kiss.

My knees went weak and the only thing holding me up was Liam's embrace. I knew I had to push him away. My thoughts were so muddled at the moment. I couldn't allow myself to be swept up in the moment. But yet I couldn't pull away from his kiss either.

When the doorbell rang, it was like being saved by the bell. I wasn't sure if that was a good or bad thing though. Liam pulled away from me and looked at the door. The bell ringing at LaVeau Manor meant trouble and he knew it. Sometimes that meant gorgeous men showing up, but that still equaled nothing but trouble.

I raced over to the door and peeked out the little hole. The night was clear and the light on the veranda illuminated the men's faces. The man from the bar stood on my doorstep. He wasn't alone though.

"It's that strange man from the Bubbling Cauldron, the one who was smoking outside, and there's another man with him," I whispered.

Liam hurried over and opened the door. It was funny how I thought things couldn't get stranger, and yet they always did. This place was like the vortex for all things strange. And I was now queen of the weirdness.

"What do you want?" Liam asked as he opened the door.

I peeked around to get a better look at the men. They were peering over Liam's shoulder at me. What did they want with me?

"I've come to see Halloween LaVeau," the man said in a professional tone.

Obviously he meant business. He wore a gray suit that matched the sprinkles of gray in his otherwise dark hair. He had icy blue eyes and incredibly pale skin.

"I'm afraid she's not accepting visitors this evening," Liam said, pushing the door closed.

From the expression on this man's face, he didn't seem to care whether I was receiving guests or not. He didn't look like the follow-the-rules type.

The man stopped the door with his foot. "You're Liam Rankin," he said. "Aren't you Nicolas Marcos' brother?"

The only thing that saved this man's foot from being smashed was the mention of Nicolas' name. Liam eased his stance and opened the door again.

"Why do you ask?" Liam said, as his expression changed.

In spite of everything, was Liam genuinely concerned for his brother? I wasn't sure if the tension between them had gone too far to the point that they'd never be like brothers again.

"Have you see Nicolas?" he asked.

"Who are you? Did you follow us home?" I asked, pointing at the cigarette guy.

This was incredibly frustrating and I wasn't about to let them get by without telling me exactly what they wanted with Nicolas.

"When I told him that I'd talked to the new leader of the Underworld, he insisted that I follow you home, so yes, we did follow you," the cigarette man said with a gruff voice.

Liam stepped in front of me. "What the hell do you want? You have about two seconds to explain yourself."

I tried to ignore the thoughts in my mind, but it was hard not to think about how sexy Liam was when he was angry. Plus, Liam had stayed here when the times were tough. Nicolas had thought it was best to leave. I wasn't sure how I felt about that.

"I haven't seen Nicolas and I wonder if he's in trouble," the man said.

"Why don't you tell me who you are before I give you any information regarding Mr. Marcos?" I said, crossing my arms in front of my chest.

"My name is Gilford Harris. I am the leader of the Baton Rouge Clan of Vampires. I've been looking for the leader of the New Orleans Clan. It seems he is missing. That's when I heard of Nicolas' troubles. I saw the clan leader and Nicolas together about two weeks ago."

"The leader is missing?" I asked.

"For how long?" Liam asked, as if he'd read my thoughts and asked my next question.

"It's been almost a couple weeks now," he said.

I wasn't sure if Liam had read my thoughts this time or what, but he looked at me. I knew we were wondering the same thing. All of this with Nicolas had happened two weeks ago. Could it somehow be related?

"So if you're looking for the leader, then why do you need Nicolas?" I asked, almost afraid of the answer.

"May I come in?" His expression darkened.

I still wasn't sure I should trust this man. After all, they had followed us and that was beyond creepy and stalkerish. But with Liam there, I supposed it would be okay. I nodded at Liam that he could open the door further and allow the men to enter. As the men stepped inside, they glanced around. Were they looking for something? I glanced up toward the second floor. Was my newest guest still there? He had been awfully quiet.

The men followed me into the parlor. Liam walked behind them just in case they wanted to try any funny business.

"Please have a seat." I motioned toward the sofa.

The men sat down, taking in the full view of the room.

"I knew your great-aunt," the man said. "She was a lovely woman."

"She had a lot of friends," I said.

I didn't want to exchange pleasantries with this man. I just wanted him to get to the reason for his visit. "So, tell me exactly why you decided to pay me a visit."

"There are rogue vampires out there and I need your help stopping them. I need your help in finding the New Orleans leader. To be honest, I may be next, so I have to know why he's gone." The lines of worry deepened around Gilford's eyes.

"So you suspect that the rogue vampires had something to do with the leader's disappearance and you think they'll come after you next?" I repeated.

I had to make sure I had this story straight. It really didn't make sense and at the moment I was a bit confused.

"Yes, I do believe they had something to do with it. I have good reason to believe that too," he said.

"Do you care to share that with us?" I asked.

He leaned back in his seat. "It's simple really. The New Orleans leader threatened to eliminate the bad ones. He didn't want to tolerate their behavior, so they wanted to get rid of him."

"And they want to get rid of you for the same reason?" Liam asked.

He nodded. "That is correct."

The cigarette guy looked like he really didn't want to be here. He had been caught in the middle of this when all he probably wanted was a beer.

"When did the vampires start acting this way?" I asked.

"It's been going on for about six months. There's a dark force at work. A demon has been trying to come through for some time." The strain in his voice was palpable.

I exchanged a glance with Liam. Since I'd just dealt with a demon, I really didn't want to hear the word again anytime soon.

"What kind of demon?" Liam asked.

The cigarette guy shifted in his seat. I knew he was uncomfortable with the topic too.

"I don't have expertise with this demon, so I can't offer much information other than I know it is somehow connected to the witches and the vampires."

That was odd. How would I find out what that connection was? It was my job to find out what that connection was, right? I needed an assistant. I'd barely had time to look at the Book of Mystics, much less research demons.

"You said a demon had been trying to come through? What do you mean?" Asking the question sent a chill down my spine.

"A demon has been unleashed. I don't know what he is capable of, but it's best not to find out the hard way. Don't you agree?" He fixed his gaze on me.

"Well, yeah, I don't want to deal with a demon," I said.

"Ginny Love told me you were in the New Orleans bar. I heard you were looking for Nicolas, but I didn't figure you knew the full extent of what's been going on."

"I am aware of the charges against Nicolas, but I didn't know about the clan leader. But rest assured, I'll try to help you any way I can," I offered.

"Do you think the charges against Nicolas are related to the actions of all the rogue vampires?" Liam asked.

He shrugged. "It seems like it could be, but I know Nicolas is a decent person, so I don't think he could be involved with these vampires."

I didn't think so either, but Nicolas was now with the bad witches in New Orleans. I'd have to go to Nicolas and confront him about the new details I'd learned. And I also needed to find out who this demon was. I couldn't fight something I knew nothing about. I'd done that once and I'd come really close to losing the battle. I didn't want to repeat that.

As we contemplated the conversation, the click of the front door opening carried across the room. The sound of the wicked wind whistled through the house. Loud laughter followed that, echoing through the foyer. I jumped up and ran over with Liam following on my heels. When we reached the foyer, he jumped in front of me. Catherin and Claude were strolling arm in arm through the door. Apparently, they'd met each other and had become the best of friends.

When they spotted the four of us staring at them, they stopped dead in their tracks. Maybe it was just me being suspicious of everyone around me, but they looked guilty of something. What had they been doing?

"Oh, I didn't know anyone would still be awake," Catherin said in her sweetest voice.

"I didn't know where you'd gone, Catherin. Are you okay?" I'd thought for sure that I'd gotten rid of her when I reanimated Claude.

"Oh, I just stepped out for a while. You didn't need me hanging around so much. When I came back Claude was here. I made him a batch of cupcakes, I hope you don't mind."

What was the deal with cupcakes? "No, I don't mind."

"We made sure to clean up our mess. You'd never know we were in your kitchen." Claude flashed a sly smile.

How did Catherin become close to the people around her so quickly? She certainly was charismatic. Well, in their eyes at least. I wasn't falling for her charms though. It would take more than a few cupcakes for her to convince me she was as sweet as she wanted everyone else to believe. I needed to get rid of both of my guests now.

CHAPTER TWENTY

After the vampire leader had gone and everyone else had retired to their bedrooms for the night, I picked up the phone and called Annabelle. She'd left me a message while I was at the Bubbling Cauldron, but this had been the first chance I'd had to return her call. If the bodyguard Liam had sent her home with turned out to be a jackass, there would be hell to pay. Mostly from Annabelle because she could unleash a tongue-lashing when someone made her really mad.

"How's it going?" I asked in hushed tones so that no one would hear me.

"Do you know that we really have a lot in common? We even like the same ice cream, mint chocolate chip. And did you see his smile? Oh, and those gorgeous eyes," she said dreamily.

"Yeah, he sounds like a real loser." I laughed. "But have there been any problems?" I asked.

Annabelle obviously liked this guy and she hardly ever liked any guys. She always found something wrong with them. Either their shoes were dirty or their hair was out of place or they didn't like the right TV shows. She was always looking for an excuse not to like the guy. It looked as if this one had finally been able to meet her crazy standards.

"Oh, we're getting along wonderfully. I even made us dinner," she said.

"Okay, now I know you have it bad for him if you offered to cook." Annabelle was a great cook, but she never prepared food for a date. She didn't want to set the precedent.

She snorted. "I will admit that I can't find anything wrong with him, but that could change in a heartbeat, you know."

Unfortunately, I knew all too well how things could change in a heartbeat. After briefing Annabelle on what had happened since we'd last talked, she agreed to come over in the morning with her hot bodyguard, but only if she could make breakfast. That was fine by me, although I wasn't sure if it was because she wanted to show off her cooking skills in front of the new guy or if she just didn't want me to embarrass myself in front of him by burning pancakes again.

As I lay in my bed, I couldn't stop the rapid succession of thoughts from running through my mind. I worried about Nicolas and what he'd gotten messed up in. I knew this wasn't like his character, but I had to find out what type of spell he was under and who had done this to him. Because there was one thing I was sure of and that was that Nicolas had been put under a spell. The logical people to blame were Sabrina and her brother Jacobson, but what had they done to him? It would be impossible to stop it if I didn't know what type of spell I was dealing with.

After tossing and turning, I crawled out of bed and grabbed the Book of Mystics. If I studied it long enough, maybe something would make sense. I needed to perform a spell for clarity, so I clutched the book to my chest and made my way out into the hallway. The manor was quiet, but something hung in the air. It was that same foreboding that I'd felt when Liam and I had pulled up earlier in the night.

Once in the kitchen, I inhaled a deep breath and soaked in my surroundings. The more I performed the spells, the more comfortable I became in the manor's kitchen. Even though the spells didn't always work as I'd intended most of the time, the place was starting to feel more and more like home. Now if only I could banish that strange vibe that was hanging over the place.

As I moved around the kitchen collecting my spices and herbs, it felt more and more like the normal routine I should be in… as if this really was my calling, just like Aunt Maddy had said. But how could this be my calling when I was obviously so bad at it?

For a spell of clarity, I'd call to the elements. Facing north, I recited the words: "Element of Earth, I call to you. Empower me with your energy to see clearly." I turned to face the west, and recited the words: "Element of Air, I call to you to push the negative that surrounds me." I shifted to face the south and recited the words: "Element of Fire, I call to you for warmth and protection. Help me have the knowledge." Completing the spell, I moved again to face the east and recited the words: "Element of Water, I call to you for force and tranquility. Give me the force to make the right decisions."

When the energy from the spell began to fade, another blast of wind stirred. The foreboding feeling swirled within the wind. The book opened to a spell just as it had when I'd found it. The problem was that I didn't know what this spell was for, so it couldn't help much. I was blindly casting the spells without knowing what or why. But what other options did I have at the moment? Maybe the clarity spell was responsible for what was happening now. The pages flipped rapidly until finally coming to rest, then the wind stilled.

Again I began to recite the words: "Element of Earth, I call to you. Take away negativity and keep me safe." I sprinkled salt in the cauldron, then faced west and recited the words: "Element of Air, I call to you to push the unnatural force from this place." I dumped more salt into the cauldron, then turned to the south and recited the words: "Element of Fire, I call to you to receive and burn all the negativity. Allow me to cleanse the manor from the wicked." Another dash of salt into the cauldron, and then I turned to the east, reciting the words: "Element of Water, I call to you for power. Give me the power to fight the evil."

The book had to be giving me the correct spells, right? It was just up to me to discover their meaning and put them to the right use. According to the Book of Mystics, it was my duty to shut down the New Orleans Coven if I felt there was a problem. And as far as I could tell, there was most definitely a problem. But what would I do to shut down the Coven? There had to be a spell to hamper the Coven's powers, right? It might require more energy than I had at the moment though. Why did I feel as if my energy was being drained? Was someone stealing it again? The image of Catherin flashed in my mind with her sweet face and big brown eyes. Surely a relative wouldn't do such a thing, right?

The clarity spell I'd performed must have worked because an idea came to me. Why hadn't I thought of this before? Since I couldn't get a spell to work to bring back Nicolas' mother to help me, then why didn't I send someone to talk with her? I didn't mean literally send someone to the afterlife, but use a medium to speak with Gina. If the medium could channel Nicolas' mother, perhaps I could get answers to some of my questions. Luckily, I knew just the person who could help me. She just so happened to be in New Orleans too. Tomorrow we would visit her, then find Nicolas.

I'd fallen asleep with my head resting on the counter again. At least that was where I remembered falling asleep. However, that wasn't where I woke up.

CHAPTER TWENTY-ONE

Annabelle and Jon were standing over me when I opened my eyes. He had a slight smirk on his face and Annabelle's mouth hung open. The blue sky was painted with white fluffy clouds. The smell of grass and earth surrounded me. When I glanced down at my body, I saw that I was covered in dirt again. My neck and back hurt.

"Hallie, what the hell are you doing out here?" Annabelle's voice was so loud it sounded more like a screech.

I sat up and rubbed my head. "I don't know. The last thing I remember was sitting at the kitchen counter."

I was now not far from the backdoor leading outside from the kitchen. Had I blacked out again like when I had been in the cemetery? Was something seriously wrong with me? Other than having a stiff neck and achy back, I felt fine. My energy felt depleted though. I had a suspicion that something was zapping my energy again. Had the demon Isabeau returned? Or was it some other force at work? Could it be related to the demon that the vampire leader said had been unleashed?

Jon stretched his hand out to help me up.

I jumped up as quickly as my achy body would allow. "Come on. We have to hurry. We're going to New Orleans."

"I take it we're not going to New Orleans to collect beads," Annabelle said as she followed me inside.

"Not on purpose at least. I have other plans," I said from over my shoulder as we entered the kitchen.

"You get dressed. Jon and I will make breakfast," Annabelle said, tossing an apron at Jon.

"It looks good on you." I pointed at Jon as he tied the apron around his waist.

"The little blue flowers match my shirt, right?" he asked as he slipped it over his neck.

After a quick breakfast, the four of us were in Liam's car headed back to New Orleans. Liam didn't seem sold on my psychic medium idea.

"I worry that we may be opening ourselves up to entities that we don't want around." Even he couldn't hide the worry in his voice.

"Honestly, do we really want any entities around? We'll have to talk to Gina in order to get rid of whatever bad may be hanging around. Besides, my friend knows what she's doing. I promise," I said, crossing my heart.

"Regardless of what she tells us, we still need to know who this demon is that Gilford Harris was talking about." His voice was full of with concern.

I offered a faint smile. "One thing at a time."

We made it to the outskirts of New Orleans in record time. The house where Sierra Gray lived was down a small dirt road. We pulled the car in front of the white clapboard house. Wind chimes hung from the porch and a couple of white rocking chairs sat by the front door. One swayed back and forth as if someone had just gotten up.

"How do you know this woman?" Liam asked.

"We went to high school together," I said.

"She was always spooky, if you ask me," Annabelle said from the backseat.

Annabelle thought Casper the friendly ghost was scary, so that wasn't saying much.

"Annabelle and I can wait outside," Jon said while winking at Annabelle.

That was a sure-fire way to win her heart—keep her away from spooky things.

After Liam and Jon got out of the car, they stepped off to the side and spoke for a moment, whispering just out of earshot.

I let out a deep breath, then said to Annabelle, "I'm sorry for dragging you into this. I've said that a million times over the past few days, huh?"

"Hey, I got a bodyguard. How cool is that?" Annabelle chuckled.

I laughed. "That's a good point."

When the men joined us again, the suspicious look still covered Liam's face.

"Liam, just trust me on this. I really think she can help." I touched his forearm.

"If you say it'll work, then we have to give it a try," Liam said as he walked up the porch steps beside me.

I didn't tell Liam that I couldn't think of any other options. After lightly knocking on the door, it swung open and Sierra smiled broadly.

"It's good to see you, Hallie." Sierra grabbed me in a hug.

"It's been too long. Sierra, this is Liam Rankin." I gestured toward Liam.

Liam's cheeks turned red when Sierra grabbed him in a hug too. He wasn't the hugging type, which was exactly the opposite of Sierra. She'd never met someone she didn't like. Although if she'd met some of the people I had recently that would probably change.

"Please come in," she said gesturing over her shoulder.

The house was small, but decorated just as I'd remembered Sierra's personality—eccentric and full of whimsy. I'd always envied Sierra's zest for life.

169

"Please, everyone have a seat." Sierra gestured across the room.

Liam and I sat on the oversized floral sofa. It took up most of the space in the room.

"So tell me what's been going on." Sierra sat cross-legged on the floor across from us.

I'd filled her in over the phone about my new leader of the Underworld status. Talk about an awkward conversation. How did you tell people something like that? When they asked what it meant, I had no clue what to tell them. Should I describe my title as babysitter to the paranormal crowd? That was what it felt like at the moment.

"I need help figuring out what the spells in the book I inherited mean. I thought if you could help me talk to the previous leader, then I could ask her questions. I've been reanimating the dead, but it's never who I want to come back," I said with a wave of my hands.

Her face turned white. "You've been bringing back the dead?"

I nodded. "Not on purpose. Well, other than the one time, but the spell I cast didn't bring back the person I wanted."

"It doesn't matter how good at the craft you are, that's a tricky spell. There's so much opportunity for something to go wrong." She shook her head and looked out blankly across the room, as if she was lost in her thoughts about all the horrible things that could happen.

Now she told me. If someone had written that out in the Book of Mystics I never would have had this problem. Of course if I could actually read all of the Book of Mystics, I wouldn't have had this problem either. But that was neither here nor there.

"It's a little too late anyway now," I said.

"How many spirits have you returned?" Sierra asked in a shaky voice.

"Well, let's see. There was the demon Isabeau, but I banished her back to hell. At least I hope I did. My magic is a little iffy, you know," I said as I used my fingers to count the spirits.

She grimaced and nodded.

"Then there was Catherin and now Claude. I tried to bring back the last leader, but she vanished before I could complete the spell." I folded my hands in my lap. "So, that's it, just the three. There are plenty of spirits hanging around though."

"I bet," she said, wide-eyed.

"Do you think you can help me?" I asked.

"I highly recommend that you don't bring any other spirits back," she said with an ominous tone.

"Trust me, I don't intend to," I said.

The bracelets on her wrists jingled as she spoke with her hands. "Well, I can probably speak with the person you want, but it would be best if we have a séance."

"A séance?" I asked.

She nodded. "Yes, but it's better if we do that tonight. And I'll need a couple more people to complete the circle."

Oh, Annabelle was not going to like this one bit. I wasn't sure how I could convince her to participate. Maybe the new hunk bodyguard could talk her into it.

"I think that can be arranged," I said, hiding the uncertainty in my voice.

Liam coughed, but I ignored his warning. Everyone knew by now that Annabelle wanted no part of the creepy stuff. Now it was up to me to convince her to do it. I was such a terrible friend. But I had technically introduced her to Jon. That counted for something, right?

CHAPTER TWENTY-TWO

While we waited for night to fall and the séance to begin, we had only one mission to accomplish—find Nicolas. If we found him, as the leader, did I have the right to order him to come with us? Probably not.

We'd decided to check out the most logical place first, Jacobson's plantation. On our way there, I had to convince Annabelle to take part in the séance. That would be like getting a cat to take a bath. I'd probably end up with a ton of scratches before it was all said and done.

As we drove along, I peered out the car window and casually said, "Annabelle, have you ever been to a séance?"

Okay, that was far from casual and I knew the answer to that question. In fact, it hadn't been so much a question, but more like my stupid passive-aggressive way of telling her about the séance. It was better than saying, *Hey, do you want to conjure up some spirits in the dark?*

Annabelle released a nervous snort that quickly turned into a loud chortle. "Hallie, you are insane if you think I'm going to have a séance with that woman."

She knew me so well. This was going to be harder than I'd thought.

"You really wouldn't have to do much other than hold hands with us," I said, trying to sound breezy.

When I glanced over at Liam, he gave me a 'good luck' smile of pity.

She shook her head. "Yes, then a spirit can take over my body."

"That rarely ever happens." I waved my hand.

She snorted again. "Rarely is not the kind of odds I was looking for."

I'd have to work on her before nightfall. If she didn't agree to it I didn't know what I'd do.

My apprehension grew as we neared the plantation. By the time we pulled down the long tree-lined driveway, my nervousness was off the charts. I didn't want another fight, but it would probably be unavoidable. Spanish moss swayed in the wind as it dripped down from the old oak trees. The massive white mansion dripped with southern ambiance. Liam pulled the car right up in front of the place.

We weren't even making an attempt to be surreptitious. Jon and Annabelle didn't offer to stay in the car this time as we opened the car doors and climbed up. I scanned the area, then stared up at the magnificent place. Yet again there were no other cars and no signs of anyone around.

"It doesn't look like anyone is here," Annabelle said.

I didn't have the heart to point out the strange vibe hanging around the place. It felt just like the vibe at LaVeau Manor as of late. That couldn't be a coincidence. Jacobson had probably been trying to cast spells around the manor and I was probably feeling the residue of his magic here.

As we moved up the front steps, Liam walked beside me, and Jon and Annabelle followed behind us. Once in front of the massive entrance, Liam knocked on the door. We waited for several seconds, but just as I suspected, no one answered.

"If they're not here we should just leave," Annabelle said with a shaky voice.

Liam didn't pick up on her apprehension when he said, "We could do that, but I think we should go in."

Annabelle shot him a venomous glare.

"I doubt they'd leave the door open again. Not after we told them that we'd been in the house," I said.

"There's only one way to find out." Liam twisted the knob and the door opened. "There's our answer."

I shrugged. "Hey, if they keep leaving the door open…"

Annabelle grabbed Jon's shirt as they followed us through the open door. The fact that Jacobson kept leaving the door open was odd though. Maybe we were walking into his trap. That was the price I'd have to pay. I had too many unanswered questions and I needed to find Nicolas.

"Hello?" I called out. "It's Halloween LaVeau. Your friendly Underworld leader."

Annabelle chuckled. At least she wasn't so scared that she'd lost her sense of humor. I stepped over to the staircase and peered up. Annabelle's anxious breathing was audible from across the foyer. When Liam walked over to the parlor, I followed close behind. It looked as if someone had cleaned up since the last time we'd been there.

"At least we know they've been here since our last visit," he said, pointing at the empty table.

I stepped around the room, picking up a small metal statue on the table near the window. It was an abstract piece that didn't quite fit in with the inside décor or outside façade of the plantation. I placed the piece back on the table and stared out the tall window. Movement in the flower garden at the edge of the property caught my attention. It must have been a bird, I thought. The others were talking as I stared out the window. Their voices became muffled. It was as if I was in another world, on the outside looking in. The walls seemed to be closing in on me and the room grew smaller by the second. My vision turned black, and after that, I remembered nothing.

When I opened my eyes, everyone stood over me, their expressions filled with worry.

"Are you okay?" Liam asked.

"Hallie, what happened?" Annabelle knelt beside me.

"Let's sit her up," Jon said.

Rubbing my head as I sat up, I remembered being overcome with the strange sensation again, but this time it had been amplified by about one hundred.

"This weird feeling came over me and the next thing I knew I was on the floor." I tucked a strand of hair behind my ear. "I've felt the same at the manor recently. You know, when you found me outside?" I said to Annabelle.

Jon nodded. "I've seen this before. The witches are casting a spell and taking away Hallie's powers. It happened to a witch from Baton Rouge not too long ago."

"What happened to the witch?" Annabelle asked.

"They never found out who was doing it to her." Jon shook his head.

I hadn't been messed with this much since I'd botched that spell in high school and my teacher's hair had been green for a month. The Coven had really come after me over that one. How was I supposed to know that my teacher was the coven leader's sister?

Liam's expression was filled with worry as he helped me to my feet. "We need to get you out of here."

I nodded. "We should go back to The Graveyard and ask Ginny Love if she has any updates."

Liam helped guide me toward the foyer. As we moved across the small space, I couldn't help but look into the room across from us. The strange drawings and words were still on the walls. Without saying a word, I stepped away from the group and entered the room.

"Where are you going?" Liam called.

They hurried after me, probably worried that my energy would be zapped again and I'd end up flat on my face. I just had to take a look at the wall one more time before we left. What did it all mean? How would I discover its meaning? Since the painting and markings had been in the house that had supposedly belonged to Sabrina too, I knew whatever its meaning, it couldn't be good.

I paced the length of the room, staring at the wall. Stopping in the middle of the room, I pulled out my phone and snapped a picture. Maybe I could match the writing on this wall with words in the Book of Mystics. It might be a long shot, but it was all I had.

"Come on, Hallie, we need to get you out of here before you black out again." Liam touched my arm.

I nodded and put the phone back in my pocket. As I turned to walk out of the room, something shiny on the floor in the corner of the room caught my attention. I glanced over and noticed a gold object on the floor. It looked like a necklace.

"Hold on a second," I called to Liam.

He paused at the door as I reached down and picked up the necklace, holding it in the palm of my hand. The chain was gold with a gold pendant. In the middle of the pendant was a symbol that looked familiar. That was when I realized I'd seen the pendant before. Holding the necklace up, I studied the wall painting again. Just as I'd thought—the symbol on the necklace was on the wall too. How strange was it that the necklace matched the painting?

By this time Liam had stepped back over to where I stood. "What is that?" he asked.

I held the necklace up for his inspection. He stared as the chain swung back and forth, the gold sparkling in the glint of the sunlight.

"The symbol on this pendant is the same as the one that's on the wall." I pointed.

Liam grasped the necklace in his hand. He looked down at it, then up at the wall. "It does match. But what does it mean?"

I shook my head. "I don't know, but we should go back to the house while we wait for nightfall. I want to see if this necklace matches the painting on that wall too."

"What if it does? Do you think there's any connection?" he asked, handing me the necklace again.

I touched the pendant. "Yes, I think there is a connection. Whatever this means it has to be significant to the Coven. Why else would they go to the trouble to make a necklace with this on it?"

"That's a good point. Come on, let's get over there," Liam said, grabbing my hand.

After showing Annabelle and Jon the necklace, we hopped in the car and headed for the abandoned house. It was a good thing I'd kept that napkin with the directions on it. A nagging voice in my mind had told me that I'd need them again.

"Hallie, if you really need me, I'd be happy to do the séance with you." Annabelle leaned forward in the seat.

Wow, I hadn't expected that from Annabelle. But instead of making me feel better, it just made things worse. I shouldn't have asked my friend to do something that made her feel so uncomfortable. But on the other hand, I really did need her in order to make the séance more powerful and to ensure that Nicolas' mother came through. I had quite the dilemma.

When I looked over my shoulder at Annabelle, she held up her hand. "I know what you're thinking, Hallie, and before you say no, I understand what I'm getting into and if I didn't want to I wouldn't volunteer. I won't take no for an answer." She waved both hands through the air.

I let out a deep breath and reluctantly said, "Okay… but I'm going to owe you a huge favor, aren't I?"

"I'm keeping a list of all the favors you owe me." She crossed her arms over her chest.

I grimaced. "That bad, huh?"

Liam laughed. "You owe her big time for saving you with the burnt pancakes."

They'd never let me forget about those blackened disks that I called pancakes.

CHAPTER TWENTY-THREE

A short while later we were driving down that dirt drive again. My head still reeled from that strange vibe—I had to fight it off. As the quiet little house came into view, I wondered how long it had been since someone had lived there. And who had brought Nicolas there? Had he come here on his own?

Liam cut the engine. We were silent as we stared at the house. It definitely gave off a creepy vibe. Any sane person would give pause before entering the place. And I'd thought LaVeau Manor had been creepy. What was even more shocking was that I'd been able to get Annabelle within a hundred miles of this place.

With the necklace clutched securely in my hand, I hopped out of the car. "Well, let's see what we can find."

Annabelle and Jon followed us up the rickety steps. Jon hadn't been with us last time and I wondered if he could offer insight into the mysterious drawings. After all, he'd seen a witch succumb to the same strange pull as me. Could it be related?

When Liam rapped against the wood door, it swung open. Something scurried across the floor in the dimly lit room and I jumped back, clutching my chest. Annabelle leapt off the porch in one giant motion, making it half-way back to the car before Jon caught up to her.

"It was just a mouse," Liam said with a chuckle.

"Are you okay?" I asked Annabelle.

She smoothed back her hair and stood up straight. "I'm good."

Annabelle climbed the steps again and grabbed the back of Jon's shirt as we stepped inside the house. The surrounding trees shaded the sun from coming in the window, making the space dark and spooky. The space looked the same as the last time we'd been there. Unfortunately, as far as I could tell, there was no sign that Nicolas had been there again.

"Who lives here?" Jon asked as he looked around the space.

"That's not entirely clear. I've been told that a witch owned the house. But based on the layer of dust, I'd say she hasn't been here in a while. Either that or she's a very bad housekeeper," I said, stepping through a stream of dust motes.

"And why are we here?" Jon took in the full view of the room.

I motioned for him to follow me down the hallway. "I'll show you."

Annabelle hesitated, but ultimately shadowed us down the short hallway into the back room. The hardwood floor under our feet had many dings and dents. The walls that I assumed had once been white had yellowed with age.

Once everyone was in the room, I pointed at the far wall. "That's why we're here. They're the same markings that are on the wall in the plantation."

Everyone stared at the paintings on the wall as I pulled the necklace from my pocket. I held it in the palm of my hand, then looked up at the wall. The symbol on the necklace matched the markings on this wall too. This place was obviously connected to the plantation since I'd found the necklace there. A thought nagged at the back of my mind, but I couldn't place my finger on it. I knew that I'd seen this symbol before... but where? Then it hit me. Nicolas had been wearing this necklace.

"This is the necklace that Nicolas had on last night at the Bubbling Cauldron," I said breathlessly.

Liam looked at the necklace. "Are you sure?"

"I'm almost positive," I said almost apologetically. I wished I wasn't so sure.

"We could cast a spell to see if it'll give us a glimpse of what happened in this room," Jon offered.

Liam gestured toward Jon. "He's got a point, but a spell might allow us to see things we might not want to see."

My stomach turned. "Like bad things that happened... possibly to Nicolas?"

Liam looked down. I knew the answer was yes. No matter what I saw though, I had to know the truth. We'd have to cast the spell. Perhaps with the help of Liam and Jon, I wouldn't mess this one up.

"Let's do it," I said with resolve.

Liam stared at me. "Are you sure?"

I nodded. "It's about the only option we have right now."

Annabelle shifted from one foot to the other. "Oh, what the hell. I've helped you with a spell before."

I smiled. "Thanks, Annabelle."

"Let's join hands." Jon motioned for us to form a circle.

Once we'd all joined hands, I began to recite the words: "Element of Earth, we call to you. Empower us with the energy to see." Liam and Jon repeated my words. I continued, reciting the words: "Element of Air, we call to you to push the unnatural forces from this space." Once again, Liam and Jon repeated my words, but this time, Annabelle joined in too. I recited the words: "Element of Fire, we call to you for protection and deep perception."

Reciting the last words of the spell, I said: "Element of Water, we call to you to allow our eyes to see."

With my eyes shut, I waited for a vision of what had happened in the room. But instead of having scenes painted in my mind, there was nothing but black. There was no action, no life in the past of this room.

"It's completely black," I said.

We released hands and I opened my eyes. It was hard to hide the disappointment on my face as they stared at me.

"Sorry, Hallie," Annabelle said.

"I guess it wasn't meant for the spell to give us answers." I shrugged.

Jon's eyes widened with concern. "Maybe the blackness means something. This stuff is black magic, so there could be a black cloud over this room, so to speak."

After the others had stepped out into the hallway, I snapped a few pictures of the wall. I'd compare them to the photos of the other wall later. The same symbols and words adorned both walls, but I figured I might discover a pattern or spot something that I hadn't before.

When I walked back to the front room, they were waiting for me by the door.

Annabelle rubbed her arms. "This place gives me the chills. Let's get out of here."

"We should get dinner, then head over to your psychic friend's house for the séance," Liam said, casting a glance to Annabelle.

Luckily, she didn't react by running away. That was a good sign.

I nodded. "Yeah, I guess that's all we can do at this point."

I took one last glance over my shoulder, then headed outside. My thoughts were going a million miles a minute, but I had a few ideas of what I needed to do next.

CHAPTER TWENTY-FOUR

Liam pulled the car down the gravel driveway toward Sierra's house. The overgrown bushes surrounded her place, shielding the house away from the world in its own little cocoon. The house was a white cottage style with splashes of color from the vast amount of flowers she'd placed in pots along the porch and sidewalk.

Liam parked the car out in the drive. Luckily, I didn't have to drag Annabelle out of the backseat. If she was having second thoughts about the séance, she didn't mention it and her behavior seemed surprisingly calm.

"Annabelle, if you don't want to do this then just say the word and we'll stop, okay?" I said.

She nodded. "I'll be fine."

A bird fluttered from a treetop, making me jump. I looked over at Annabelle, but she didn't meet my gaze. She had a laser-like focus on Sierra's house, as if she'd change her mind and run away if she looked over at me. The sun was setting quickly and darkness would surround us soon. Once that happened, would Annabelle retain her bravery? Would I?

I knocked on the door and waited as Sierra unlocked and opened the door.

"You made it back," she said with a smile.

"You've already met Liam," I said, gesturing toward Liam. "This is Jon."

"It's nice to meet you," she said with a nod.

"Likewise." Jon stretched his hand toward her.

"And you remember Annabelle." I gestured.

Sierra smiled. "Oh yes, how are you, Annabelle?"

"I'm okay," Annabelle stuttered as she looked around at Sierra's eccentric décor. "How are you?"

Annabelle's eyes widened and I followed her stare to a skull that sat on the bookshelf. I knew what Annabelle was thinking and I hoped it wasn't real too.

"I have to ask if everyone is mentally ready for this? We don't want to allow any negative spirits to come through because of our own negative thoughts," Sierra said.

I looked around at everyone for a sign that they wanted to back out. "We're ready."

"Okay then, we can get started." Sierra pointed at the table and chairs set up in the middle of the room.

If I hadn't thought I'd mess up a spell again, I would have tried to reanimate Nicolas' mother one more time, but I didn't need another lively ghost with a spell gone wrong. There was probably something written in the rules about how many mistakes a witch could make with one spell. So Sierra was the only option. But could she really bring Gina back via a séance?

"Why do we need the round table and candles?" Annabelle whispered.

She'd directed the question to me, but Sierra overheard and answered, "It's part of the ritual and it's what allows the spirit to channel our energy."

Annabelle nodded but by the look on her face, I didn't think Sierra's answer was all that comforting.

Sierra placed three white candles in the middle of the table, then lit them. We all pulled out a chair and sat around the white fabric-covered table.

"Will you be able to communicate with her?" I asked.

"I'll give it my best shot." Sierra sat at the table, then said, "Please, if you'll all join hands, we'll get started."

My hand tingled when I grasped Liam's strong hand. When I felt his gaze on me, I surreptitiously looked over at him. I'd tried to play it cool, but my attempt was mostly pathetic. His stare sent a shiver through my body.

To my right, I held Sierra's hand. The room fell silent as she closed her eyes and began to summon Nicolas' mother's spirit.

"Gina Rochester, we bring you energy from life into death. Please come forward and communicate with us. Gina Rochester, we need your help and guidance," Sierra intoned.

Sierra's grip on my hand grew tighter, while my other hand continued to tingle with desire from Liam's touch.

"Everyone repeat the phrase with me," Sierra urged.

We chanted, "Gina Rochester, we bring you energy from life into death. Please come forward and communicate with us. Gina Rochester, we need your help and guidance."

In spite of our best efforts, nothing was happening and I began to worry that this plan would fail faster than one of my lousy spells. Opening one eye, I peeked over at Annabelle. She seemed to be doing fine, so that was one worry off my mind. If she started to freak out, I'd end the séance right away.

Just then the candles flickered, casting a glow across everyone's faces. The room was eerily still.

"Please make a sound, tap on the walls, move something, or just give us some kind of sign that you're here." A deep line furrowed Sierra's brow.

No noises came and nothing stirred in the room. Sierra shifted in her seat and I knew she was growing anxious.

"We'll have to try the Ouija board," she said matter-of-factly.

"Are you sure?" I asked. "I've never liked the idea of using one of those things."

"Well, I don't recommend novices using them, but I have a lot of experience with them. Trust me. I know what I'm doing," she said confidence.

"Okay." I exhaled slowly. "I trust you."

Sierra pulled out the board from under the table and placed it in the middle of our circle. Annabelle's face drained of color.

"Are you okay?" I whispered to Annabelle.

She nodded. That was about the only answer I'd get out of her at the moment.

Sierra placed the wooden triangle in the middle of the board. "Now please gently place your fingertips on the planchette, but don't add pressure. If the ghost is here and wishes to communicate with us, she'll be able to use our combined energy to move the planchette and answer our questions."

I reluctantly released hands with Liam and placed my fingertips on the planchette. He looked over at me and gave a reassuring smile.

"The spirit may have never done this kind of communication before, so she may not know how to channel our energy. We'll need to coax her into talking," Sierra urged.

"She appeared to be in spirit form," I offered.

"Well, that's a little different. We're calling to her now, so she won't be expecting our invitation." Sierra watched us with a serious stare.

"Please, Gina, can you use our energy to move this glass? Can you please give us a sign to show us that you're present?" Liam's voice wavered. It was evident that he wanted to speak with her badly.

I added, "We wish you no harm, we only want to communicate with you."

"We'll have to be patient and wait for her to come through," Sierra said with authority. "She may be quiet because there are strangers here."

"But she knows me," Liam offered.

"Yes, but she doesn't know me," Sierra said. "That can be intimidating."

Something told me that Nicolas' mother wasn't intimidated by anything. Annabelle shifted in her seat. When I looked over to see if she was ready to quit, her eyes rolled back, then she shut her eyelids. When she leaned back in the chair, her body twisted and turned in the seat.

"Annabelle, are you okay?" I asked in a panic.

"She's channeling the spirit. It's coming through her," Sierra said calmly, trying to ease my fears.

Uh-oh. I was going to be in so much trouble for this. If I thought I owed Annabelle a favor before, I hadn't seen anything yet. This was beyond a simple favor. It was Annabelle's worst nightmare.

I knew I shouldn't have allowed her to participate. The spirit always attached to the one who didn't want it the most. Nicolas' mother should have known that.

"What do we do?" Jon asked.

How would a bodyguard protect her from something we couldn't see?

"We allow the spirit to talk. Once she's done, she'll move along and we'll get Annabelle back," Sierra said.

She tried to act calm and professional, but I knew by the look in her eyes that she was freaking out a little.

"That had better be the way this works," Jon said.

Annabelle finally opened her eyes and looked directly at me. She remained expressionless for a moment. I stared, unsure of what to do or say next. Annabelle's eyes had changed to a dark brown hue instead of her usual cobalt blue. I hoped that the spirit was that of Nicolas' mother and not something sinister.

"Halloween LaVeau," Annabelle spoke in a suffocated whisper.

My eyes widened. "It's me."

"Thank you for bringing me back here tonight." Her voice was low.

"Are you Nicolas' mother?" I asked.

Annabelle nodded. "My energy is weak tonight, so we have to speak quickly."

"I need to find Nicolas. We need to know about the witch who is accusing him of stealing her magic," I said, rushing my words.

She placed her hands on the table. "Nicolas is in danger. He is with people who shouldn't be trusted."

Well, I knew that much. "We know who he's with," I said.

"Your spells are being blocked and they're trying to stop you from helping him," she said.

"Who are they? The people who he's with now?" I asked.

"I don't know the answer to that question, but there's someone strong behind this. I can feel it," she said in a voice that seemed to come from a long way off.

"What can I do? I don't know how to be the leader," I said with a little too much excitement.

Her eyes widened and she locked her gaze on my face. "You have the Book of Mystics. The answers are in there."

Again with the book! "That's just it. I can't understand the writings. When a spell appears, I usually do it incorrectly," I said.

"You're not performing the spells incorrectly, but you have to have faith in your abilities. Other witches are placing spells against you." Her voice wavered as if she was having a difficult time coming through.

"Is that why I've had the blacking out episodes?" I asked.

"Yes…" Annabelle closed her eyes.

"Are you still here?" I asked.

Annabelle popped open her eyes and blinked at me. "You need to find the other necklace. The pendant is larger than the other necklaces. It's in the house. It will unlock the writings of the book."

"Where in the house?" I pushed.

Annabelle shut her eyes again, then leaned her head back against the back of the chair. After a second, she opened her eyes again. The blue shade had returned.

Gina was gone. How would I find the necklace now?

"Annabelle, is that you?" I asked.

Annabelle wiped her forehead with the back of her hand and looked around. "Why are you all staring at me like that? Aren't we going to do the séance?"

She didn't know. It would be so easy not to tell her, but I knew I had to. She needed to know the truth.

"It's over," Jon said.

Annabelle shrugged. She didn't seem to mind that it was over, but she did look suspiciously at us. I was positive that she knew something strange had happened.

"We need to break the circle and extinguish the candles." Sierra waved her hands through the air.

Once we broke the circle, Sierra blew out the candles, signaling the end of the séance.

"Thank you, spirit, for joining us," Sierra said.

A whisper of a breeze blew across my skin. Had Gina's spirit left the room?

CHAPTER TWENTY-FIVE

When I opened the car door, I spotted the single rose resting on the seat. My breath caught in my throat.

"How did this get here?" I showed the flower to everyone.

Annabelle scrunched her brow. "That's odd. Where did you find it?"

"It was on my seat." I pointed.

I looked to Liam and Jon, but there only response was a shrug. Where were the roses coming from?

As we drove back to LaVeau Manor, I knew I had my work cut out for me. Now there was a necklace to find? Why had no one told me about this to begin with? Hadn't the Coven known about this? Weren't they supposed to know about all this witchcraft stuff? They always acted so superior. As it turned out, they didn't know half as much as they thought they did.

"I've made at least one decision tonight," I said.

"What's that?" Liam asked while keeping his focus on the road.

"I'm asking Jacobson to step down as the leader of the New Orleans Coven. It's something I should have done when I met the jackass," I said.

Liam's eyes widened when he glanced over at me. "He's not going to like this at all."

"He won't have a choice," I said with forced confidence.

"Who will you get to take his place?" Liam steered the car around a slight curve.

I shrugged. "I have no idea, but one problem at a time."

"When do you plan on doing this?" he asked.

"I'd like to do it tonight, but I'll have to find him first. When I get back to LaVeau Manor, I have to look for this necklace." I leaned my head back against the seat.

"I'll help you look," he said with a smile.

I met his gaze momentarily. "Thank you. I'd like that. Do you think this necklace is related to the one I found at the plantation?"

"I hadn't thought of it, but it's possible," Liam said.

The car's engine faded into a meaningless drone, making me drowsy. I must have drifted off to sleep because the next thing I knew we were pulling up in front of LaVeau Manor. Night had settled over the manor and I knew that searching for the necklace tonight would be pointless. As I peered up at the stars, I wondered where Nicolas was and if he was okay. I inhaled the sweet perfume from the rose. Was he thinking of me too?

After filling Annabelle in on what had happened at the séance, I figured she'd never speak to me again, but she did. It seemed like I kept dishing out bad things to my friend, and she just kept rolling with the punches. That was true friendship. Luckily, she knew I'd do the same for her.

I said goodbye to Annabelle knowing that she was in good hands. Jon seemed like a nice guy and I felt like I could trust him. Okay, I'd only known him for two days, but he gave off a good vibe. But now that Annabelle had pulled out of the driveway with Jon, I was alone with Liam. At least I thought I was alone because there were no lights on in the manor. I figured that the new best friends

Catherin and Claude had stepped out for more cupcakes or friendship bracelets. They were probably out celebrating my pathetic witchcraft skills and their good fortune because of it.

As soon as Liam and I stepped through the door of LaVeau Manor, in one swift movement, Liam grabbed me in his arms and planted a kiss on me. He caressed his tongue over my lips and I momentarily gave in to the pleasure. Nothing could have prepared me for this mind-blowing lip lock. As his mouth moved from my lips to my neck, his fangs whispered over the exposed skin. If my head hadn't been spinning before, it definitely was now. It was hard to resist Liam Rankin.

What if Nicolas really did want to be with the witches now? I couldn't really wait around, right? Since I was having a tough time resisting Liam, I melted into his arms and kissed him back. As my mouth moved across his, my legs went weak. Unfortunately, as magnificent as the kiss was, his lips weren't the reason for my weakened state. I knew that someone had unleashed a spell against me again. The room darkened and I fell to the floor.

When I woke, I was on the sofa in the parlor. I scanned the room, trying to remember what had happened. The single rose was on the table across from me. Liam must have placed it there. He knelt down beside me as I tried to sit up. "What happened?"

Liam grabbed my arms and lowered me back to the sofa. "Just lie there. Don't try to get up. You're being attacked with a spell again."

"I blacked out again?" I rubbed my head.

He nodded. "We have to find this necklace."

I tried to get up again. "We need to look through the house. Gina said it was in the house."

He gently pushed me back again. "You need rest. We'll find it in the morning. Just try to relax. You're safe here with me tonight."

I wasn't so sure. I'd been attacked with a spell in my own house. Nowhere was safe. Without warning, Liam scooped me up in his arms.

"Where are you taking me?" I asked breathlessly.

"To your bed." Liam carried me in his strong arms with ease.

"Will you stay with me?" I whispered in his ear.

"I won't leave," he said in a low voice.

A knot rose in my throat. Had there been desire in his words?

As we turned the corner of the second floor landing, Catherin appeared from her room. Liam sat me on my feet, wrapping his arm around me for support.

"I didn't think you were here," I said with surprise.

"Is everything okay, dear?" she asked with a quirk of her eyebrow.

"I'm just really tired and Liam is helping me." I gestured toward Liam.

Catherin quirked a disapproving eyebrow, then shrugged. "Well, I guess it's your home now and you can do whatever you like."

"Is Claude here? I didn't think you all were home because all the lights were out." I gestured with my hand.

"Yes, he is," Catherin said snippily. "I'm going to talk with him now." She marched down the hallway, releasing a loud huff in her wake.

Was she going to tattle on me? At least I had Claude to keep Catherin occupied while I figured out this other mess. As soon as I had time I'd find a way to get rid of both of them.

***

When I woke, Liam's arms were wrapped around me. I paused for a moment, wondering if this was a dream. Nope. It was all too real. He'd kept his word and slept in the bed with me all night. I hadn't wanted to be alone. Not last night. Liam was still fully clothed though, so he'd been a perfect gentleman. I still hadn't decided if that was a good or bad thing. One thing was for certain, I was thankful I hadn't drooled on him while I'd slept.

When I turned to look at Liam, he opened his eyes and smiled. "Good morning," he said.

I stretched, trying to add as casual as possible. "We should start looking for the necklace."

Liam nodded. "Your guest will probably want to know what we're doing. She wasn't very happy with you last night."

"She doesn't seem happy about anything," I said, pulling the sheet up tighter around my body.

Liam climbed out of my bed. I looked up at his powerful set of shoulders and let my gaze drift, studying every inch of his muscular physique as he moved. Maybe it was my imagination, but he seemed as if he was in a hurry to get out of the room.

"I'll leave so you can get ready." He paused with his hand on the doorknob. "If you need me I'll be in my room."

I nodded, but didn't say anything. For once I was at a loss for words. How could I possibly know what to say when I didn't even know what I was thinking? He stepped out of the room without looking back. I hoped that I hadn't hurt his feelings.

When I stepped out into the hallway, I noticed Catherin's room door was open. I peeked down the hallway. Claude's door was open too. Had they already gone out? Where were they headed off to all the time? Maybe they were already downstairs and Catherin was making breakfast. It was obvious that she didn't trust my cooking abilities.

After heading downstairs, I searched every room on the first level, looking for my guests. They were nowhere to be found. When I stepped into the kitchen, there was no sign of Catherin or Claude there either. I'd expected to see remnants of cupcakes or some other delicious breakfast that Catherin had whipped up with her magic.

As I peered out the back window, contemplating my next move, someone touched my back. I jumped and spun around with my fists in the air.

Liam stood behind me. "Whoa. Settle down, killer. I didn't mean to startle you."

I clutched my chest. "It's okay, I guess. I was expecting to find Jacobson behind me when I turned around."

"Where are Catherin and Claude?" Liam asked, looking over my shoulder out the window.

I shook my head. "I don't know. They must have left."

Liam opened his full lips as if he wanted to comment, but he obviously changed his mind because he didn't utter a word.

"What?" I pushed.

Finally, he asked, "Don't you think they are acting weird? What do you think is going on with them?"

I leaned against the counter and tucked a strand of hair behind my ear. "I don't know, but you're right." I couldn't deny that I'd become suspicious of their behavior. "They're always together now. I mean, maybe they just have a lot in common, or they share a bond because I brought both of them back…"

His eyebrows rose inquiringly. "Or maybe it's something more than that?"

"How will I know?" I searched his eyes for an answer.

"Have you snooped in their rooms?" Liam asked.

"I can't do that. That's against the bed-and-breakfast proprietor code," I said. Technically, I had snooped in Liam's room and I had checked out his underwear, but I had a perfectly valid excuse for that. Okay, and I had snooped in Catherin's room too, but I digress.

"Well, it's not like they are paying guests." Liam shoved his hands in his pockets and leaned on the counter next to me.

Liam's sexual magnetism invaded my personal space. I stepped away from the counter and motioned for him to follow. "That's true. Come on. Let's see what's going on, although I doubt we'll find anything."

He didn't allow me to move too far before grabbing my hand and guiding me out of the room. "Maybe we'll find out where they've been going every day."

I tried to throttle the dizzying current racing through me as Liam guided me through the manor. "Let's hope so."

We made it to Catherin's room first. The room was tidy and nothing seemed out of place. She'd even made up the bed with military precision.

Easing into the room, I headed over to the closet and peeked inside. Several pieces of clothing hung on the rack and a couple pairs of new shoes sat on the floor. Apparently, Catherin had been shopping.

I held up a bright pink sweater from the closet. "She has a lot of new clothes. That might explain what Catherin and Claude have been doing. It's nothing more than hanging out as friends, I guess. But I'm not clear on where she got her money."

Liam walked across the room and looked out the window. "I'm still suspicious. There's just something about them that I don't trust."

When I scanned the room, something caught beside the bed. The item was gold and shiny. "There's a necklace," I said, pointing across the room.

Liam followed me across the room. I knelt down and picked up the necklace. When I saw the pendant attached to the chain, it was as if someone had punched me in the stomach.

"It's the same symbol as the necklace we found at the plantation," I said with shock in my voice.

Liam took the necklace from my outstretched hand. His expression tensed as he studied it. "I can't believe it. It's the same damn thing."

"Do you think the necklace is Catherin's?" I asked.

"I can't imagine why it would be in her room if it wasn't," Liam said.

"It can't be the necklace Gina told us about because she said it was larger. I've never seen Catherin wear this." I scanned the room to make sure we were still alone. "We have to find out what that symbol means. Come on, let's check Claude's room, then we'll look for the necklace that Nicolas' mother was talking about," I said.

After searching through Claude's room and finding nothing, I headed for my room to grab the Book of Mystics. I wanted to see if it would present a spell to me. What kind of spell, I wasn't sure, but at this point I was out of ideas. If I got lucky, I'd cast a spell that would help lead me to this necklace that Nicolas' mother was talking about.

After grabbing the book, I joined Liam in the kitchen where he'd been waiting for me. He was still studying the necklace that I'd found in Catherin's room.

"I brought the necklace from the plantation so we can compare them," I said, handing him the other necklace.

He placed both of them on the kitchen counter, stretching both out side-by-side.

"They look like an exact match," I said.

"You're right, they look alike and that isn't a coincidence. This must be some kind of special witchcraft symbol. They share some kind of common bond," Liam said, as he ran his hand through his thick hair.

"But why was Nicolas wearing this necklace? Do you know if he was involved with any special magic?" I asked.

Liam shook his head. "No, not that I know of. Of course, we haven't been the best of friends lately."

"Well, I know one thing for certain. I'm calling a meeting of the New Orleans Coven today and removing Jacobson as the leader." I felt as depleted as my voice sounded.

"You know I'll support you any way that I can." Liam touched my hand.

The doorbell rang, echoing through the house, and my stomach dipped. The last thing I wanted was another unannounced guest. I exchanged a glance with Liam.

"I'll see who it is," he said, walking out of the kitchen toward the front door.

He reached the door before me and opened it immediately for the person. The open door blocked my view of the unexpected guest.

"Oh, it's you," Liam said.

CHAPTER TWENTY-SIX

When I stepped into the hallway, I finally got a view of who'd been at the door. Annabelle and Jon stood in the foyer, holding hands.

"I didn't expect to see you two here so early." I gave Annabelle a knowing smile.

If this mess was ever finished, I wanted full details from her on what had led to the quick handholding.

Annabelle returned a bashful grin. "We figured you needed help looking for that necklace."

"Yeah, well, we already found one necklace today." I displayed the found object.

She quirked her eyebrow questioningly. "What are you talking about?"

I let the necklace dangle from my hand. "We found this in Catherin's room."

Jon took the necklace. "It looks just like the one you found at the plantation."

I looked at him. "Yeah, I'm surprised you remembered."

"It's a unique symbol. Hard to forget something like that," he said.

I shook my head. "It's not that unique. We've found two. I still have to figure out what it means."

"That's why we're here to help," Annabelle offered.

"I have a plan for the day. Number one: find the necklace that Nicolas' mother told us about and number two: call a meeting for the New Orleans coven," I said.

Before anyone had a chance to respond, the strange vibe fell over me again. I knew by now what was coming on when it hit me. The walls were closing in on me and the room grew darker and darker. My legs grew weak and I fell to the ground again.

When I woke, I was on the sofa again with everyone standing around me. This was becoming a routine—one that I wasn't fond of either.

"Are you okay?" Annabelle reached down and touched my forehead.

Liam paced beside the sofa. "This is beyond out of control."

"I'm feeling fine now," I said, rubbing my head.

"Since Jon is here he can help us cast a counter-spell. You can draw on the elements from us," Liam said, gesturing toward Jon.

"I'll help if I can," Jon said with a shrug of his wide shoulders.

It was about the only shot I had. If I could cast a spell to help lead me to the necklace, then I could unravel the puzzle. There had to be a reason why Nicolas was with the witches. What spell had they cast on him and how would I reverse it? Would I need to find him first before I cast a spell?

"Do we need to find Nicolas in order to help him break whatever spell he's under?" I asked.

Liam's frown burst my bit of hope. "Yes, I'm afraid so," he said.

"I feel so useless," Annabelle said wrapped around a heavy sigh.

"Annabelle, no. What would I do without your support?" I asked. "Plus, you have more paranormal skills than you know. After all, you allowed Nicolas' mother to channel through you at the séance." I gave a lopsided grin.

Annabelle gave a little smile. "That's true, I did do that."

I nodded. "See, you helped. Now come on. Let's go to the kitchen and try a spell."

We gathered around the cauldron and held hands as Annabelle watched. With any luck, the spell would lead me to the necklace and block whatever junk someone was throwing my way. If it didn't work, then I wasn't sure what I would do next. I was at the end of my witchy rope. LaVeau Manor was a gigantic place and it would take forever to search every room. Although I'd try the attic first since that was where I'd found the Book of Mystics. My great Aunt Maddy was eccentric and she could have hidden the necklace or buried it in the backyard for all I knew.

Once the water bubbled, it was time to add the spices. The room began its dazzling show. Annabelle grabbed the counter for balance as the wind whipped around her. The energy zapped from Liam and Jon to me.

I tossed in the last of the spices. "Bring back the spirit near, it should not cause fear. So mote it be." That wasn't good enough for me though. I decided to add my own words to the spell. After all, calling to the elements had helped me use the magic to my full potential before. I needed all the help I could get for this important spell. "Element of Earth, I call to you to allow the spirit to rise again. Element of Air, I call to you to push the spirit back to the manor. Element of Fire, I call to you for warmth and protection. Help me have the knowledge. Element of Water, I call to you for force and tranquility. Give the spirit the power to return."

Blue and red lights swirled up and out from the cauldron and began to make a circle around me. The wind whipped my hair as a fiery wind blew through the kitchen. Smoke bellowed up from the cauldron as the water bubbled up to the top.

Finally, the smoke settled, the water boiled no more, the breeze stilled, the lightshow in my vision stopped, and the smell of Mother Earth vanished.

I released a deep breath and looked around the room. It was the calm after the storm. Had the spell worked? As if on cue, footsteps sounded in the library again. My heart beat faster. With any luck, the spell had worked and Nicolas' mother had now returned from the dead.

The spell pulled at me, like a giant magnet, willing me to move out of the kitchen and through the house. My whole body tingled from the tips of my toes to the top of my head.

"I feel weird. I think the spell is working," I said, shaking my arms as if that would make it go away.

"That's a good thing. Let it lead you to the necklace," Liam said with confidence in his voice.

As if being guided by an unseen force, I walked through the parlor, then the library and toward the foyer. Everyone followed behind me, anxious to see where this spell was leading me. I hoped it didn't make me take a wrong turn right out a window because it didn't seem as if I could stop myself from moving forward at this moment. I turned to the left and moved up the stairs to the second floor.

When I glanced over my shoulder, I was shocked to see that Annabelle had followed me. She never came upstairs. The only way she would have come upstairs was if the house had been on fire and she had to save me. Even then she'd try to recruit a gorgeous firefighter to do the job.

"Annabelle, what are you doing? I can't believe you're coming up the stairs." I glanced over my shoulder to gauge her panicked expression.

She shrugged. "I made it through being possessed. I figure I can make it through a little trip upstairs."

Wow. She did have a point though. I was proud of her. She was facing her fears—something I should do more often.

When I reached the second floor landing, I turned to my left and continued up the next flight of stairs. This was the top floor of the manor. There was nowhere else to go from there, other than the roof. *Please don't let this spell take me to the roof.* I was terrified of heights and that was one fear I was not ready to tackle. We moved up the last flight of stairs and then down the long hallway, finally coming to a stop in front of the little attic door.

"This is where I found the Book of Mystics. Apparently, this was a go-to hiding spot for my aunt," I said, placing my hand on the tarnished brass doorknob.

As I turned the knob and pushed on the little wooden door, it creaked out as if welcoming us. With a slight pause, I stepped into the stuffy room. Dust motes flooded through the air as I disturbed the space. I'd caught Liam looking for the Book of Mystics in there one night. A lot had happened since then. Liam, Annabelle, and Jon followed me into the room. The men had a harder time fitting through the door, but they twisted their way inside.

"Wow, this place is creepier than I imagined," Annabelle said with a tense smile. She rubbed her arms to ward off a chill.

There had always been rumors that my great-great-great-grandfather's bones had been hidden up in the attic. But that was just urban legend, something the kids told each other during Halloween. At least I hoped that was the truth. It did make me wonder what had actually happened to him. I knew very little about him other than that he'd been a famed alchemist. Had he been the leader of the Underworld way back then? That was something I filed away in my mind to look into if I ever got the time.

"I cleared out most of the things. I did find a map of with all the books' locations marked on it under the floor," I said.

"I wonder if there are more hiding places under the floor." Jon scanned the area.

I shrugged. "Your guess is as good as mine."

"Is the spell still pulling you?" Liam asked.

I shook my head. "Sadly, no. I don't feel anything now. But it brought us to this room. That has to mean something, right?"

"All we can do is look." Liam raked his hand through his hair.

"We could break up and look in sections," Annabelle said as she fidgeted her hands.

"That's a good idea. How about you and Jon do the front half and Liam and I will do the back half," I said, pointing around the space.

"Sounds good," Jon said, clapping his hands. "Let's get to work."

Liam and I moved to the back section of the room.

I flashed Liam a nervous smile. "This is crazy, right?"

"I've seen a lot crazier," he said.

"I'll look on this side and you can look on that side." I gestured around the room.

I pulled out the boxes and painstakingly went through each one with no luck. They were full of old clothes with feathers and silk. My Great-Aunt Maddy had everything in there from utensils to teddy bears. It was a good thing she hadn't been a hoarder or I never would have finished sorting through her items.

When I reached the last box, it was full of postcards from people all around the world. I flipped through a few, but nothing seemed out of the ordinary. She sure had a lot of friends. The last postcard caught my eye though. It had yellowed with age, but the front displayed a photo of The Eiffel Tower. My hands froze when I flipped it over and saw the writing. It was in the same strange language as the Book of Mystics.

The postcard had been addressed to my great-aunt from Catherin. What was going on? Catherin had acted as if she had been dead and never returned from the dead. If she had died in the 1800s and the postcard was marked 1938, then how had that happened? She had to be lying to me. If she was lying about this, then what else was she lying about?

"Look at this," I said, holding up the old postcard.

Liam stopped searching under the loose floorboard and stepped closer. "What is it?"

"Look at the back. It has some of the same strange writing as the Book of Mystics. But more importantly, look who signed it," I said, tapping the postcard with my index finger.

Annabelle and Jon had stepped closer. "What did you find?" Annabelle asked.

"Catherin sent this post card to my great aunt in 1938, but according to Catherin and the tombstone in the graveyard, she died in 1865. She is lying to me. But what else is she lying about? She had the necklace that connected her to the New Orleans Coven. When she comes back, I will demand answers," I said.

Annabelle's face turned a couple shades lighter.

"What does the postcard say?" Annabelle asked straining to look over at the aged paper.

"It says she'll be back soon." I looked up at everyone. "That doesn't say much, huh?"

"Where is the postmark?" Liam asked.

"Far away in Paris." I pointed at the postmark.

"May I see it?" Liam held out his hand. After studying it for a moment, he said, "We'll have to ask her about this."

"I'd like to hear her explanation." Annabelle shook her head.

The likelihood that there was another Catherin who knew my Aunt Maddy was slim.

"She has a lot of explaining to do." I felt stupid for falling for her games.

"I have a feeling that she'll just make up another lie." Liam handed the postcard back to me.

"We may never know what secret she's hiding," Jon said.

Sadly, Jon was probably right.

"Liam was a part of the New Orleans Coven. Didn't you know what was going on in that plantation?" Jon said.

Liam glared at Jon. The last thing I needed was for them to get into a fight.

"When I was there nothing was on the wall. It must have been a new thing," Liam said through gritted teeth.

"When we were there the other night I didn't notice it," I said in Liam's defense.

Of course it had been dark... but still.

"We shouldn't argue about what happened in the past, let's just worry about right now," Annabelle said.

"She's right. We don't have time to debate this. Let's get back to looking for the necklace." I had little patience for playing the blame game right now.

As I stacked the boxes back into the corner where I'd found them, Liam broke the silence.

"I think I've found something," Liam said, drawing my attention away from the boxes.

This place was a treasure trove of hidden secrets. Liam held the linen cloth in the palm of his hand. It had been tied with a piece of jute. A tiny gasp escaped my lips when Liam untied the string and unfolded the cloth. I hadn't meant for that reaction, but it was hard to hide my shock at what I saw. The item was unmistakable. Inside the fabric was a wooden stake. The pointed end was sharp and looked as if it had been used... more than once.

"Is that what I think it is?" Annabelle asked. Her eyes looked like they would pop out at any second.

"It's a stake used to kill a vampire," Liam said softly.

I knew that wasn't something Liam wanted to see.

"Was it used on someone?" she asked.

"Probably, yes. That's why it was bound. The vampire who was killed by this stake was not a pleasant person. The witch who did this was trying to bind the spirit of the vampire from ever returning." Liam seemed transfixed by the object.

I exchanged a glance with Liam. There was never a dull moment at LaVeau Manor.

"What do you think that means?" I asked, looking over his shoulder.

"By the look of the cloth, I'd say it's been here for a while. I'm not sure if it came from my Aunt Maddy. It may have been before her time. Although she'd lived many years, so it was possible she'd performed the spell when she was younger."

Liam folded the stake back in the cloth.

"Let's finish looking so we can get out of here." I trudged back to the corner that I'd been scrutinizing.

After searching through the last box, and not finding another postcard like the one from Catherin, I closed the boxes and looked around the room. I'd exhausted all my options.

"I found it," Annabelle yelled.

She ran over with the necklace clutched tightly in her hand. "It's the necklace, right?" she asked breathlessly.

I took the necklace from her outstretched hand. How would I know if this necklace was right one? My aunt could have had a hundred pieces of costume jewelry hidden away. There was only one way to find out if it worked.

CHAPTER TWENTY-SEVEN

The necklace was similar to the one I'd found at the plantation and the one I'd found in Catherin's room. However, the symbol on this one was a little different. It had a circle in the middle with small circles running through it, then scrolled patterns at the top and bottom.

Like the other necklace, this one was gold and had the same gold chain. Unlike the other necklaces though, this one had an energy emitting from it as I held it in the palm of my hand.

"I have a feeling this is the necklace," I said as I studied the necklace.

"It has a lot of magic around it," Liam said.

"Well, there's only one way to find out if it's the right one. I'll see if the magic works when I'm wearing it. And the first spell I plan to cast is a call to meeting, just like the Book of Mystics said." I tried hard to keep the insecurity out of my voice.

Liam smiled as if I'd just learned how to ride a bike or figured out how to tie my shoelaces.

"Let's get out of this creepy room before we find something that I don't want to see," Annabelle said.

Annabelle and Jon hurried down the stairs, but Liam grabbed my arm as we headed toward the staircase. I stopped and spun around to face him.

"Are you sure about calling the meeting? Things are unpleasant with Jacobson now, but when he finds out what you want to do, it will get a lot worse," Liam said.

"So I'm supposed to allow him to continue to be a bully? You are the last person who I thought would want to put up with that." I fixed him with a stare.

Liam exhaled. "No, I don't want to allow him to get away with that, but I don't want him to come after you."

"That's just the chance I'll have to take. It's my job now. Besides, I have to get Nicolas back," I said.

Liam looked down. I knew he wanted to say something, but was currently having a debate in his mind about whether to speak up or keep his mouth shut.

"Don't you want to help your brother?" I asked.

He looked up and met my gaze. "No, I do want to help him."

There was more to that sentence. Liam wasn't telling me everything. After all that had happened, I didn't know what my feelings were for Nicolas and Liam. I was more confused than ever, but I knew I had to help Nicolas.

Liam grabbed my hand and we headed downstairs. I couldn't deny the way his hand felt in mine. I couldn't lie and say that the thought of calling a Coven meeting didn't leave my anxious, but it had to be done. I had to put on my big girl witch panties and do the right thing for once.

Liam and I gathered around the cauldron while Jon and Annabelle stayed in the parlor. I thought she needed a break from the magic for a few minutes. Besides, if things went as planned and the necklace worked—I know, my plans never worked out—then I wouldn't need anyone's help performing magic from this point forward. I'd get rid of the spell-blocking someone had placed on me and find out who was doing it in the first place.

As I placed the book on the counter, I didn't even have time to search for the spell before the book started turning pages on its own. The pages flipped with the wind until finally stopping. When I glanced down at the page, the spell was written in English. Another spell that I could understand. I'd have to check the other pages and see if the language barrier was finally broken.

"It stopped on a spell," I said, glancing up at Liam.

"Let's do it before it disappears," he said, tapping the page.

Liam and I ran around gathering the items listed on the page. Finally, I began to recite the words: "Element of Earth, I call to you. Strip the power that is binding me." As I threw herbs into the cauldron, I recited the words: "Element of Air, I call to you to push the unnatural force from this place." Grabbing more herbs and tossing them into the water, I recited the words: "Element of Fire, I call to you for warmth and protection while I oversee the call of witches." With the last of the herbs, I splashed them into the water, and said: "Element of Water, I call to you for force and tranquility. Give me the force to change the power and banish the evil."

When the herbs hit the water, flames flicked and crackled from the cauldron. The necklace vibrated around my neck. Only time would tell if this spell had worked.

"If this spell worked, then they'll be here tonight," I said, touching the pendant around my neck.

"Where do you think your guests are?" Liam asked.

I'd been so distracted that I'd forgotten we had to find Catherin.

"I don't know, but I have an idea whatever they're doing isn't good," I said with a click of my tongue.

"We could look for them, but I wouldn't even know where to start," he said, peering down into the cauldron.

"Which reminds me, I have to check to see if I can read the rest of the Book of Mystics." I moved over to the book and flipped the pages.

Everything was written in English, not just the instructions on how the Underworld was structured, but the rules that I had to enforce. It would take hours, if not days to figure everything out.

"Where do we start?" I asked.

"From the beginning," Liam said, touching my chin. "We have all day."

CHAPTER TWENTY-EIGHT

We'd just reached the section in the book that might contain the mysterious symbol when we ran out of time. The Coven members would be arriving at any second. As part of the ritual, I lit candles around the room.

I'd just lit the last candle when the doorbell rang. Liam squeezed my hand as I sucked in a deep breath and walked to the door. I was bracing myself for the worst—anything less than that would be a success.

Misty, my mother, and a couple of Enchantment Pointe Coven members stood at my front door. I figured I'd never hear the end of it if I hadn't included my mother and a few Enchantment Pointe Coven members in on the meeting so I'd invited them too. It really didn't concern them though.

After hugging my mother, I said, "We'll be starting the meeting soon. Please have a seat anywhere."

I gestured over my shoulder toward the parlor.

"Hallie, are you sure of what you're doing?" my mother asked.

I shrugged. "It's what I have to do."

Before she could ask another question, the doorbell rang again. My heart sped up. Without looking, I knew it was the New Orleans Coven members. I took a deep breath, then forced myself to walk over to the door and open it.

Just as I'd thought, Jacobson and Sabrina stood in front of me. Behind them were the other members who I'd met that first night. The other person standing behind them was a total shock though. I hadn't expected Nicolas to show up. He didn't look up at me as I stared at him.

"Hello, Halloween. I'm surprised by the emergency meeting tonight." Jacobson showed off his dazzling white smile.

Yeah, because he'd probably figured I didn't know how to call the meeting. I guess I'd proved him wrong.

"Good evening. Won't you please come in? I'm glad you came. I'm sorry I had to call the meeting like this, but it is very important." I stepped out of the way and gestured for the group to enter.

Jacobson and the others filed in, but when I looked at the group Sabrina was missing. I knew she'd been standing at the door with Jacobson, but where was she now? Nicolas had entered the foyer behind the others. He still hadn't looked up at me. Did he think he could ignore me all evening? I was getting to the bottom of this once and for all. They couldn't ignore my questions now. I had them right where I wanted them.

The Enchantment Pointe Coven members exchanged pleasantries with the others.

As I entered the parlor, Jacobson looked at me with his usual sly grin. "What, no refreshments? I get the feeling that this isn't a pleasant social call."

"Well, this meeting is all business. I'm sorry if you feel I'm being a bad hostess." I flashed a fake smile.

He chuckled. "I really didn't expect anything else."

Okay, now he was insulting my hosting skills. I wouldn't have that. Those were fighting words.

"Please everyone have a seat. This won't take long." I gestured toward the various seats in the room.

I looked over at Nicolas. He still didn't look at me. And where was Sabrina? I knew without a doubt that I'd seen her when I opened the door, but after that she'd vanished. I hoped she wasn't snooping around in the house.

There was no time to waste, so I got right to the point. "As you know, things haven't gone as I'd planned since I accepted the leader role."

Jacobson smirked, but didn't offer a response, so I continued.

"Nicolas has been accused of attacking your sister, so tell me, Jacobson, why would you forgive him now? Why accept him into your Coven again? You wanted me to punish him before." I crossed my arms in front of my chest, happy with my line of questioning.

Jacobson shrugged. "Everyone makes mistakes. I guess we worked things out."

"I don't believe that. There is no truth to that statement and I know it. And considering Nicolas won't look at me and acts as if he doesn't know me, I know you've done something to him. I plan on finding out what that is and reversing it. You can't play with him like that. He is not your toy." I looked around at the glares and frowns of the New Orleans Coven members. I knew whose side they were on with this one. "Can't you all see what he is doing?" I asked while looking at them. They just continued glaring at me.

Jacobson feigned a look of surprise. "I have done nothing of the sort and I don't appreciate you accusing me of something I didn't do."

I snorted. "So now you know how it feels."

"You were so quick to just assume that he was innocent. You had no proof other than you wanted to go to bed with him." Jacobson smirked.

I stepped closer to Jacobson. So close that I felt his breath on me. "Don't ever talk to me that way again. I based my decision on what I knew of Nicolas, but I tried to be open to the facts. If it had been true, then I would have done something about it. You didn't give me a chance to find out if it was true."

He shrugged, but didn't speak. I got the impression he was stunned that I'd actually confronted him and not backed down.

"Now, if that's settled, there are a few questions I want to ask." Jacobson's glare didn't falter, but I continued anyway. "We noticed the paintings on the plantation wall with the symbols and writing. They're also at the abandoned home that I believe is your sister's place." I glanced around for Sabrina, but she was still nowhere in sight. "Do you want to tell me what you are doing?"

He stared at me for a moment, then said, "You're getting around a lot. It's nice to see a leader who is so concerned for others. But I can tell you that I have no idea what you are talking about."

"I want to know what the paintings mean." I fixed my gaze on him.

He shook his head. "I have no answers for you."

"What does the symbol on this necklace mean?" I held the gold necklace up, letting it dangle in the air.

He watched the necklace move back and forth for a moment until I thought perhaps I'd hypnotized him.

Finally, he looked up and glared at me again. "Again, I have no answers for you. I've never seen that necklace before."

Clearly he wasn't going to budge with this question. I'd have to move on to the next topic.

"Fine, if you won't answer, then I can explain the purpose of this meeting." I placed my hands in front of me in my most professional leader of the Underworld stance.

"I'm glad you're finally getting to the point. I have another party to attend." Jacobson glanced down at the gold watch on his wrist.

"As leader of the Underworld, I am stripping you of your Coven Leader position. As a matter of fact, you are no longer a member of the Coven. You are relieved of all your duties," I said with a wave of my hand.

His face grew instantly red. I'd never been looked at like that before. I knew he was wishing me dead at that moment. I prayed he wouldn't try a spell, but with the necklace, I hoped I had my full powers to fight it.

"You can't do that." One of the women stepped forward, but Liam blocked her.

"I can, and I did," I said without allowing my voice to waver.

"Where will he stay?" she asked, almost in tears.

I frowned. "What do you mean?"

My mother handed me the Book of Mystics and pointed at a paragraph on the page in front of me. I glanced at her and scowled.

"Read it," she said, tapping the page.

I looked down and read the paragraph. "You mean you don't own the plantation?" I said, looking up with wide eyes.

According to the book, the plantation belonged to the Coven, not Jacobson. The leader was the one in charge of the home and only allowed to live there. Once Jacobson was no longer the leader, he wasn't allowed to live in the home. He'd have to get out.

I looked up at Jacobson's angry face. He knew what I was about to say.

"You can place the keys to the plantation on the table." I tapped on the wood in front of me.

"I'm not going anywhere," he said through gritted teeth.

Was there a spell for evicting witches? I glanced down at the book and wondered if I had time to check. No, there was no time. I'd have to improvise.

With my gesture, Liam and Jon grabbed Jacobson by the arms. The others reluctantly followed as they escorted him out the door.

"You won't get away with this." Jacobson's lips twisted into a snarl.

I didn't know what he had in mind, but I knew he wouldn't give up this easily. Nicolas followed the others toward the front door.

As he stepped through the foyer, I grabbed his arm. "Nicolas, aren't you going to talk to me?"

He turned and looked me straight in the eye. "There's nothing to say."

I stopped in my tracks when I saw the necklace around his neck. It matched the other necklaces that I'd found. The far-off look in his eyes sent a chill down my spine. This wasn't Nicolas.

"Who are you? What have you done with Nicolas?" I asked.

Without speaking another word, he walked out the door… whoever *he* was.

CHAPTER TWENTY-NINE

Once I reached the veranda, I stopped. The Enchantment Pointe members stood beside me, looking on in shock. What? Hadn't they ever seen witches out for revenge before?

"What are they doing?" I asked.

Liam shook his head. "They're casting a spell."

This couldn't end well.

"What do you think it is?" I asked.

"I think we're about to find out." He gestured with a tilt of his head toward the jilted Coven members.

The group joined hands, making a circle in the front driveway. They weren't even trying to hide the fact that they were casting a spell. It was unnerving to say the least to realize that they were trying to cause harm to me. Sabrina stood beside her brother. How had she gotten out there? I'd never seen her walk out of the house. Maybe she'd been outside the whole time. But why? What had she been up to?

The group chanted as the wind blew around them. The trees swayed wildly in the wind. When they'd finally completed their task, they simply climbed into the car and drove off down the driveway. I hadn't seen Nicolas' imposter in the group, and I wondered if he'd been a part of the spell.

After we stepped back inside, it took me a while to calm my mother down.

"I can't believe they had the nerve to do that. Who do they think they are?" she fumed.

"It's okay, Mom. I found this necklace now, and it's helping me fight any magic that they throw at me." I pointed out the gold chain.

She touched the necklace around my neck. "Where did you find it?"

I paused. Did I really want to recount the whole story?

"To cut a long story short," I said, "we went to see Sierra and she channeled Nicolas' mother through Annabelle. Anyway, his mother told us about the necklace, then I came home and found it." I'd tried to keep my voice as calm as possible so as not to freak her out.

It didn't work.

My mother swayed again. I was giving her dizzy spells. Literally. "Annabelle let a spirit come through her?"

"Well, she didn't do it willingly," I said.

Annabelle gave a half smile and waved at my mother.

"Anyway, we'll talk about this later. I have to get to work right now," I said.

"Thank you for including us," Misty said softly. "And I promise we're going to destroy all the pamphlets we made on how to avoid bad witchcraft that reference your name."

"You're welcome and thank you." I offered a faint smile.

I tried not to hold a grudge. It was good to forgive and forget, right?

"We'll be taking off now. Call us if you need anything. Come on, Annette, I'll drive you home," Misty said, motioning over her shoulder.

I hugged my mother and waved to the others.

"We're leaving too." Annabelle squeezed my shoulders.

"Are you okay?" I asked.

"I feel fine." She smiled and waved off the question.

Her expression didn't offer much confidence, but I'd take her word for it.

When Annabelle and Jon walked out the door, Liam stepped close and grabbed my hands. "You did a great job tonight," he said.

"Thank you," I said softly.

"We'll get to the bottom of this." He touched my chin with his index finger.

"I just hope it's not too late," I said, looking down.

"At least you haven't had any more of the blackouts." He brushed hair from my cheek.

"Yeah, I guess there was something to this necklace after all," I said, touching the pendant.

Liam looked down at his shoes. "Um, do you want me to stay in your room with you tonight?"

Wow. I hadn't expected him to ask. The thoughts whirled in my head, but I knew I had to turn him down. I didn't need him to babysit me. I didn't know what I needed.

I picked at the hem of my shirt, avoiding his persistent stare. "I think I'll stay up and look through the book more. I want to know everything about my duties now that I can read and understand the book. I'm not saying that I'll know what it means, but at least I can try now."

He nodded. "You'll come get me if you need me?"

I nodded. "Of course. Thank you."

Liam placed his lips against mine and kissed me softly. I closed my eyes and lost myself in the moment. When I opened my eyes, he turned around and walked up the stairs without looking back.

CHAPTER THIRTY

At some point in the night I'd fallen asleep sitting on the stool at the counter while reading the book. Looking around the room, I wasn't sure what had startled me awake. Something seemed off though and a chill ran across my body.

A strange vibe hung in the air again. I'd thought I'd moved past the blackout spells thanks to the necklace. The sound of footsteps caught my attention, so I eased over to the kitchen door, looking out into the parlor. I saw nothing, but I thought I heard voices. Was it Catherin and Claude? Had they returned?

Adrenaline pulsed through my body. I'd have to confront them. If the Coven wouldn't tell me what the necklace meant, then I expected Catherin to give me a straight answer. She'd obviously known my great-aunt.

I followed the sound of the voices. When reached the foyer, I spotted Catherin and Claude. They stood side by side, watching me as I moved toward them. It was as if they knew what I was about to ask them.

"I've missed you two," I said, trying to sound as casual as possible.

I didn't sound very convincing though.

"Hello, dear," Catherin said as they stared at me. "Is everything all right?"

There was no time to be wasted. I'd get right to the point.

"I'm sorry I was in your room, but I found this necklace." I pulled it from my pocket and flashed it at them.

Catherin's eyes narrowed. "Thank you for finding it. I'll take it back now." She wiggled her fingers.

Claude and Catherin stepped closer, until finally they surrounded me. Liam had said to get him if I needed him, but I couldn't get past them. And by the looks on their faces, I was sure now was the time I'd need him.

"Are you going to tell me what this necklace means?" I asked. "I've seen it at the New Orleans Coven. Plus, I found the postcard you sent to my great-aunt back in 1938. You said you hadn't been back until now. You lied to me." I gave her my most evil glare.

Neither Catherin nor Claude answered as their faces darkened. Who exactly was I dealing with?

Catherin reached out and snatched the necklace from my hand, then ripped the necklace from around my neck. "The necklace is mine and I'll take it back," she said with venom in her voice.

As much as I wanted to grab the necklace back, I couldn't. It was like I was unable to move at anything other than a snail's pace.

Without being able to stop myself, I moved across the foyer and to the front door. Just then, out of the corner of my eye, I spotted Liam as he walked down the stairs. Thank goodness he'd be able to help me now.

"Liam, I can't stop," I said as I reached the front door.

The next thing I knew, I was on the veranda. Liam walked out the front door too. Something had pulled me outside. A force beyond my control. I couldn't stop the pull. The front door slammed shut with such force that it rattled the wood. I ran over to the door and turned the handle, but it wouldn't budge. Liam ran rushed behind me and tried the door. It still wouldn't move.

I threw my hands up in the air. "They've locked us out. I think they cast a spell that threw me out of my own house. They took my necklace. I can't believe this."

Liam pounded on the door, but it was no use.

"That thing is solid, there is no way it's coming down," I said.

"Is the back door locked?" Liam asked.

"Yes, and so are all the windows. Safety, you know?" I shrugged.

Liam grabbed my hand. "Come on. We have to stop them."

Liam and I raced down the steps, but stopped when we reached his car.

"What do you suggest we do now?" I asked.

"You can try a spell that pulls energy from other witches," he said matter-of-factly, as if this would be the easiest thing in the world.

"You make it sound so easy, but we'll need to get another witch here," I said, blowing hair out of my eyes.

"My car keys are in the house." He pointed toward the front door.

Of all the luck. What would we do now?

"We'll have to walk somewhere and use a phone. There's a shortcut through the woods," I said, pointing at the line of trees at the edge of the property.

He blew out a deep breath. "Okay. I'm getting a bad vibe from this idea, but I don't think we have any other options."

I looked up at the house one last time. "What are they doing in there?"

Every light in the house had been turned on, but other than that, there was no sign that Claude and Catherin were even still in there. Liam grabbed my hand and we took off across the yard into the dark woods. We could have traveled down the road, but since it looped and curved, the distance through the woods was much shorter. The nearest house was about a quarter mile away. With any luck, the neighbor would let us use the phone.

I considered myself somewhat of a brave person, but being surrounded by the tall trees and darkness was unsettling. If you'd told me a month ago that I'd be running through the woods in the dark of night with a vampire warlock, I would have told you that you'd been drinking way too much. Fallen branches snapped under our feet and the rustling of leaves stirred high in the treetops.

Up ahead under the screen of overhanging branches, I spotted movement. If it was some kind of wild animal I would freak out. Witches, vampires, demons, I could handle. What if it was a werewolf? No, I didn't want to think about it.

"Did you see that?" I asked Liam as we continued our trek.

"See what?" he asked without looking at me.

"That!" I pointed.

It was that moment that I realized Nicolas was walking up ahead. How had he gotten there? Was it the real Nicolas? "It's Nicolas… at least I think it's him," I hurried forward in hopes that I'd catch him.

"Nicolas," Liam yelled.

We ran ahead after Nicolas, but within a couple seconds he'd turned to the right. When we reached the spot where he'd turned, we paused and searched for any sign of him. He was nowhere in sight.

"Where did he go?" There was nothing but trees as far as I could see.

Liam shook his head. "I don't know. Do you know who lives in the house next door?"

"No. I never met them. I haven't been here long, you know."

"Hey, you don't have to explain to me why you haven't been neighborly. Come on, we'll continue and see if he shows up there." He reached out, gently lacing his fingers with mine.

CHAPTER THIRTY-ONE

When we came out into the clearing, I spotted the house in front of us. We paused under the shadow of the sizeable red brick house. Cupolas, spires, and scrolled balconies decorated the façade. Each window was completely dark. Just what I needed, it looked as if they weren't home.

"I don't even want to think about what we'll do if no one is home," I said as we crept across the lawn like cat burglars.

"We'll stay positive. Maybe they're just sleeping." Liam tried to sound optimistic.

"Good point. It is late. What if they call the police because we knock on the door this late?" I asked while glancing over my shoulder.

Liam grinned. "That would be a good thing. The police could give us a ride."

We made our way up the front steps and to the front door. Liam rang the bell and I cringed at the loud noise. If someone was sleeping in there they wouldn't be after that racket. After I was ready to give up on anyone answering the door, a shuffling sound came from inside the house.

"Who is it?" the little voice croaked through the wooden door.

"Oh no. We woke a little old lady. There's no way she'll answer the door for us," I whispered.

"You talk to her. She'll be more likely to speak with a woman," Liam said.

"My name is Hallie LaVeau and I live next door. I'm afraid I locked myself out of my house. We need to use a phone," I yelled through the door.

I would have attempted a spell to call someone, but it probably wouldn't have worked anyway. Plus, I didn't want to send out the magic, allowing Claude and Catherin to know where we were.

"Did that sound sincere?" I whispered to Liam.

He shook his head. "Not really. You sound like you're the big bad wolf trying to talk your way in."

I poked him in the side.

"LaVeau… Oh yes," she said as recognition hit her.

The rattling of the lock made me flash Liam a smirk.

"Don't get too cocky," he said with a grin.

She opened the door just a little and peeked out. All I saw was an eye and a little bit of white hair piled on top of her head. She looked us up and down but the door didn't open any further. If she didn't let us in, I'd have to take back that smirk I'd just given Liam. Finally, she opened the door wider. She wore a blue robe and white slippers.

"I've meant to come visit you for some time," the old woman said.

I supposed I hadn't been a good neighbor. Maybe I could whip her up a batch of my magically made cupcakes if I ever got my magic mojo back.

"I'm sorry I didn't stop by and introduce myself earlier. This is my friend Liam Rankin." I wasn't about to tell her he was my bodyguard. That would scare her to death.

She waved off my statement with her bony hand. "Think nothing of it. My name is Estelle Fairchild."

"It's lovely to meet you," I said, looking around trying to avoid the awkwardness.

"Again, we are sorry for disturbing you at this late hour. Is it all right if we use your phone?" Liam said, looking over her shoulder into her home.

She stared at him for a moment and I thought she was ready to tell him to get lost. Instead, she said, "I do have some things that belonged to your aunt's. I think you should have them."

I hadn't expected that. What could she possibly have of Aunt Maddy's? "What kind of things?" I asked.

"Come inside and I'll get them for you," she said as she shuffled out of the way and motioned for us to enter.

The inside of Estelle's home was dark except for the faint glow of light from a room in the back. The house was large like LaVeau Manor and had a lot of the same details. I imagined it had been built around the same time—maybe even built by the same architect. Estelle held up her index finger, then shuffled down the hall, disappearing into a room.

"What do you think she has?" Liam whispered.

I shrugged. "With my aunt it could be any number of odd things."

When Estelle returned, she handed me a wooden box. Unlike the box that I'd found hidden outside of LaVeau Manor, this one didn't have a lock. I looked up at her and she just gave me a knowing smile, motioning for me to open the box. By her expression, I assumed she'd already looked inside the box at its contents. I'd never seen Estelle at the Coven get-togethers, so I was almost positive she wasn't a witch.

"When did she give this to you?" I asked.

"Hmm. Well, I guess I don't know. My memory isn't what it used to be," she said with a wave of her hand.

Apprehension ran through me as I eased the lid of the box open. My stomach turned when I saw that inside was another bound item, tied in the fabric with the same jute cord as the stake we'd found in the attic. I glanced over at Liam, but his expression remained resolute. In addition to the bound item, a small leather-bound book lay inside as well. It looked well-worn and the gold letters on the front had faded years ago. Without even peeking at the bound item, I shut the lid of the box. I'd look at the items later. Right now we needed to use the phone and get out of there.

"Is it all right if we use the phone now?" I asked.

"Oh, please help yourself." She gestured toward the small walnut-colored table in the corner of the room.

Liam picked up the receiver on the outdated phone and dialed the number. It took forever with that rotary spinning each number.

Estelle and I awkwardly watched each other.

"You look like your Great Aunt Madeline." She pointed at my face. "You have the same clear blue eyes and small button nose."

"Thank you," I said softly.

After a minute, Liam placed the receiver back and returned to my side. "Jon and Annabelle are on their way."

"Would you care for some tea?" she asked as she stood.

I waved my hand. "Oh, no. We've taken up too much of your time already. We'll just wait for our ride outside."

She frowned as if I'd just given her the highest insult possible. "It will only take a moment."

Liam shrugged.

"Okay. That would be lovely, thank you." I flashed a giant smile.

Estelle shuffled off to the kitchen. I couldn't believe we were drinking tea when we needed to be looking for Nicolas. I felt Liam staring at me.

"What could I say?" I whispered after she left to make tea.

"I don't even like tea." Liam leaned back in the chair.

I lowered my voice and said, "Pretend to drink it."

After placing the water on the stove, Estelle returned, sitting directly across from us in the white wingback chair.

The room was packed with an assortment of furniture—cherry, walnut, and mahogany pieces covered almost every available space. Massive wood bookcases took up the wall across from us. I wondered if she had spell books too.

She placed her hands in her lap. "I am sorry about your great-aunt. She was a delightful woman."

"Thank you," I said softly.

"So are you enjoying your new home? I heard you had a party the other night." She eyed me suspiciously.

"Um, yes. It was just a one-time event though." I shifted in my seat.

Her relentless stare made me feel as if I was in the principal's office. I hadn't been there since I'd accidentally changed his suit into a dress in the middle of the school assembly. High school had been a tough time for me. Thank goodness that had been years ago now.

I was already making excuses for wild parties and I'd only just moved in. There was no way she'd heard the party. It was too far away.

The headlights from a car spilled through the window and flashed across the room.

I stood and said, "Well, there's our ride. Thank you again for everything."

Estelle was a lovely woman, but I was ready to get out of there. She followed us as we walked toward the door.

"Your aunt used to bring me her homemade desserts." One corner of her mouth twisted into a little smile.

I glanced over at Liam and he smiled. I took her comment as a hint. "I'd be happy to make you something if you'd like. It would be my way of saying thank you for holding on to my aunt's belongings."

She grinned bashfully. "Well, don't go to any trouble."

I was unable to hold back a chuckle. "Oh, it's no trouble. Thank you again for the box."

I waved as we stepped off the porch and climbed into Jon's waiting car. Annabelle was sitting in the front seat.

When I jumped in the backseat, she said, "What happened? What's going on?"

"As it turns out, Catherin and Claude aren't so nice after all," I said, buckling my seatbelt.

"They actually locked you out of your own place?" Jon asked as he backed the car up.

"Yes, and they stole the necklaces. Catherin ripped it off my neck. I would have snatched it back, but they'd placed a spell on me. I did nothing but walk right out the door while they slammed it in my face. Liam was affected too. He walked right out the door with me." The more I spoke the louder my voice grew. Excitement had a way of causing that reaction from me.

"So you didn't get to ask Catherin about the postcard?" Annabelle asked.

I ran my hand through my hair and let out a deep breath. "I asked, but she didn't answer. I did get this box from the neighbor though. She said it was my great-aunt's."

"What's in it?" Annabelle twisted in the front seat and looked back at us.

I opened the box and unfolded the fabric from the item. It was just as I'd suspected.

"It's another stake. Plus there's a small book that I haven't had a chance to look at until now." I pulled out the little leather book.

When I flipped open the cover, I realized that it was my great-aunt's journal. Written in cursive, the pages were yellowed and very fragile. It consisted mostly of simple spells for gardening or baking. I'd almost given up on finding anything interesting written in the book when I flipped through a few pages and saw the symbols.

"It has the symbols," I said breathlessly.

"What?" Liam leaned over in the seat.

"Look, it talks about the symbol we found on the necklace from the plantation and from Catherin's room.

It's part of a demonic cult. They were vampires and apparently staked."

Liam's face turned white. "It's all coming back to me now."

"What's all coming back to you?" I asked. What dreadful thing was I about to discover? I wasn't sure how much more I could handle.

Liam paused, then finally said, "Nicolas and his mother, Gina staked the vampires who turned us. I was supposed to be there that night to help him, but I didn't make it in time." Liam gazed out the window for a second before continuing, "The vampires who turned them were part of a demonic cult. The cult was led by a vampire and he vowed revenge if anything ever happened to them. I guess that means he came back as a demon. Gina's sister, Mara… claimed she wasn't a part of the cult, but we know how that turned out."

Jon glanced at us in the rear-view mirror. "So they've come back for Nicolas? Then why is Nicolas acting this way?"

"Jacobson and his sister have to be a part of this cult. And so do Catherin and apparently Claude," I said.

"We haven't seen the real Nicolas since the night he left," Liam said.

"What does that mean?" Annabelle asked.

"Someone is using a spell and pretending to be Nicolas. We just need to find out what happened to the *real* Nicolas." Liam exchanged a worried glance with me.

I flipped a page and saw another name that I recognized. Sabrina Stratford's name was mentioned as a vampire. She had been turned by the same group who had turned Nicolas and his family. I couldn't believe that this information had fallen into my lap, so to speak. Poof, it had appeared at just the right time. I didn't think that was a coincidence. There was some other magic in play.

As I continued to leaf through the book, I realized one thing. "Wait. I think we're going to need more witches to fight this thing. Annabelle, can I use your cell phone?"

"Sure," she said, handing me the phone.

With a shaky hand, I dialed my mother's number. "

Hallie, what's wrong?" she asked with panic.

My mother always thought something was wrong when I called at that time of night. So what if she was right this time.

"Mom, I'm fine. Take a deep breath."

I heard her take a couple deep breaths, then she said, Okay… I'm calm."

Now that I'd calmed her somewhat, I laid the big whammy on her. "Can you get the Coven members together and come to LaVeau Manor right away?"

"What's the problem?" she rushed her words.

"I've been locked out of LaVeau Manor by a couple of demon witches," I said.

Coming from me, I knew that wasn't such an odd admission.

CHAPTER THIRTY-TWO

Within a minute, we were pulling up in front of LaVeau Manor. A chill ran down my spine at the thought of Catherin and Claude taking over LaVeau Manor. In the short time I'd owned the place, I'd grown attached. The thought of someone harming the manor made me furious.

"Are you sure you want to take on these witches?" Jon's voice seemed less than confident.

I fixed my gaze on him and answered with as much assurance that I could gather up. "I don't have a choice."

"Jacobson and Sabrina will probably be here soon if they know Catherin and Claude are about to battle it out with you," Liam said.

"I hope there is no battle." I released a deep breath and opened the car door. "We'll sneak up and try the door again while we wait for the Coven members to show up," I said as we all climbed out of the car.

The four of us stood in front of the house, peering up at it. Silvery light from the moon pierced the thick cover of darkness. A night wind ruffled the nearby trees as if sending us a warning. The open veranda stretched the width of the house as the four towering columns rose skyward, gleaming in the moonlight. The manor's lights shone brightly in the night sky, but there was no movement from inside.

"Maybe Liam and I should check the door while you all stay down here and keep an eye on the place. Yell if Catherin or Claude come from the back," I said.

"You got it," Annabelle said in her bravest voice.

When Liam and I made it to the front door, he turned the knob, but it still wouldn't budge. Using the strength of his body, he pushed on the door, but it was no use. I stepped over to the window and cupped my hands over my eyes, peeking in the parlor. The bright lights made it impossible to see anything.

"They have to come out sometime, right?" I asked, peering in the window again.

"Yeah… at least I think so." His eyebrows drew together in an exasperated expression.

When we turned around and headed back down the veranda steps, Annabelle or Jon weren't standing where we'd left them.

"Where did they go?" I asked as we neared the car.

Liam scanned the area. "I don't know."

By the look on his face, I knew he was concerned. They wouldn't have just walked off.

"Someone took them, didn't they?" I asked, searching Liam's eyes for a truthful answer.

Finally, he nodded. "Yes, probably so. I can't imagine where they'd be, but let's check the back of the manor."

As we eased around the house, I peered in each window, but still couldn't see any sign of Catherin or Claude.

"I don't think they're in there. They must have taken my keys and left," I said.

"They probably went to the plantation," Liam said.

As we rounded the corner and came back to the front of the manor, the Coven members pulled up behind Jon's car. We'd have to cast a spell that would get rid of this demon once and for all.

My mother was the first to climb out from the van. "What's happening?"

As I filled her in on what had happened to this point, the other Coven members joined us.

"We need to cast a spell that draws them out of the house if they are still in there." The level of panic in my voice was a dead giveaway to my current freaked-out state.

"You think they're not there anymore?" Misty asked.

I shook my head. "No, I don't think they're in there and I think they took my friends too."

The worry line deepened between Misty's eyebrows. "Tell us what we need to do."

"I have to find Annabelle," I said.

A terrifying cloud of the unknown hovered over me.

Jacobson had attacked Annabelle once. I knew he wouldn't think twice about using her to get to me again.

"We'll find her." My mother's bracelets jangled as she patted my hand.

"We'll join hands and cast the spell. I need to pull off of your energy," I said.

I was glad that I could finally count on the Coven for help. There would probably always be some hesitation about me as far as they were concerned, but right now I really did need them.

We formed a circle by holding hands on the front lawn. Without hesitation, the words for the spell came to me.

I held my mother's hand to my left and Liam's hand to my right. The words for the spell flowed as if I'd known them all my life. Tapping into the energy from the other witches was the only chance I had to find Annabelle and Nicolas. With the help of the Coven members, I could call to the elements and tap into the full potential of the magic. This was the most important spell of my life—people's lives depended on me.

As I concentrated on the spell, the world around me changed. I had no idea if the wind was blowing, if the clouds zoomed past, or if it was even raining. It was as if I was contained in my own bubble.

With a steady voice I said, "Element of Earth, I call to you to cast back the evil, we have no fear. Element of Air, I call to you to push the bad away through wind and the dark of night, we have no fear. Element of Fire, I call to you for warmth and protection. Help me have the knowledge. Element of Water, I call to you for force of the sea, bring us the power against those who mean us harm."

Finally, the bubble around me broke, and I opened my eyes. The spell had been cast, and we looked toward the house. Nothing was happening. It remained the same as when Liam and I had been kicked out.

"It looks as if they weren't in there after all," my mother said.

I was about to agree with her when the lights in the house flickered. "Did you see that?"

Liam nodded. "I get the feeling it wasn't faulty wiring that did that."

The front door opened with full force and Catherin and Claude appeared. They did not look pleased with what we'd done. The frowns deepened on their faces as they moved down the steps and stopped in front of us.

"So nice of you to join us." I faked a smile.

Catherin glared at me. "You had to call in your friends."

"Why don't you tell me who you are," I said.

"Why don't you guess?" Claude answered for her.

"I'm not much for games. It's better if you just tell me now because I'll find out sooner or later. And I'm thinking it'll be sooner." I warned with a wave of my hand.

Before they answered, Catherin and Claude changed right before our eyes. I let out a gasp when I saw who they really were. They had revealed their true identities. Sabrina and Jacobson stood before us. They had fooled me all along. Once again, I had had the enemy right under my nose the whole time. I really needed to check out my guests better.

"Why did you pretend to be Catherin Butterfield?" I asked.

Sabrina laughed. "At first it was totally random, but then I discovered that Gina had reanimated Catherin years ago because Catherin specialized in binding vampire stakes so that the vampires couldn't come back as demons. What are the odds that I would pick her? Obviously Catherin hadn't been great at binding because the vampire Darkess, who turned Gina and her family, came back as a demon anyway."

"Are you surprised it was us?" Jacobson asked.

"You tricked me. Good for you. I bet you are really proud of yourself," I said.

He nodded with a smirk. "Actually I am happy with how well we pulled it off. But then again, you aren't that hard to fool."

He loved to insult me. But who would have the last laugh? I was going to try my hardest to make sure it was me.

"How did you appear at just the right time when my spells had gone wrong?" I asked.

"We cast a spell so we'd know exactly what spells you were trying and when. It just happened to fit perfectly into our plan. We couldn't have asked for anything better."

"Why did you do this?" My tolerance level for his antics had vanished ages ago.

"Nicolas was here with you. We wanted to take him down and steal his soul for the demon. We figured while we were at it we could take your soul too." Jacobson held one arm behind his back. I probably wasn't going to like whatever he was concealing.

"And I'll be the leader of the Underworld." Sabrina flipped her cola-colored hair off her shoulder. A satisfied gleam sparkled in her dark eyes.

Jacobson whipped around and glared at her. "I thought we agreed that I would be the leader."

"Neither of you will ever be the leader," I snapped.

Jacobson pulled the Book of Mystics out from behind me. "That's where you're wrong. I have the book now."

A sneer of satisfaction covered his face.

My stomach sank. How would I get the book back? I'd really screwed up now.

"That was why you banished me from the house." I glared at him. "You made me have the blackouts too, didn't you? You were trying to take my soul?"

"We would have succeeded if you hadn't discovered that damn necklace. But now that we have it back…" He smiled.

"What have you done with Nicolas and Annabelle?" My anger surged and I felt the blood drain from my face.

"I don't know anything about anyone named Annabelle," Jacobson said.

"Tell her the truth," Liam demanded.

"You do know. She was here. You attacked her earlier," I said.

He snorted. "She serves no purpose to me."

"You are a liar. Where is Nicolas?" I demanded.

"He's with the demon where he belongs," Jacobson said with that familiar smirk.

Jacobson was out of control and I had had it with him. With all the energy I could muster I raised my hand and pointed at Jacobson. He had made me furious. Some way or somehow I would force him to tell me the truth. As the words popped into my mind, I spoke them out loud. I had no idea if they were right or would even work, but with my anger, there would be no stopping me.

I recited the words, "I freeze your power. You will not work magic. No harm will come from you. So mote it be."

A wave of energy flowed from my fingertips and hit Jacobson. As he stumbled backward, Sabrina flashed her fangs and hissed at me.

"You lied about Nicolas attacking you. That vampire turned you years ago. Why did you do that?" I asked.

"We wanted you to deliver Nicolas to us. He needs to suffer for what he's done." Jacobson's face was hard and unyielding.

"Why now? Why didn't you do something years ago?" I asked.

"We just became aware of what Nicolas and his mother did. So we decided to fight for the demon. Besides, what better time to become the leader of the Underworld? We could get rid of Nicolas and you, then I would be the leader," Jacobson said.

"That doesn't even make any sense," I said.

"To you maybe it doesn't make sense. To us it makes perfect sense." He gave an evil grin.

Misty stepped forward slightly, as if she hated to interrupt. "Um, we can cast a spell that will help reveal where they are keeping Nicolas and Annabelle."

"Cast the spell and use our energy again," Liam said.

I nodded and then repeated the words. "I freeze your power. You will not work magic. No harm will come from you. So mote it be."

The wave of energy flew from my fingers again as I pointed both hands at Jacobson and Sabrina.

They fell to the ground. Their movements were sluggish as they attempted to get up from the gravel drive. It was no use though. Their powers were bound—for a short time at least.

Liam pointed at the incapacitated witches. "They won't be out long. We need to reach Nicolas and Annabelle before it's too late. If we can get rid of the demon then we can save them."

"In the book it says we have to destroy the symbols. I'm guessing that was what my great-aunt had tried to do all those years ago when she bound the stakes so that the bad vampires wouldn't come back as demons." I grabbed the book and waved it through the air for emphasis.

"It's an hour's drive to New Orleans. Does anyone know a spell to help us not get a speeding ticket?" I asked.

I snatched the necklaces and the Book of Mystics from Sabrina and Jacobson. "Y'all won't need these."

CHAPTER THIRTY-THREE

Was Nicolas really at the abandoned house where we'd found his wallet? Was he really being held there by the demon vampire who had turned him and his family? Talk about holding a grudge. I mean, get over it already. Nicolas had killed the vampires who had turned his family—he was clearly the winner in that situation.

Liam had taken over driving the van. I was just glad my mother hadn't insisted on chauffeuring. She was as blind as a bat at night, yet she still insisted on climbing behind the wheel every chance she got. As we cruised down the road, I repeatedly glanced at the clock on the van's dashboard. Those green numbers sure seemed to be moving extra slowly. I nervously tapped my fingers against the seat—anything to keep my mind off what was happening.

The hour-long drive seemed to take forever, stretching out as long as the endless road in front of us. The chatter of the Coven members filled the inside of the van. They discussed their favorite spells and which was the best style of cauldron to use. Liam grew uncomfortable when the women began discussing shirtless men—anything to take their minds off the dangerous situation, right?

Finally, we pulled up to the dirt driveway hidden by the tall moss-covered oak trees. Liam wheeled the van in and drove down the driveway. The house soon came into view. I couldn't help but notice the eerie fog that purled across the ground and hovered around the place like some evil haze from Hell. What lurking horrors waited for us? My nerves were on edge, but I had to be strong. I inhaled a deep breath to prepare myself for what I might find inside that house.

As soon as the van had come to a stop and before Liam had even cut the engine, I jumped out and headed in a rush toward the house, wading through the swirling fog. To say that I was anxious would be a vast understatement. There was one thing on my mind: my mission to save my friends. I had no idea what I was walking into, but I had to save Annabelle and Nicolas. When I stepped up onto the porch, an invisible force blasted me backward and I landed at the bottom of the steps with a thud. I groaned as I attempted to move.

Liam raced over. "Are you okay, Hallie?"

"Oh dear, are you all right? What happened?" my mother asked as she helped me up.

I rubbed my head. "Something knocked me on my butt. I'm going out on a limb and guessing it's the aforementioned demon."

Liam and my mother helped me to my feet. Once I'd gotten my footing back, I straightened my shoulders and mentally prepared myself to give it another shot.

The other Coven members gathered around as we looked up at the house. If that was the power this thing possessed, then I was terrified to find out what it had done to Annabelle and Nicolas. Anger mixed with fear boiled inside me.

"I thought Jon was supposed to be her bodyguard? Why did he allow this to happen?" I asked with disappointment in my voice.

Liam looked stricken. "I don't know, Hallie. I'm sorry."

Jon had a lot of explaining to do. Some bodyguard he'd turned out to be. I knew Liam felt bad for recommending him, but the fact was he'd failed at his job.

"We have to get in the house," I said.

My mother grabbed my arm as if she wanted to drag me away from the house. "Hallie, you can't try to get in the same way you just tried. The same thing will happen again."

She had a point. How would I break through the invisible force that this demon was using to shield the house? That was when I remembered I had the necklace again. Had my new magic skills returned enough with the necklace? There was only one way to find out.

With the necklace clasped between my fingers, I recited a spell to protect us. "I call for the power of three to conjure protection for all that surrounds me."

After chanting the phrase several times, a whirlwind of energy engulfed me. When I popped open my eyes, the energy was invisible. The sensation stayed with me though and I knew it was time to move forward.

I released a deep breath, then said, "I'm going in."

"I'm going with you," Liam said, grabbing my arm to slow me down.

"Liam, I don't know if the spell will protect you too," I regarded him with a worried stare.

"Well, I have to give it a shot," Liam squeezed my hand.

"What should we do?" my mother asked, flashing me a look of concern.

Unfortunately, I wasn't sure there was anything the coven members could do to fight this demon. It would probably turn into a one-on-one battle between us.

"Stay out here and perform a spell for protection. Just keep doing it over and over until we come out," I said, hiding the fear in my eyes.

I didn't want to think about if we didn't come out of the house. Negative thinking wouldn't help me out of this predicament.

"Hallie, I don't want you to go in there," my mother grabbed me again.

I touched her arm. "I kind of have to now, Mom. It's my job."

A witch's work was never done, right? I didn't give my mother a chance to protest. If she had time, she could probably talk me out of it. That would be something I'd regret for the rest of my life. So without another word, I forged ahead, making my way up the stairs onto the porch. It had worked. I wouldn't lie and say that I hadn't expected to be thrown off the porch again. I'd fully expected to land on my butt. Liam joined me at the front door. He glanced over at me and I knew by the expression on his face that he was shocked that the spell I'd cast had actually worked. I couldn't take credit for it—the necklace had done all the work. When I turned the knob, the door wouldn't open.

"Stand back," Liam warned.

He moved back several steps, putting distance between his body and the door.

After rushing forward, he kicked the door with full speed and it swung open with a loud crash. Impressive. As I stepped over the threshold, a force of wind smacked me in the face, almost knocking me down again. I managed to steady myself, but walking into the space was like treading through cotton. It had felt the same way that first night at the plantation.

As I looked around the room, I realized that there was no one in sight. Undeniably, the air was heavy with powerful magic.

"I have a feeling I know where they are if they're in this house at all," I said, pointing down the hall toward the room with the paintings.

Liam and I headed down the narrow hallway, stopping in front of the bedroom door where we'd found the strange paintings. In front of the room, the magic was even stronger now. It was oozing out from underneath the door.

"Do you hear anything?" I whispered.

Liam shook his head. "Not a peep."

I twisted the knob, but of course it was locked too. When I couldn't get the door to open, I pounded on the wood with both fists. It rattled, but no one opened up for me. Go figure.

Liam placed his hand on my arm. "Stand back again and I'll knock it down."

I stood back and watched as Liam ran toward the door, kicking it like he had the front door. With one giant rush, the door slammed open, rattling the entire wood frame. He was getting really good at that.

My feet wouldn't move fast enough as I charged into the room like a bull. Annabelle, Jon, and Nicolas were all bound and sitting on the floor in the middle of the room. The fear in Annabelle's eyes made my stomach turn. Fear erupted through my body when I saw another Nicolas standing by the window.

CHAPTER THIRTY-FOUR

"Which one is the real Nicolas" I whispered to Liam.

Liam looked just as confused as I felt. "I don't know," Liam stammered.

"Hallie, it's me. I captured my imposter," the Nicolas standing near the window said.

The pleading look in the gaze of the Nicolas on the floor gave me pause. Magic filled the room until I thought the walls would burst.

"How can I trust you?" I asked the Nicolas by the window.

Something about his voice seemed off. I'd have to go with my instinct on this one and pray that I had it right.

"You can trust me," his voice wavered.

Without asking me, Liam rushed toward what I believed was the imposter. Liam slammed him into the far wall. He immediately fell to the floor. As he lay there, limp and unmoving, the transformation began. Before our eyes he changed and soon the Nicolas on the floor had morphed into the woman from the bar. The one who had sent us here in the first place. Her spell had worn off.

I stared in disbelief. "What are you doing here?"

"Jacobson paid me to lead you here." She said, then drew her lips drawn back in silent snarl.

My opponent looked confident that I wouldn't win this battle.

"Why did you send us here? You're not very organized with your plan."

She bared her fangs, but didn't answer.

"You were the one who turned the waitress. Did Jacobson pay you to do that?"

She scowled. "That was an added bonus. No charge."

Liam pointed at her and magic jumped from his hand. She hissed and tossed the magic back at him. When he fell to the floor, I knew I had to do something quickly. I spotted the gold pendant around her neck.

"Liam, I need her necklace." I pointed.

With Liam struggling to get the necklace from her, I knew I needed to get Annabelle out of the room. She didn't deserve to be drawn into this mess.

"Annabelle, are you okay?" I asked.

She shook her head and spoke only with her eyes. Something held her attention. I followed the direction of her stare. When I turned around, I gasped at the huge creature standing in the corner of the room. So that was what the demon looked like. It was the most hideous thing I'd ever seen. My first instinct was to run, but I quickly remembered why I was there.

The creature that I assumed could only be a demon responsible for this whole mess looked at us. Its eyes glowed red and it bared its yellowed fangs. The thing was a huge humanoid-like beast. This was what the vampires and witches had been a part of? They really were sick.

I was shocked that I was able to somewhat keep my cool. There was only one way I was going to get rid of this thing. I'd have to destroy the necklaces with the symbols. If I could get rid of them while casting this spell, the demon would be banished.

When Liam finally stumbled to his feet, I realized that he had necklace clutched tightly in his hand.

I held my hand out to him. "Give me your hand."

"Hallie," Nicolas said with a weak voice, "take this necklace." Nicolas ripped the gold pendant from around his neck and threw it in the air.

Liam reached and caught the necklace faster than a blink of an eye. Liam and I joined hands while I clutched the necklaces tightly. I recited the words for a banishing spell. "Element of Earth, I call to you to banish the evil forever. Element of Air, I call to you to push the spirit back, never to return. Element of Fire, I call to bind the evil to the fires of hell. Element of Water, I call to you for vision and force."

A shadow fell over the room. The darkness inched and snaked its way across the walls and ceiling. Liam and I grasped our hands tightly and continued to recite the spell. As the darkness grew, my hope faded. We were losing the battle. I'd given up hope, when a loud wail sounded from the demon. The dark cloud engulfing the room reversed and was sucked back into the belly of the beast.

After a fury of twisting black flames, the demon collapsed into a pile of ashes. Instantly, the heaviness lifted from the room. Liam wasted little time running to Annabelle and releasing the rope from her hands.

I raced over to Nicolas. "Are you okay?"

He nodded. "Thanks to you all." He exchanged a glance with Liam.

"Annabelle, are you okay?" I asked.

She nodded and offered a grin as Jon helped her up. "What took you so long?"

And to think she'd just started to get over her fear of the paranormal. This would set her back ten years.

Nicolas stumbled to his feet and grabbed my hands. "Thinking of you all this time was the only thing that kept me sane."

That was one of the sweetest things I'd ever heard.

"Did you get the roses I sent? It took all the energy I had and it was the only spell I could push through. But I wanted you to know I was thinking of you."

"That was you?" My lips parted in surprise.

"I'm sorry it wasn't more. The spell they'd placed over me wouldn't allow me to cast spells, but I did the best that I could." Nicolas leaned down and in one swift movement covered my mouth with his own. I kissed him with all the pent-up stress from the last several days, allowing myself to be lost in the moment.

"The roses were perfect," I said softly.

Nicolas placed a gentle kiss on my forehead. "I'm glad you liked them."

How long have you been here?" I asked, wiping a smudge of dirt from his cheek.

"Too long," he said, running his hand through his hair. "I'm glad I was finally able to rip that necklace off."

"That was the former vampire turned demon who turned you and your family. And that woman was pretending to be you," I said, pointing at the witch across the room.

Nicolas rubbed his wrists where the rope had been secured tightly. "I figured that out after a while. Jacobson and Sabrina brought me here."

"We came by here and found your wallet. You weren't here then," I said.

"I was here the whole time with the leader of the New Orleans Clan of Vampires. Jacobson staked him." A troubled look crossed his face, remembering the scene. "Jacobson and Sabrina cast a spell so that you all couldn't see me. I called out to you, but I was completely invisible." Nicolas stared at the witch who had slipped over by the door.

That sent chills down my spine. "I'm so sorry that I couldn't help you."

I didn't want the witch to get away, so I motioned for Liam to grab her. But before he realized what I wanted, she'd slipped out the door and ran down the hallway.

"I'll try to catch her," Liam said, as he dashed out of the room.

Nicolas focused his attention on me again. "I guess you'd given up on me."

"No, we didn't give up on you." Seeing the flash of joy in his eyes made my insides dance.

Nicolas glanced over at Liam as he spoke with Annabelle and Jon. I knew he was wondering what had happened between us since he'd left LaVeau Manor. My feelings were more confused than ever. Liam was so kind and gentle, but Nicolas was sweet and caring too. I needed to stay far away from both of them, but I knew myself well enough to know that I wouldn't be able to pull that off.

Helping everyone out of the house, we joined my mother where the Coven members were still casting the spell.

I stepped up to my mother. "The demon is gone. It's over now."

She whipped around. "Oh my goddess. I was so worried about you."

She wrapped her arms around me and squeezed tightly, then released me to grab Annabelle.

"I don't think I can handle you being the leader of the Underworld," my mother said.

That was a topic for another day. Right now I had to get everyone back to some sense of normalcy.

"What happened in there?" Misty asked.

"The demon was holding Nicolas, Annabelle and Jon. The demon had used the power from all the witches he recruited, but it had to be a slow and steady process. Once I destroyed the necklaces with the symbols, he could no longer fight us. He's nothing more than a pile of ashes now," I said with a sense of satisfaction.

"Wow, that's impressive," Misty said.

I couldn't believe she'd actually complimented me. "Thank you," I said with a proud smile.

Movement from behind me caught my attention and I turned around. Liam was walking toward me. His expression was grim. I hoped he didn't have more bad news.

"Well, I guess my work here is done." Liam looked down to avoid my stare.

I looked around for Nicolas, hoping that he hadn't vanished again. He stood at the bottom of the steps, pretending not to watch us.

"What are you talking about?" I asked softly.

Liam continued to focus his attention on his shoes, not meeting my stare. "You're not in danger any more. Nicolas can be with you now," Liam said.

I was a little insulted that he just assumed that I wouldn't want him around. But in fact, I didn't know what I wanted. Nicolas was back in the picture, but as far as I was concerned he'd never been out of the picture.

Without thinking, I blurted out, "I want you to be in charge of the New Orleans Coven."

"What?" he asked while looking me in the eyes.

"Now that Jacobson isn't in charge, I'll need someone there. You are already a member of the Coven. Naturally, you're the perfect person for the job," I said, handing Liam the keys to the plantation. "I'm going to ask Nicolas to lead the New Orleans Clan."

With both men in New Orleans, maybe I could work through my thoughts.

He glanced down at the keys, then back at me. "That would mean I'd be living in New Orleans."

I took his hand in mine and said, "We'll have to be in contact every day though."

He smiled. "It doesn't sound like you're confident I can do the job if you think I'll need guidance every day."

I shrugged. "Well, it's not an easy job."

How would Liam restore the New Orleans Coven? He would need my help, right?

"No, I guess it isn't. You're right… I could use the help." A broad grin split his face.

"Does that mean you'll take the job?" I smiled. "I could really use your help."

He leaned down and kissed my lips softly. Was Nicolas watching us? Of course he was. I felt his eyes on us.

After a moment, Liam leaned back and said, "I'd be happy to help you, Ms. LaVeau."

He had the softest lips.

Liam glanced over his shoulder at Nicolas. "I think a conversation with my brother is long overdue."

I nodded. "I think you're right."

As Liam walked toward Nicolas, headlights caught my attention. Who could that be? No one other than Jacobson and Sabrina would know we were here. It was too late now. Their powers would be gone since the demon was finished. The only thing left for them to do was apologize.

The fog still rolled across the ground, swirling around the wheels of the black car as it inched toward us, adding to the mystique of the scene. The car proceeded down the dirt driveway, finally coming to a stop next to the Enchantment Pointe Coven van. The car had black tinted windows, making it impossible to see who was inside. For all I knew, there could have been one or six people in there. Everyone turned their attention to the mysterious vehicle. I held my breath waiting for what was about to happen.

After a few seconds, a man climbed out from the back seat and approached us. He was looking straight at me, so I knew this wasn't a chance encounter. He probably wasn't asking for directions. He wore a black suit with black tie. He looked like a movie star from the 50s, immaculately dressed and groomed.

Once he'd stopped in front of me, he said, "My name is Giovanni St. Clair."

He held his hand out to me and I reluctantly shook it.

"Um, hello," I said, as I raised an eyebrow at him. "May I help you?"

"Are you Halloween LaVeau?" he asked, looking me up and down.

I wasn't sure if I should answer that correctly. Now that I was the leader, it was bringing out all the crazies. Go figure, right?

Finally, I nodded at him suspiciously. "Yes, I'm Hallie LaVeau. What can I do for you?"

After just battling another demon I really wasn't in the mood for pleasantries. At this point Liam and Nicolas had walked up behind me. Now I had two bodyguards. I wouldn't lie, that felt good.

"I hear you're the leader of the Underworld now," he said.

"Yes, that's correct," I said. This guy needed to get to the point.

He looked around. "Well, I'll get to the point of my visit. I heard you relieved the New Orleans Coven leader of his duties."

"Yes, that's right," I said.

"It wasn't your job to do that. You see, I am next in line to be leader of the Underworld," he said.

Well, I hadn't seen that one coming.

ABOUT THE AUTHOR

Rose Pressey is an Amazon and Barnes and Noble Top 100 bestselling author. She enjoys writing quirky and fun novels with a paranormal twist. The paranormal has always captured her interest. The thought of finding answers to the unexplained fascinates her.

When she's not writing about werewolves, vampires and every other supernatural creature, she loves eating cupcakes with sprinkles, reading, spending time with family, and listening to oldies from the fifties.

Rose suffers from Psoriatic Arthritis and has knee replacements. She might just set the world record for joint replacements. She's soon having her hips replaced, elbows, and at least one shoulder.

Rose lives in the beautiful commonwealth of Kentucky with her husband, son, and three sassy Chihuahuas.

Visit her online at:
http://www.rosepressey.com
http://www.facebook.com/rosepressey
http://www.twitter.com/rosepressey

Rose loves to hear from readers. You can email her at: rose@rosepressey.com

If you're interested in receiving information when a new Rose Pressey book is released, you can sign up for her newsletter at http://oi.vresp.com/?fid=cf78558c2a. Join her on Facebook for lots of fun and prizes.

50861700R00159

Made in the USA
Lexington, KY
02 April 2016